THE ONLY WAY HOME

Jeanette Minniti

Paperback ISBN: 978-1-7355669-0-0
Ebook ISBN: 978-1-7355669-1-7
Library of Congress Control Number: 2020918480

Published by

Penning
Press
Penning Press, Monument, CO

Book cover design: Lindsay Heider Diamond
Interior layout: Veronica Yager, YellowStudios

First Edition.

Printed in the United States of America.

To my husband, Bill and my children, Renee and Gregory

1

The heat in the Georgia courtroom that morning in 1933 was stifling. The ceiling fan was loud, doing little to cool the room. Robert sat on a courtroom bench watching men get sentenced to time working on nearby peanut farms or sentenced to jail for theft or assault. Making his way across the country looking for work over the last four months, he'd felt much older than fifteen until now. Life got serious for him fast.

Hopping off a freight train the day before as it slowed to make a stop in Macon, he'd followed the scent of fried chicken to a small cafe on Main Street to try his luck at finding something to eat. When he'd entered the cafe, he'd slid his hands into his trouser pockets, staying near the doorway to see who was behind the counter. A middle-aged waitress walked out of the kitchen carrying two platters of food and set them down at a nearby table. Noticing Robert standing at the back of the restaurant, she nodded and then turned toward the kitchen. Sensing he might not get thrown out, he'd moved toward the counter, waiting for her return. Catching her concerned look as she stepped behind the counter and saw him, he became uneasy to ask if he could trade doing work for food. He'd spent the last of his change on breakfast that morning.

"Howdy, I'm Ada. What can I do for you, son?"

Uncertain now, with his voice shaky, he tried to speak. "Well, ma'am, I was wondering if I could do some dishes or help clean up for something to eat?"

A number of times over the past months this approach had worked, ending in some type of work, but a seriousness crept across her eyes, showing she was thinking it over. Just as he was expecting her to ask him to leave, a slight smile slipped across her lips. "We don't need any help, but you can have dinner if you eat at the table outside behind the restaurant."

"I don't want a handout, ma'am. I can do any kind of work, and I'd rather work for my supper if you don't mind."

"That's okay, kid, just have your dinner at the table out back. I'll be just a minute." She walked toward the kitchen, cutting off the chance to say anything more.

She swung back around the corner with a plate of fried chicken, mashed potatoes, a steaming hot biscuit, and a dish of fried apples. The serious look was back on her face as she handed him the plate of food, but it softened slightly as she popped open a soda. He was sure her changed expression came from his eyes widening and his sheepish grin as she slid the cold bottle of cola across the counter.

Finishing the last bite of fried apples, he sipped the end of the cola. Just as he stood to take the plate inside, a police car pulled up coming to a quick halt a few feet beyond the table. A young police officer jumped out, expressionless as he stood staring at Robert for a moment. The officer took swift strides toward him, stopping just a foot away. "What are you doing in Macon?"

"Just passing through. The waitress was kind enough to give me some food. I'm leaving tonight."

"On the freights?"

"Well, I . . ." Robert looked away, not knowing what to say.

"Come on, boy, get in the car." He drove directly to the jail.
Robert was put in a crowded cell. He'd settled his body
against the wall like a fly, repulsed by how the cell reeked from
body odor and the smell of urine. A pool of urine was sprawled
in front of wooden benches that lined the walls.

After the night in jail, it frightened him to think he could
spend months with the shoddy-looking men sitting around him
in the courtroom. Taking a quick glance at his wrinkled trousers
and threadbare shirt, he brushed away his thick brown hair that
had fallen down over his face, realizing his appearance wasn't
much different. Like him, some had been picked up for
vagrancy.

The sheriff walked to the front of the court room and
addressed the judge. "Your Honor, I'll take responsibility for
him," he said as he glanced over at Robert. The judge shuffled
through the papers in front of him, raised his eyes, and gave him
a slight nod. The sheriff moved toward Robert and sent a clear
message to rise and follow him out of the courtroom.

The dust from the peanut farms hit their faces as soon as
they stepped out the door and started down the cement steps.
The midday heat clamped down as if a wool blanket had been
yanked tightly over their heads, keeping any tease of air from
them. Robert hopped into the back seat of the police car and
quickly tipped his head down to hide his distress about where
the sheriff was taking him, worried it might be another jail
somewhere. He pushed his hands down hard on both his knees
to stop them from shaking.

Once they pulled away from the courthouse, Robert glanced
up to see the sheriff's deep-set hazel eyes peering at him through
the rearview mirror, but he said nothing to him. He drove north
out of town. Signs for peanut farms began to appear.

As he tried to take his mind off the previous night in jail,
Robert glanced out the window to focus on the countryside.

Not a moment later the thought stormed through his mind that the waitress must have let the policeman know he was behind the restaurant. Now he understood the seriousness of her glances, wavering from annoyance to concern for him, her eyes drifting into a dazed thought, holding back a reply for such a long, awkward time.

A comforting breeze swept across Robert's forehead when the sheriff rolled his window down farther, signaling the day was starting to cool off. Dark overcast skies ahead gave off a hint the weather might change soon.

The sheriff began driving west. It wasn't long before he turned on to the main street of a small town that had nothing but a filling station, a diner, and grocery stop. Standing in the open doors of freight trains over the past months, watching towns like this one pass by, Robert always pondered what life was like in what seemed to be the middle of nowhere.

"We're stopping for lunch," the sheriff announced tersely.

Conversations halted at once when they walked through the door of the diner. As they crossed the room toward a table, Robert noticed people gawking at them, probably wondering why he was with the sheriff.

The sheriff nodded to the waitress as she came toward the table. "The usual, Ruby."

"Grilled cheese and baked beans for the both of you, right?"

"You got it."

Robert sat without knowing what to say. The sheriff didn't offer any conversation. He was anxious about where he would end up and wanted to ask about where they were going, but the sheriff's demeanor invited no questions.

"Looks like you're done," the sheriff said abruptly as he rose from the table. "Let's get moving. Take a piss if you need to."

When they pulled away from the restaurant, he noticed a couple of boys about his age walking along the road with rucksacks hanging from their shoulders. Robert began thinking about what might have happened to his neighborhood pal,

Johnny Tominello. Two years older than Robert, they'd been inseparable growing up. The morning Johnny suggested hopping a freight train to see what kind of work was out there, it didn't take much time for Robert to start talking about plans of where they would go. The dire economic downturn in the country hit his widowed mother especially hard, and finding work to help her support his five siblings was important to him.

They'd headed west from Illinois first to check out the coal mines northwest of Denver. When that didn't work out, they traveled in different parts of the country still trying to find work.

But then things fell apart. They had separated a month ago in St. Louis after Johnny got discouraged when four guys on the same day labor job waited for them to collect their wages, followed them out to the road, and rolled them for their money. Johnny headed home to Illinois the next day, urging Robert to come with him. But when it came to hopping on the train, Robert couldn't face going back empty handed. He regretted not staying with Johnny now. It was four months to the day since they had left their hometown of Elmhurst, on February 7, 1933, one week after his fifteenth birthday. Their big plans to find work to help things out at home felt foolish now.

As the sheriff continued to drive west, Robert tried to figure out where he might be taking him. Spending the morning in the courtroom ran through his mind again. So many of the men got sentenced to labor. If he was being taken to another jail, maybe he was being put on a chain gang somewhere. He'd overheard guys talking on the freight train to Georgia about them and mentioning there were chain gangs in all parts of the state. They'd shared stories about the labor the men were forced to do for hours and hours out in the heat, shackled together at the ankle. His hands started to tremble from not knowing what was going to happen to him. *It could be months before I get home now.*

Leaning his head back against the seat, he closed his eyes for a moment to calm himself about what might lie ahead. When he opened them, Robert saw the sheriff's eyes in the rearview mirror looking at him again. Shifting his head quickly toward the window to escape his glare, he noticed the scenery around them was beginning to change from miles and miles of flatland and farmlands with row upon row of planted fields to rolling green hills directly ahead of them. The sheriff pulled in to a gas station. An elderly man sitting in front of the station jumped up, slid the newspaper he was reading onto the chair, and sauntered toward the police car. As he bent his head into the side of the window to greet the sheriff, he glanced back at Robert, showing some surprise as he sized him up.

"Fill it up, Sheriff?"

"You bet, thanks."

The sheriff opened the door to step out, and then turned to Robert. "If you need to use the toilet, you can do it now."

Robert slid out of the car but didn't move until the sheriff signaled for him to go ahead.

"Is that kid a criminal?" the man asked as Robert walked away.

"No, just a boy trying to get home."

Once they headed west again, he could think of nothing but home now. A sadness draped him as he pictured returning with nothing to show for his travels after leaving his mom to worry about him like he did. Trying to get his mind off what his mother would say or do once he got back, his thoughts shifted to his father. He'd been sick for a long time. Robert didn't know what cancer was, but people always whispered when they talked about it, so he figured it was something really bad. Nothing had been the same since his dad died, especially where they lived and how they lived. Sitting by his dad's bedside playing the violin his father had bought for him swept through his mind, but he pushed it away as fast as it appeared. The pleasure of hearing each note as he moved the bow across the violin, and the smile his music always brought to his father's face were memories too painful to let in.

The striking beauty of the sun setting to the west over the foothills caught his attention, bringing his thoughts back to where the sheriff was taking him. As they came over the ridge, the road began to flatten, making the sun seem as if it were dangling in the horizon ahead. Hours had passed since they'd left Macon. Signs for Alabama started to appear.

A feeling of relief rushed over him when the sheriff pulled off the road just before the sign for the state line. He shifted his body around to face Robert. "You're free to go, but you better never come through Georgia again." He held out two dollars. "Here, son, take this. Put it in your sock or a deep pocket. Get yourself home and don't trust anybody on the way there. Do you understand me? Well, do yah?"

Robert's mouth dropped open as he reached for the dollar bills. It had been awhile since he saw that much money all at once, making only enough doing labor along the way to have maybe two meals at most until the next day job came along. Glancing down to hide the emotions welling up from the sheriff's kindness, he could only nod a reply. He opened the car door but paused before stepping out. With a crackly voice he said, "Thank you, sir."

"Well, good luck to you, boy."

Eying a small town just ahead, he started down the road and suddenly stopped, spinning on his heels to look behind him. The sheriff had already turned around, leaving a trail of dust spitting up from the gravel underneath the tires as the car pulled onto the road.

Turning back toward the town, he tried to swallow away the lump in his throat as he wondered what would happen now.

2

"Hey, kid. What are you doing here all by yourself?" Robert focused his eyes on a man who could've been his dad's age. The man wasn't as scroungy looking as the rest of the people in the freight car, definitely not as grimy looking as he was after so many days on the road. The night before he'd ripped his trousers at the knee on a nail when he slipped into a barn to sleep. A code carved on a fence post by others traveling through signaled it was supposed to be a safe place to use as a shelter. He borrowed some of the horse's water from a trough to wash up but knew he probably still smelled like the horses in the barn.

"So, what's your story, kid? I didn't see anyone hop on with you. You could get in lots of trouble traveling alone. You on the run or something?"

Robert couldn't think of what to say. His small frame made him seem even younger than he was, so he figured that's why people had been staring at him on the trip from St. Louis to Georgia and now back.

"I'm not in any trouble. I'm just going home, that's all."

Someone in the car slammed one of the freight doors shut, giving him the opportunity to turn away. The man seemed out of place on the freight train, his light-brown hair trimmed, clothes clean, boots barely scuffed, leaving Robert to wonder if he was with the law or something.

Most of the people on the freights stayed to themselves and didn't talk much except if the guys started playing cards. Then sometimes there was shouting. Two families in the corner of the boxcar had small children, one with a baby. Families tended to look down and not around, as though they were scared or maybe ashamed.

The man's stare felt piercing, so he tried not to focus his eyes directly at him.

"Where you headed?"

"Illinois."

"I'm headed up north, too. By the way, my name is Al. What's your name, son?"

Holding back from answering his question for fear it might lead to him pressing for more information, he leaned forward, wrapped his arms around his knees, and then took the risk.

"Robert."

The man didn't say much after that. Robert glanced out the side of the other freight car door, trying to remember the route he took to Georgia, not sure about all the stops or what route he and Johnny had taken to St. Louis.

The train started slowing, then jerked to a stop. In an instant, the freight car door slammed back open. Someone in the car bellowed "Raid!"

Chaos was immediate as everyone jumped up, grabbing what little belonged to them just as three burly men with rifles walked alongside the tracks shouting at them to get out. Robert snatched his rucksack and moved toward the family across from him to try to help them with their kids just as Al pulled him out the other side of the train. They slipped through rows of freight cars sitting on another track, squatting to look underneath the cars for signs of railroad detectives who might have noticed them.

"Come on, kid, this way."

Robert followed, grateful that he wasn't going to spend another night in jail. That's if they didn't run into any railroad detectives waiting ahead of them. "Bulls," as everyone on the freights called them because they were so mean and rough. Robert used to watch them walking up and down the station platform in Elmhurst, just a block up from his house. The bulls stood with rifles, ready to pounce on anyone hopping on or off the freight trains coming through. He'd seen lots of people get roughed up.

He and Johnny had their first run-in with the bulls on their way to Colorado to find work in the coal mines. Neither of them knew much about hopping freights, so they hitched rides to Nebraska before trying to jump their first freight. Running out of the brush just twenty feet beyond the train station, they were prime targets for the bulls who were on top of them within minutes, pointing rifles down their throats and nudging them harshly with their thick clubs.

"You'd better get out of here if you don't want to end up in jail," a bull yelled. "There are no second chances."

They'd spent the night in a field with some hobos, the first of many who filled them in on the smarts of riding the rails and the codes to look for along the way that made their travel safer.

Robert followed behind Al as the man began to veer away from the box cars. Al took a quick glance back over his shoulder toward Robert and suddenly stopped. Robert looked around to see what was happening. A tall, lanky kid, maybe a few years older than him, stood at the end of the parked boxcars. He remembered him from the freight car because of his carrot-red hair and heavily freckled face. The kid stood with his body sideways from them, leaning away as if trying to figure out whether to run in the other direction. Then he darted forward, catching up to them. It was obvious he'd been following behind, waiting for a chance to talk to them. They stood looking at each other, waiting for someone to say something.

Al broke the silence. "Where you going?"

"I'm headed up to Missouri and maybe west. I heard you talking on the train about going north, too. Thought maybe I could join yah for a while."

The boy had a strong southern drawl, one Robert recognized from spending time in Georgia. Al started to say something but hesitated for a moment.

"Yeah, okay. Come on, let's see where we are."

They walked the last stretch of the freight yard up a narrow gravel street that wound behind a town. Robert noticed a water tower a few blocks up. Tapping Al on the shoulder, he pointed to it.

"Well, I guess we're going to see what Montgomery, Alabama, is like," Al said. "It wasn't exactly my plan, but it is now. I guess it's yours too, isn't it?"

Robert wondered who Al was and where he was going, hoping he would have a chance to ask him soon. The sheriff's words about not trusting anyone flashed into his mind.

It was about midday when they got to the edge of Montgomery. Robert was anxious to find out where to catch the next freight north, not sure whether he was heading straight for Elmhurst or if he'd try to find work somewhere. Still shaken from the night in jail and being hauled off from the courtroom by the sheriff, he knew it could've had a disastrous ending. Even thinking of not heeding the sheriff's words to get himself home was dumb. But there wasn't any work for a fifteen-year-old in Elmhurst. He was beginning to wonder if there was work anywhere paying any real wages.

Thousands of kids riding the trains were trying to get work too, and not finding it either. Only the guys eighteen or older were taken seriously when they asked about work. They were the ones to get the jobs that weren't just a day's labor and paying only enough for a meal or two. So far, he hadn't come across anything that wasn't chores on a ranch or farm, lasting a half-day or a day at most. But at least it meant food to eat. After traveling on one meal a day a couple times, he'd learned not to pass up a chance to work even if it was just for meals.

Coming to the edge of town, he was surprised at how large Montgomery appeared, sprawling for blocks in all directions. As they continued toward the center of town, Robert began thinking about Johnny again, wondering if he was sorry he went home now. After being told to come back when "they had a few years on them" at the coal mines northwest of Denver, they'd headed east again to see about work they heard of in Missouri. When the work didn't pan out, Johnny said he was going home and got irritated with him when he said he wasn't going too. Johnny called him crazy for thinking about traveling alone. Maybe it was a stupid thing to do, but at least he stuck it out to see if something better was out there. No, he wasn't ready to give up and go home with nothing, to be a burden to his mom with no way to make things easier for her.

Al stopped when he found the main street of Montgomery and stood looking from one end of town to the other.

"Well, boys, why don't we meet up later. I want to check into a few things while I'm here."

Robert stared at him, thinking he wanted to get going, not waste the day sitting around.

"I want to head north yet today," Robert said, turning his head toward the other boy. "How about you? What's your name, anyway?"

"It's Tucker. Yeah, going north is okay with me. Anywhere is okay with me."

Silence stood between the three of them until Al broke it. "Well, I want to move on north today too, but do you think it would be smart for you to hop on a train in daylight after that raid? I think the railroad bulls will be hanging around for a while. I have business in Little Rock, Arkansas, and I have something that might interest the two of you. That's if you want a chance to earn some money. Let's talk about it later." Al glanced at his watch. "How about meeting here at five o'clock?"

Robert briefly turned toward Tucker and back to Al. "Okay, sure."

Al grinned slightly as he headed across the street. They stood watching him for a while as he walked away.

"Who is he?" Tucker said.

"I don't know. I've been wondering about that too. Seems a decent enough guy though. Let's go find something to eat and then check out the train schedule."

3

Robert's mother, Lucille, found herself caught up in wondering where her son might be, and if he was safe. The mundane process of doing laundry always provided the opportunity to stray from the moment to the worries on her mind. Her eyes, quick to look up from the porch and focus on the children playing kickball in the front yard, were snapped back into the present by a loud ruckus.

It was a repetitive process, pulling out clothes from a washtub of sudsy water one by one to rub against a washboard, followed by the automated motion of running each piece through the hand wringer where they dropped into the tub of rinse water. Once the tub was full, the clothes were worked through the wringer one last time to squeeze out excess water, and then dropped into the laundry basket. She spent hours keeping up with laundry for five kids but as time consuming as it was, she wished it were for six, not five. Robert had been gone for four months, and every time her mind strayed it was about why he left, if he was safe, or what she most dreaded—was he alive?

She was abruptly brought back from thinking about Robert again when a rubber ball hit the top step of the porch, bounced up, and found its way into the middle of the rinse water. Lucille lifted her eyes to see Del, her ten-year-old, son staring down at the ball floating.

"Sorry, Mom," Del said, holding back a grin.

Trying to look serious and not smile herself, she lifted her chin to see Del's curly brown hair bending down over the tub and then watched as he sheepishly pulled the ball from the water.

"You kids need to be more careful. The ball could have broken the front porch window," she said in her strong German accent.

"I know Ma," he said, nodding as he slid his canvas shoes off the porch step and turned to join the other kids.

Within a few minutes, her mind strayed again to Robert, feeling she was at fault somehow for his leaving. He and his sister, Kathleen, had to grow up fast after their father died. Both always helping with the kids, doing chores without being asked.

When they'd moved to the small, two-bedroom home the past year just before winter came, Robert started gathering scraps of coal from around the tracks for their coal stove. It had to be demeaning for him to pick up scraps. Coal companies began white-washing the top layers of the coal with lime and water to keep people from taking it when the freights made stops passing through. Robert got upset with her when she'd told him not to do it anymore. "Everybody does it," he told her.

"Well, we're not everybody, and I won't have one of my boys thinking it's okay."

She refused to be like the other mothers and send her children to follow coal deliveries to pick up stray chunks from the road.

Glancing up from the laundry for a moment, she watched the yard full of kids playing and smiled. All these neighborhood kids lived in big houses up the street, and yet somehow, they all gathered in her tiny yard day after day. Meanwhile, the yard became more dirt than grass as each week of summer went by. Like today, the constant loud laughter from the boys always helped bring her back from thinking about Robert or her life before her husband's death.

Life had changed drastically after Nicolas died. Even with the economy taking a huge spiral downward during the late 1920s, life had been manageable. Nicolas's commercial painting business was sought after because people in Elmhurst trusted his work. The business was well established. Many of the customers were Italian and German immigrants, supplying a steady stream of work even through the extreme economic ups and downs.

Their previous home on Beech Street was gloriously finished in the latest baroque wallpapers, accented with the newest shades of paint. Five-inch wide, hand-carved oak wood trim across the top and bottom of every wall, seemed to sweep itself up along the banisters and walls to the second floor.

There were no banisters, no walls to paint, no wallpaper, in their small wooden home finished inside with the same bleak, plank wood that framed the outside.

"Ma, could we please have some apples with cinnamon and sugar?"

She looked up to see her thirteen-year-old son, Marty, with an angelic expression pasted on his face. Taking a moment, she tilted her head, shifted her eyes sideways and scrunched her lips together as if thinking about it.

"Oh, please Ma, can we?" Marty said. His brown eyes were imploring her.

Every few days the kids sent someone different to ask the same question. They hadn't figured out they always got apples and cinnamon because it gave her so much pleasure to see them delight in the one thing that was abundant in their lives. Thank

God for the apple trees next door and the neighbor who gets just as much joy from the children eating them.

"Hmm, okay, Marty. You kids can have apples with a little cinnamon, but you don't need the sugar. Ask Kathleen to come help cut them up. You'll have to be in charge outside for a bit."

Running a few more shirts and cotton underwear through the wringer to finish up for the time being, she walked to the front door, catching a glimpse of herself in the window. Pieces of her light brown hair had dropped down on the right side from her updo onto her angular face. The wispy look of her fallen hair softened her strong German features, larger and bolder than most of the American women she knew. She was self-conscious of her big bones, broad cheekbones and high forehead. A little smile caught her lips when she remembered how Nicolas found her beautiful just the way she was, always reassuring her that her German features were distinct, and reminding her she should be proud of them.

Slipping through the door, she walked over to the corner of the main room that made up the kitchen area, took one of the faded aprons off the hook, and tied it over her housedress. Kathleen came in looking sullen. She watched her daughter as she put on an apron, and pulled aside one of the flower-print cotton curtains hanging underneath the counter to get a large white metal bowl for the apples.

Next to Robert, Kathleen resembled Nicolas the most. Her deep brownish-black wavy hair and dark brown eyes that complimented her olive skin, were just like her father's face.

"You don't look so happy," Lucille said.

"No," Kathleen replied.

"Well, what's the trouble?"

"I don't want to talk about it, Ma."

"Well, it seems like you should."

Noticing Kathleen was about to cry, she decided not to say anymore, waiting, hoping her daughter would share what had happened on her own. Standing silent next to her, Lucille quartered the apples and handed them to Kathleen to slice, listening for something more than the edge of knives hitting against the cutting boards.

"Well, Margaret just told me she made friends with the girl that lives in our old house on Beech Street. She has Emma's and my bedroom. Margaret was in it today and said it has new wall paper and curtains."

"Oh." Lucille didn't know what else to say. Her lips tightened. How devastating it must have been for her to hear about this development. Nearing seventeen, Kathleen was experiencing growing pains and was old enough to remember life the way it was, longing for it, just as she did. Looking over to see a tear run down her daughter's face, she waited a few minutes, giving her time. She wanted to give herself time too. Covering her face for a moment, she was suddenly saddened by the discussion of the family in their house on Beech Street.

They continued slicing apples on the wood block slabs, tossing them in the bowl between them in silence, the sounds of cutting apples growing louder with each slice.

"I heard Johnny Tominello has decided to stay here and live with his dad," Lucille said. "Did you hear?"

Kathleen kept her head down but whispered, "Yes."

"I'm sure it was hard for Johnny to get back home to find out his mother was taking his sisters to California to live with her family."

Kathleen nodded. Silence stood between them again.

"Kathleen, sweetheart, I know how difficult it's been for you since your dad died, having to move out of our house into such a small home."

Lucille stepped away to pull down the cinnamon from the shelf behind them, giving herself a moment to think about her next words. "There was a time when people were telling me that it would be better for you kids if you went to live with other families for a while. I didn't want that to happen because then you might not know each other so well. It's got to hurt to hear about someone else in your beautiful bedroom. That makes having to share a room and a bed with me and your sister even harder."

Lucille paused to take a deep breath as her own hurt of having to let go of her home rose up. "We haven't been able to keep much of what we had when your dad was here, but we've been able to keep us as a family together. It's still hard to give all that up though, isn't it?"

They finished preparing the apples in silence. Lucille worried Kathleen might be thinking of the piano she had to leave behind. With not enough room in their small home for all of them to sleep comfortably, bringing the piano wasn't possible. It was sold with their other cherished pieces of furniture. They all missed the music that had been so much of their life.

A few more tears dropped off Kathleen's cheek onto the apple slices. Lucille put her hand on her daughter's shoulder, rubbing it gently, wishing she could rub away the pain. Kathleen put down the knife, and tucked her hair behind her ears as she turned toward her mother. Standing silent, as if she were going to speak, Kathleen suddenly reached out, wrapping her arms around her mother's shoulders. She let her soft sobs be heard as her tears began to flow freely.

The front screen door opened and then shut. They heard Emma's rushed voice. "Hey Mom, Marty wanted me to ask if it's time for Oliver's nap yet? He's rubbing his eyes and keeps pushing me away when I try to hold him. And why are you hugging? Did something happen?"

Lucille quickly came over to Emma, her youngest daughter. She placed her arms around Emma and kissed the top of her head.

"Because it's fun to hug, isn't it? Let's get this little guy down for his nap. I'll lay with both of you for a few moments until he's settled. Then you can go back outside. Okay?"

Emma slipped her arms around her mother's waist, hugging her back. Oliver crawled on top of the bed and snuggled his nose in the pillow, drifting into sleep within minutes. It didn't take long before Lucille's thoughts wandered to Robert again. Where could he be, and was he safe?

4

As the boys headed into downtown Montgomery, Robert wondered if there might be less of a chance of being picked up again traveling with Tucker. But he couldn't shake off the feeling that he might somehow be trouble.

After pooling change to buy bread and cheese for sandwiches, they settled under a huge tree in a heavily shaded park spanning a city block.

"Why are you traveling north and leaving Georgia?" Robert asked. "You're from Georgia, aren't you?"

"Yeah, lived there my whole life. I wasn't planning on going anywhere, but my dad said it was time for me to get out and take care of myself. Said he's got five growing kids to feed and I was taking up a bed a couple of my brothers needed."

"Geez," was all Robert could mutter back.

"I told my dad I wanted to finish high school, but he said times were too tough, way too tough for me to be thinking of staying in school another year. School's a luxury for rich kids, he told me. Said he heard some schools for older grades might close anyway come fall because of the hard times the country is going through."

Tucker finished making a sandwich, and then slid the bread and cheese over to Robert.

"So how did you end up on the train out of Georgia?" Robert asked. "Did you look for work there before you left?"

"My dad handed me five bucks and said it should hold me until I found work. Told me he heard there was work harvesting in Missouri, so maybe I could check it out. Said he might have to try it himself if he didn't find work in Georgia soon, but he doesn't want to leave my ma alone with all the kids unless he has to. Says it's only the men with families getting what jobs there are in Georgia, and he can't even get one of them." Tucker lifted his sandwich to his mouth as if he were done talking but lowered it to his lap. "I sat looking at my dad, hoping he was kiddin' about me leaving but he told me I could stay until the end of the week to think about where I was going. That was the beginning of last week."

Tucker started eating, sitting quiet for several minutes before turning back to Robert. "So, that's my story. What about you? You don't have no southern accent. Where you from and why are you traveling alone? Did your dad tell you to leave, too? Seems to be what's happening, I guess."

Surprised by his frank questions, Robert took a minute to think of what to say. "I'm from Illinois. Been traveling with my buddy but he decided to go back. I didn't want to give up on finding work yet."

"So, you had any luck finding work?"

"Just jobs paying enough for food to keep me going to the next place. Sometimes not even that."

"That's discouraging to hear. You gonna keep trying?"

"Guess I'll still look for work as I head back north to Illinois."

"You ever been in one of them hobo camps?" Tucker asked. "I used to walk by the one at the edge of town back home in Georgia."

"Walked through some, but never stayed in one. I heard you could get hurt going to those places. People say most of them staying there are trying to find work just like us, though. Then again, I heard there can be real rough people in there too. Maybe even wanted by the law."

"You're kinda young, aren't you?" Tucker said. "What, you fourteen or something?"

"I'm going to be seventeen."

Tucker laughed. "When is that?"

Robert shot an irritated look at Tucker but couldn't help but grin. "In less than four months."

Tucker rolled his eyes. Robert didn't want to talk anymore and shoved the rest of the sandwich into his mouth. Scooting back about four feet to lean up against the tree, he wanted to dodge the questions Tucker might ask next. He was sure they'd be questions he tried to avoid answering in his own mind when they came up.

"You think you're gonna find any real work? Why are you still traveling around?" Tucker asked.

Shrugging his shoulders, Robert didn't answer. He felt torn after leaving home, but now his mind kept pulling him in opposite directions. When he took off with Johnny, they talked about getting money to help out their families. It felt kind of heroic then. Now he felt selfish about not going home but didn't know why.

Two girls and a boy walking across the park towards them caught his attention. They were laughing, shoving each other back and forth playfully, their laughter getting louder as they got closer. The boy must have snatched something that belonged to one of the girls because they started chasing him, reaching for it, giggling, and swatting at him. One of them lurched forward trying to grab what was in his hand, landing on the grass when he took a huge leap backward. The boy reached down to pull her up as he dangled something above her head. The girls began running in circles around him, trying to grab hold of what he had.

Robert caught himself smiling as he watched, remembering times he had spent playing just like them. It seemed a long time ago now.

Leaning his head back against the tree trunk, he was overwhelmed at how fast a sense of melancholy crept through him. Watching the kids running around reminded him of his brothers and sisters, not just before he left home but earlier times when his dad was still alive. Everything was right then. The house on Beech Street had enough bedrooms for everyone to sleep in a bed even if they had to share one. They weren't crowded in on top of each other like his two sisters were now, having to share a bed with his ma. He and his three brothers slept wedged together in small beds, and in the winter on homemade bedrolls, their bodies huddled around the coal stove in the main room to stay warm.

Before his dad died there was always enough food and enough clothes to keep warm. His mind wandered back to the annual shopping day for school clothes. It was his dad who took him because he was the oldest and the only boy in his family in school. A tradition on the shopping trip was being fitted for a new suit for church at Hensley's Haberdashery downtown. It was always one of the best days of the year, even better than his birthday because it was just him and his dad. They always went for ice cream floats at the five-and-dime store afterward.

The last shopping trip with his dad was on his tenth birthday. His dad was different when they went for their ice cream floats, serious, not playful like he usually was on his days off. Once the ice cream floats were set in front of them, his dad usually started telling him about when his father took him to be measured for a new suit in Italy, followed by more stories about when he was a boy, vividly describing the beautiful views from the mountain town of Benestare, over looking the Ionian Sea. Benestarrre he used to say, rolling the "r" an extra long time.

"Benestare is wild beauty, Robert, surrounded by rolling foothills and emerald mountains on three sides. I want you to try to imagine it in your mind. It's like being half way to heaven because you're suspended between the beauty of the lush landscapes below and the shimmering sea. The mountains plunge into miles of white sandy beaches, sweeping into turquoise blue water. And looming above, are tumbling clouds close enough to catch on to."

But he didn't tell him stories about Benestare that day. That day he sat at the soda fountain looking dazed and lost in thought, with a cloudy expression. He would always remember the look on his dad's face at that moment, leaving him with an overwhelming feeling of sadness that he didn't understand. It was much later when his dad was bedridden that he learned his father was sick with cancer.

A few months later his dad started going on trips for weeks at a time, one right after the other. When Robert asked about the trips, he'd told him they were for his business. One night he started down the stairs to the kitchen, stopping when he heard his parents talking about another trip the next week to see a doctor in Philadelphia. This doctor might have a cure for his cancer, he overheard his dad say.

By the end of the year, his dad was too tired and weak to work much. By spring, he was so tired he had to stay in bed most of the day. Three months later he died, two years after little Oliver was born.

Stretching out in the shade of the tree, Robert wanted to nap before Tucker started asking him more questions. Needing to get his mind off of his dad, he closed his eyes.

Robert woke out of a deep sleep when he felt something nudging at the side of his face. Eyes popping open, he glanced up just as a large, long-haired white dog started to nuzzle his chin. He jumped up and back a few feet all at once, hitting the tree trunk hard, ending up sprawled on the ground. Tucker broke into a huge belly laugh.

"He's just playing, that's all. He came up to me a while ago. Must of got tired of waitin' for you to wake up."

With his heart pounding, Robert turned toward Tucker. "You enjoyed that, didn't you?"

"Yeah, kinda did," Tucker said, still laughing. "First time I seen you with a smile on your face since I noticed you on the train, but now that I'm thinking about it, it's about the first time something's made me laugh since way before leaving home. It feels good. When was the last time you laughed?"

Tucker turned toward the dog as if knowing he wouldn't get an answer. "He's a spunky dog though. I've been throwing him this stick and he's been fetching it. Pretty smart dog. I just asked a guy the time. It's going on two o'clock. We're supposed to meet Al at five, aren't we? Do you want to hang out here until then?"

Robert reached down to pick up his rucksack and threw on his cap. "Let's go check the train schedule. Then we'll know when to head up the tracks so we can catch out on the evening train, if there is one."

"So we can catch out?" Tucker had a puzzled look on his face. "What's that, some railroad talk or something?"

"Yeah, it is. Was that the first train you hopped?"

Tucker shook his head, a huge grin showing his pride. "Yep, I just grabbed right on and climbed into a boxcar passing by. Thought it would be harder than it was, but the people inside scared me more than the leap on. I mean being so grungy and all, and not speaking much either."

"We need to do some talking since you're new to the rails. It might keep you alive when we split up."

Grinning to himself, it made Robert feel older to be in the position of looking out for someone else after learning the ins and outs of riding the rails. After their first attempt at catching out, he and Johnny started getting the scoop on the dangers of riding the rails from hoboes who'd been traveling the rails for years. Some of the hoboes, as creepy as they looked sometimes, watched out for young kids on the road. Just before crossing the street to the train station, Robert signaled Tucker to stop. "I don't see any bulls hanging around outside, do you? Maybe they're getting lunch, so let's take a quick look at the train schedule."

"No bulls?" Tucker turned toward Robert, laughing. "Bulls? Al said something about railroad bulls. Is that who you mean?"

"Yeah, bulls. No one told you about them? Well, you got lucky following Al and me off the side of the train, or you would have come face up with them. I'll tell you more about them after we look at the schedule."

Two men came out of the station carrying rifles, took a quick look around, and began walking in opposite directions. Bolting toward the steps of the station, Robert waved his arm for Tucker to follow, then scanned the schedule.

"I guess we'll be hanging around for a while yet. The next freight train out and the last one leaving today isn't until six-thirty. That's okay though, because it won't be dark by then. It's safer to catch on before dark. Only thing is, it's headed southwest for Jackson, Mississippi, but it looks like there's a good route north from there to Arkansas."

Stepping in to take a closer look at the schedule, Tucker started rubbing his chin. "We're gonna go south to go north?"

"It's the long way around but it'll get us out of town tonight. There's just too many mean-looking bulls around here. Best thing about the ride at six-thirty, Tucker, is it's a Red Ball. It won't stop until it gets to Jackson, so it cuts our chances of getting caught in another raid. I'd rather try getting some sleep on the train than out in a prairie around here. I don't have a good feeling about these bulls or this place after almost getting caught in a raid this morning. How about you? What are you going to do?"

"If you're going tonight, I'm going."

Two rough-looking men inside the train station turned to look at them as they walked past the station windows.

"Let's go," Robert said, increasing his stride to almost a run.

At the end of the block, Robert shifted his body around to look behind him, easing his pace to a walk when he saw that the men hadn't come outside.

"By the clock at the station, we've got almost three hours before we meet up with Al, if he shows up," Robert said. "I saw a stream running behind town as we came in. Let's head over to it. Might be a good time to tell you about the bulls."

5

The stream was running high, with water gushing against the bank on the other side, while shooting over exposed roots of giant cottonwoods. The late afternoon sun enveloped the water and trees with a mystifying glow, triggering Robert to take deep breaths in and out, allowing his shoulders to relax for the first time in days. Moments like this seemed the only good part of the long waits for the next train to leave. Spotting a group of teens standing by the edge of the water, he began walking in the opposite direction farther down stream.

"Hey, where are you going? Let's see who those kids are. They look like they might be waiting for the train, too."

Robert glanced over his shoulder but kept walking. "Let's not. It's better to stay away from other people traveling."

"Well, ain't you the snob. I'm going to see who they are."

Robert watched as Tucker moved toward them, still not sure if he should travel with him. After spending a night in jail, he wanted to stay away from anything or anyone that might get him into more trouble.

Getting a good distance away, Robert sat at a slow-moving edge of the stream where the water was calm, spinning rocks across the water. He was trying to get lost in the rhythm of the rocks skipping over the top to avoid troubling thoughts about what was coming next with Tucker, Al, or the decisions he had ahead of him.

As the sun's radiance began to seep away, a slight coolness signaled the end of the day. Robert pulled out of his trance when he noticed shadows looming across the water in front of him. He turned to see Tucker. The other four kids stood just behind him. Standing up to get a better look, he noticed in a glance that two were girls disguised in boy's clothing. He wondered if Tucker had figured it out yet.

"Hey Robert, they wanted to meet you. This is Jake, Orson, Ollie, and Danny."

"Where you from?" Robert asked.

"My brother Orson and me are from Louisiana," Jake said. "Ollie and Danny, they're from Texas. Tucker says you're from Illinois."

Robert replied with a nod. "Good to meet you guys." He fixed his eyes on the two girls. When his eyes caught theirs, they were quick to look away.

"They're all going into town to see if one of the cafes will give them some food," Tucker said. "I'm thinking about going with them to see how they go about it. Why don't you come with us? It's getting close to that time."

"No, you go. I'll catch you later. I'll meet Al and then let you know what we're doing."

"I guess I forgot about Al. Maybe I should stay here with you so we can both meet up with him."

"No, go ahead," Robert said, hoping he could get away from him for a while longer, or better yet, lose him altogether. Tucker was starting to worry him. He had money, so why hang with these kids when he'd just warned him to stay away from strangers.

"I'll be there at five though," Tucker said. "You can be sure of that."

Settling back down on the bank, Robert noticed their shadows still reflecting off the water. They disappeared one by one, except for one tall shadow. After a moment, he saw Tucker's semblance back away and retreat.

Relieved, Robert picked up a few more rocks and spun them across the water. He sat a while longer to leave them time to get some distance away before starting back to where he was supposed to meet Al. His curiosity was up about the work he'd mentioned. Focusing on the soothing sounds of the stream, he gave himself a few more minutes before leaving.

Approaching the spot where they parted, Robert looked around for Al; not seeing him, he sat down against a boulder just off the gravel path to wait, wondering if Al would show up.

"Hey kid, sorry I'm a little late but I wasn't sure you would wait anyway," Al said, coming up on him by surprise. "Where's the other boy? What was it, Tucker?"

"Yeah, Tucker. He's supposed to be coming. I checked the train schedule. The first evening train is at six thirty. It's a Red Ball. We'll have to go south to catch a train north."

"I know, I checked it too. How long do you want to wait for Tucker?"

"He hooked up with kids that were going to beg supper. Said he'd be here though."

Al sat down next to him. "You mentioned you were heading home. I hope that's true. Nothing good comes of young kids riding the rails. Too much bad stuff to run into, especially traveling alone. Boys your age are getting hurt on the rails everyday. Many are losing their lives trying to hop on trains. Numbers keep piling higher."

Robert just stared back at him not knowing what to think, still wondering about his appearance that seemed out of place on the train. Betrayal began to speed through his mind, not sure if he should take off. Curious, he decided to wait a bit longer. After a moment, he worked up his nerve to speak.

"You said something about some work we might be interested in. That's why I stayed to wait for you. If there is none, I'll go look for Tucker."

Feeling alarmed by the rising rush of disappointment crawling across his chest, Robert sat and zigzagged a stick across the gravel in front of him. Keeping his eyes on the ground, he waited for an answer.

"Look, Robert, I wasn't playing with you. I heard yesterday before I boarded the train that there's work in Little Rock, Arkansas, helping with the harvest, but you probably know they'll take the men first and tell you to get lost. There's nothing much out here for a kid your age. You said you were going home, so stick with that plan."

Tilting his head forward as he pressed his lips tight, Robert let his disappointment show. "Who are you, anyway? You don't look like someone that's going to do harvest work in Little Rock. Why did you start talking to me, anyway? Why did you pull me off that train, and have me wait here for you?"

"Lots of questions, huh? No, I'm not going to the harvest, and I pulled you off the train so you wouldn't get robbed or beat up by the railroad detectives. Can't believe you haven't run into them before. They're everywhere. You must have, right?"

Looking away, Robert offered nothing.

"Not talking, huh?"

Determined to get an answer, Robert fixed his eyes on Al's. "Well, who are you?"

Al hesitated for a moment as he let out a sigh. "I work with a government program President Roosevelt just started to put youth to work. My job right now is to promote the program so local agencies will send boys to sign up. I hop trains sometimes as I travel to get the pulse of how many youth are just joy riding and how many might be eligible for the program."

Shifting sideways to face Al, Robert shot him a grin. "So how do I get signed up?"

"Sorry, Robert, you're too young for the program. I just finished reading the Montgomery Advertiser and got the update on kids killed on these rails, many of them your age. I regret mentioning the work. Wish I could help you, but your best bet is to go home."

Robert watched as Al got up abruptly and walked toward town, and then suddenly stopped a bit up the road. He began walking back toward him.

"Why don't we get a quick supper on the way through town? It'll be my treat."

He extended his hand to pull Robert up.

Leaping up by himself, he gave Al a nod of thanks. "Appreciate the offer. Will you tell me more about the work in Arkansas and the work program for youth? I know a little about the program because I've been reading the Hoover blankets while traveling, when I could find a newspaper in one piece, that is."

"That's just great, kid, reading the Hoover blankets." Al let out a laugh. "I wonder if Herbert Hoover is laughing at the slam to his name. I'll have to say the name fits after seeing people wrapped up in newspapers on the trains, trying to keep warm. Hoover is the man of too little too late, they say. So, did they keep you warm?"

Robert glanced up with a smug grin. "Well, warm no, but they might of kept me from shivering some nights."

"As to telling you more about the harvest work, I just told you to go home. Nothing good is going to come of a kid your age on the road. You've had to see some rough goings on by now, haven't you?"

Al stopped, turning directly toward Robert. "Still nothing to share, huh?"

"No, nothing that makes a difference. Here comes Tucker, looks like."

They both raised their hands to their foreheads to block the sun to the west. Tucker began running toward them.

"Boy, am I glad to see you two. Was afraid I missed my chance to hook up with you."

Tucker bent over and gasped to catch his breath from the run. "Is it time to hike down the tracks to catch the train?" he asked, taking a quick look at Robert. "Oh, catch out I mean."

"No, we've got time. We're getting some supper. Did you get lucky?"

"Yeah, the waitress gave us some tomato soup and old bread to dip in it. She was real nasty to us though, looking at us as if we were dogs, calling us bums. Wasn't what I thought it would be first time askin' and all."

"How long have those kids been on the road?" Robert asked.

"Just a few weeks. They're on their way up north to see the World's Fair in Chicago. After that, they're going on to see Colorado and California. Told me it was their chance to see the world instead of hanging around doing nothing in their hometowns. They teamed up last week at a train stop."

"You know those two short ones are girls, don't you?" Robert asked.

Eyes wide, Tucker rubbed his chin as if puzzled. "No, are you kiddin' me? You are, aren't you?"

Tucker glanced at Al. Catching his look, Al tipped his head and shrugged his shoulders.

"Why would I kid about it?" Robert said. "Girls disguise themselves as boys on the trains so they don't stand out. To be safer, I guess. I got fooled, too, the first couple of times."

"Geez, I would never of guessed, but I'll know to look a little closer next time. Just thought their voices hadn't dropped yet. But now that I think about it, they didn't say hardly nothing." Tucker smiled, "Girls, that's something. Say, can I tag along to dinner so I can head out of town with you?"

"Sure," Al said. "You can have something else to eat if soup didn't fill you up. It'll probably be a while before you eat again."

They headed west after dinner, taking the backstreets. Working their way behind the train station, they squatted down in heavy brush about forty feet from the tracks. Dusk was just moving in when the first blast of the train whistle blew, signaling the train had left the station.

Everyone in the brush stood up, moving toward the tracks. Al was just in front of them. Robert walked along side Tucker. "Hey, the train will be approaching in minutes. Don't wait too long to pick a car so you don't miss your chance to load. You want to grab onto the first boxcar that you can before the train gets going too fast."

"Yeah, I watched a bunch of people before I tried it my first time."

"We didn't get a chance to talk, so listen. You don't want to end up trying to load at the back of the train. That's dangerous. So keep up. Got it?"

"Yeah, I got it."

Al turned around. "What, you just started riding the trains? How many times have you loaded?"

"Once."

Al shot him a look of concern.

The train exploded into sight. Al ran out from cover first. Robert was right behind him. Lining up, they gauged their distance apart as they waited for an open boxcar.

As they moved forward, several men ran out of the brush in front of them, cutting them out of the chance to hop on the car directly in front of them. Forced to wait for the next car, they kept moving along side of the tracks.

The speed of the train was picking up. If another open car didn't come along quick, they would have to catch on even farther back or hop the ladder at the back of a car, then climb on top of the train.

They kept their momentum until another boxcar came along side of them. Al latched onto the opening first and swung himself in, swiftly looking behind him. Robert, next in line, was running alongside the car, trying to grip the floor. Al grasped Robert's left hand as he pushed his weight up with his right hand, then took hold of his trousers to slide him into the car.

Rolling up onto his feet, Robert looked down at Tucker just as he reached the midpoint of the opening. Al reached for Tucker's hand then gripped his elbow and pulled him up just as he pushed his belly onto the floor. Robert took hold of Tucker's right leg, flicking him into the car. Once Tucker was in, they leaned out all at once to see if anyone needed help. No one else was running along side the car.

Tucker poked Robert's arm, pointing to the four kids he was with earlier trying to catch the boxcar behind them. All four were reaching for the floor of the car to grab onto it, but the two girls in front were losing their momentum, while their companions were still behind them. The opening started to pass by, along with their opportunity to board. Pushing to increase their pace, they closed back in on the opening. The two girls in front grabbed onto the floor of the car, but too far back, and blocked the way for the two boys to grip the opening in time. Several hands reached down hoisting the two girls inside. Two men came back to the opening to help the two boys still running along side the train, but they slipped back beyond the opening, making it impossible to grasp their hands and pull them in.

"Looks like the two girls got inside," Robert shouted. "The two guys are too far back to board. I hope they don't try to catch onto the ladders. The train is going too fast now."

They watched as one boy latched onto the ladder at the back of the car and ran part way up, then reached down to clutch the other kid's wrist. Once he locked onto him, he moved up the ladder, pulling his friend behind him, allowing his feet to grip the lower step.

"Hey, they made it onto the ladder," Tucker yelled.

Just as the boys got settled, the train jerked sharp to the right. Both boys lost their footing, leaving them dangling, and desperately trying to get their feet on the ladder again. The boy at the top got one foot grounded just as the train shook hard to the left. Then as speed picked up, the train broke again to the right. Both bodies were flung loose of the ladder, dropping directly beneath the train.

"Did you see what happened?" Tucker yelled. The scream from the girls as they watched the boys fall was so loud its shrill pitch carried back to their car.

Arms reached out, trying to pull the girls in, away from the opening, but they were fighting with all their strength, screaming to get loose, trying to lean back out. Their bodies were yanked back into the car. The door slammed shut.

Al pulled Robert inside, nodding to him to get Tucker. He took hold of Tucker's arm, and tried to pull him in. Tucker tugged away, keeping his head leaning out, finally surrendering to his grip.

Robert dropped down against the back wall and slid his hands over his head, glancing back up for a moment to make sure Tucker wasn't leaning out again. He watched him pace in circles with his arms wrapped around his head.

"I should jump off," Tucker yelled. "See if I can help. Aren't we going to do something?"

Al seized Tucker's arm, and nudged him to the back wall of the car. "Sit. The car's moving too fast now to make a safe exit. That's why the people behind us pulled those girls inside so fast. There's nothing you can do for them. They fell directly under the train. There were a number of people left standing along side the tracks who were too late to load. They'll tell someone at the railroad station."

"Tell them what? Have them look for what's left of them?" Tucker ripped away from Al's grip, walked toward an empty corner of the train, and continued circling with his hands over his head.

Robert leaned forward and buried his head in between his knees to hide, trying to get the vision of the two boys dropping below the train out of his mind. The sheriff's face forced its way into his thoughts. He could hear his words again, "Go home, don't trust anyone." Now he wished he hadn't talked to anyone. Not to Al, not to Tucker, not even giving the "good to meet you" to the two boys who fell beneath the train. The pain wouldn't feel so strong if he'd listened about staying to himself. He shifted his eyes to Tucker, who was still circling like a mad dog trying to shake what he saw.

Over the months he and Johnny heard stories from men who had been riding the rails for a while about guys being flicked off the trains. They warned them about just such an accident happening when you grab a ladder at the back of the train after missing the opportunity to make it into a boxcar. More than a few times in their travels they heard "Better to miss that train than miss the rest of your life."

"Tucker, there's nothing you can do," Al said. "Sit down, try to steady yourself."

Robert heard Tucker's feet coming toward him and felt his shoulder brush against his as he dropped down beside him. His muffled sobs silenced the presence of other passengers.

To fend off breaking down himself, Robert tried to shake off what he saw until he could deal with it, but visions of the two bodies kept rocketing through his head like a shotgun on automatic. The kids' parents probably wouldn't even know they died. None of the fellas riding the rails carried identification with them so their parents couldn't be contacted by police if they were ever picked up by the bulls. From what he knew talking to Tucker, most parents might not really care if their child was in jail, because they probably figured they'd have a bed and some food for a while. It was probably better than what they could do for them, just like Tucker's parents, but these kids weren't thrown out. They were joy riding, seeing the world, going to the World's Fair in Chicago.

Before he and Johnny left home, they snuck inside the fences plenty of times before the World's Fair opened trying to find labor jobs. After it opened, they tried to find someone who would take them on to pick up garbage, pass out flyers, and clean up animal dung even. If there were jobs at the fair, he'd still be in Illinois.

Every kid's story who tried sneaking into the fair was the same. They were thrown out of the front gates time after time. Even the menial jobs went to men out of work with families. Can't tell anyone that though. So many kids on the trains they met were headed to the World's Fair to find work. Johnny and he tried to share their experience plenty of times about what they knew happens to those who manage to sneak in. No one listened to them though, but he and Johnny didn't listen to anyone about it either.

It was twilight when Robert woke from the few minutes of light sleep he got during the night. The train would be stopping at Jackson, Mississippi, soon. Tucker was still lying right next to him. Al was at the other end of the wall. Robert got up, trying not to disturb Tucker. He wanted to have a chance to talk to Al about the work he mentioned. Al rolled his eyes as Robert slipped down beside him.

"Am I going to be able to get rid of you?" Al said, grinning at him.

"Not until you tell me about the work you mentioned."

"What you saw last night wasn't a wake-up call? You think those boys parents are ever going to know what happened to them? They probably had no identification like most of the kids riding the rails. You have a mother and dad wondering if you're safe, or dead. A young fellow your age trying to find work over men is like a pup trying to swim across a river of alligators. What's it going to take for you to wise up?"

"I'm just wanting to know if I can pick up some work if there is some. I'm still heading north to home. Watching what happened to them last night, helpless to do anything, was a wake-up call. It's just, well, it'd mean a lot to take some money home when I face my mom."

Al shook his head, then checked his watch. "The train stops in Jackson in thirty minutes. It'd be better if we talk about it when we get off." Al tipped his head toward the mass of eyes peering at them through the twilight. Robert followed his gaze, nodding okay as he turned back to Al.

6

The loud shudder of the boxcar door sliding open brought Tucker to his feet, visibly shaken by the noise. Robert raised his hand to get his attention, realizing Tucker was trying to get his bearings after being blasted out of sleep. Sighing once he got sight of Robert, he slid down against the wall again. Burying his head in his knees, he began a slight rock back and forth, seemingly recalling the accident of the night before.

Watching him, Robert's mind raced back to the two boys dropping beneath the train. Snapping his eyes shut, he desperately tried to fix his mind onto something pleasant to remember so what happened the night before wouldn't get stuck in his head like a scratched Victrola record slipping back and forth, replaying the same annoying bit repeatedly. Grasping onto something good usually didn't take long. He just went back to one of his favorite times with his dad, sitting next to him at the soda fountain at the five-and-dime.

"Robert," he recalled as he sank into a reverie," I think you're old enough to know how I got to America." His father had spoken in such a grave voice.

"How you got here? What does that mean?"

His father laughed. "Life wasn't all that easy when I was about your age in Italy. Benestare depended on agriculture to supply jobs for families then. Still does. But life became difficult with poor crops."

"Is that why you left Italy to come here?"

His dad had sat quiet, thinking for a moment.

"Yes, Robert. America was supposed to be the land of opportunity, where you could find jobs, and get rich, if you did things right. There was a great exodus of people leaving on ships to America. Many of them tried stowing away on the ships. That's what I did when I was seventeen."

"What does stowing away mean?"

His father spun around on his stool to look at him. "Well, maybe I should have told you I bought a ticket rather than slipping onto a ship to hide away until I got to America, but getting into America wasn't easy. I would've had to wait a long time before I got approval to travel to America, given my age. There was the paper work you needed to fill out to get approved by both countries. Besides, times were tough in Italy. Saving enough money for a ticket just wasn't possible for me then."

Robert had sat smiling at his dad, thinking about what stowed away meant. "So you stowed away? Weren't you scared, coming to America alone on a big ship? I would be."

"Your Uncle Milo came first, and then I followed him once he got settled in Chicago. I knew he would be waiting for me. Families that came over from Italy, got established, then helped families that came later. That made it easier for your Uncle Milo to find work. When I got there, I took any job I could get. Then I started doing clean up work for an Italian man who started his own painting business. He'd built a trust worthy reputation and was an honest and fair man. Everything I know about painting houses, *apartments, fancy restaurants and churches, I learned from him. That's how I got the chance to start my own painting business. He took me under his wing."*

His father winked at him. "It was quite an adventure getting here, but America's been good to me. It really is the land of opportunity, but don't think I haven't missed my family in Benestare. Once you travel that far away, it's hard to get the money to go back to see your family. I've ached to see Benestare again, still do. The only way you can find out news about your family is through letters."

"Can't you stow away again?"

"The days of hopping a ship from country to country slipped away years ago, Robert. Maybe I can take you there someday. What do you think?"

Robert's eyes widened. He sat nodding his head up and down.

"Can you tell me about stowing away, Dad?"

His father winked again. "One day I will, but right now we need to get home before your mother starts worrying about us."

Playfully, his father had slapped Robert's cap on his head, slipped his arm around his shoulder, and reined him in close to his side as they walked out onto the street.

Suddenly, Robert's mind reverted to his present situation. What would his dad think of America now, of where his family had ended up? He was sad about leaving them without any money, traveling around trying to find a doctor who could cure his cancer. Maybe it was a blessing he died before the stock market crashed. He didn't have to see the America he loved gutted of the opportunities he cherished so much.

Robert didn't understand what the stock market was, or what it meant to crash, but it changed everything around him, just like that. It was as if the curtain came down on a school play for intermission and when it came up again everyone was watching a different play, leaving everybody confused about what had just happened.

The crash was all the neighbors talked about, gathering around their radios trying to find out what it meant. People acted crazy. Crowds gathered downtown, lining up for blocks in front of the banks. When kids asked questions at school about what was going on, the teachers told them not to worry about it, but everyone did worry about it. Children didn't know why parents were losing their jobs, why they were angry, saying awful things about the government. Kids were expected not to ask questions about what had happened while the world around them changed in someway everyday, whether it was their own family or their neighbors.

Robert was moved by Tucker being asked to leave home. He hadn't heard any other guys he'd met on the road telling that story, leaving him wondering how many of the guys he shared boxcars with were thrown out too. Early on, men who had been riding the rails for a long time told him and Johnny that if they wanted to keep safe on the road, they should travel by themselves, not mix with other people. Out of fear they didn't talk a whole lot to anyone, but it left him knowing little about the situations of everyone around him. What he did know from traveling the past months was that in every town they passed through, the local papers shouted headlines about poverty in the country. Headlines glared from the newsstands, screaming the destitute state of the country. The Hoover blankets Robert rolled up in gave him more information about what was happening than anyone had given him at home, maybe because they didn't understand it themselves.

When he felt Tucker's foot nudge his side, Robert was glad to be pulled out of thoughts that went sour so fast.

"Hey," Tucker said. "Seems like the train is slowing down. Is it?"

"Yeah, it is. Listen, Tucker, we're going to start unloading when the train slows enough. Remember to step off. Don't swing out or around and don't try to jump off. Got it? We have to wait until the speed is where you can step off. Keeps you from twisting an ankle, breaking a leg, or tumbling under the train. And don't forget, we need to get off as far back from the station as possible, in case the bulls are around. I'm guessing in a large town like Jackson, the bulls are gonna be waiting around the tracks. Just watch when every one in front of us starts unloading, that's a sign we're moving slow enough to get off."

Tucker nodded his head and gave him a thumbs up. Al jumped up, walked toward the door, waiting for the train to slow, glancing back as Tucker and Robert came up beside him.

"You two okay now?"

A shrug of their shoulders was the only reply he got. Al stepped off the train before them. Robert unloaded holding a small boy right behind the parents who were each carrying a child in their arms. Letting the boy down beside him, he held on to his hand until his mother took it. She gave a quick nod of thanks as the family walked away toward the brush.

"It doesn't look like any railroad guys are around, so let's check the train schedule while we're here," Al said. "I'm going to meet with some people in town about the project I'm working on while I'm here. Depending on the train schedule and yours, this might be where we part. I don't mind buying you breakfast though."

Tucker turned around to look at the girls who had jumped on the train with the boys who fell beneath it. They were not far behind them. "Maybe I should wait and talk to them."

"Yeah, I was about to mention we should see how they're doing," Al said. "Find out what their plans are. Do you know if they have money, Tucker?"

"I don't know. They begged dinner last night."

"Well, don't know if we can help them out or not, but let's go see."

Three men were walking along side the girls. The men fell back behind them once they saw Al and the boys approaching.

"Tucker," Danny shouted, increasing her pace when she recognized him.

Their faces were noticeably bloated, eyes almost swollen shut, rims red from crying.

"Did you see what happened last night, Tucker?" Danny said as she got closer.

"Yeah, we did. That's why we waited to see how you're doing."

Tearing up immediately, Danny hid her eyes under her hands for a moment.

"Do you know where those boys were from?" Al asked.

They shook their heads no, neither of them looking directly at him.

"What do you know about them?"

Danny lifted her head up, but kept her eyes down, still avoiding eye contact with Al.

"They said they were from Louisiana. That's all."

"Did they tell you their names?"

"Well, just their first, Orson and Jake."

"I guess that's better than nothing. I'll send the information forward to the train station in Montgomery so they at least have that to help trace their families. Are you two heading home?"

The girls looked at one another, and then shrugged their shoulders.

"Not sure, I guess," Danny said, tilting her head toward the men who had stopped several feet behind them. "Those men said we could travel with them for a while."

Al glanced at the three filthy men who looked as if they were a permanent part of the hobo camps. "Hmm, how about you coming to breakfast with the three of us? You can meet up with these fellas later," he said, loud enough for them to hear.

The men peered at him and immediately turned away.

"Yeah, why don't you come eat, meet with them later," Tucker said, anxiously. "We didn't get much supper last night, did we?"

The girls looked at Tucker, and then over toward Al. As if trying to read each other's minds, the girls stood facing one another without talking, while covertly glancing back at the men who were waiting for them.

"Thanks, Tucker, but we're going to be traveling with them for a while," Danny said at last.

Tucker strutted toward the girls, but before he could say anything else, they turned away, walking in a fast pace back to the men. Stopping in his tracks, he sent a panicked look back to Al and Robert.

"Come on, Tucker, let's go eat," Robert said in dismissal of the girls and their decision.

"Geez, those three old guys are scary looking. Are those girls nuts or what?"

"Not nuts, but maybe in some kind of trouble," Al said. "They might think we don't know they're girls and don't want us to find out. Well, me, anyway. Sorry Tucker, I tried."

"Yeah you did." Kicking the ground, he threw his hands up in the air, spinning his lanky body around at the same time. "Stupid girls!"

Robert put his hand on Tucker's shoulder, pushing him gently toward town. "Let's go, you can't do anything more. They made their decision, no telling why."

"I can't believe those stupid girls."

"Most likely there's a squatter's camp along side the road outside of town, probably where the men and the girls will end up," Al said. "Jackson's a big town so I suggest you hang out along the outskirts if you're catching a train out of here today. Let's see if we can find a cafe close by after we pick up the train schedule."

A police car pulled up to the side of the train station just as they reached the corner of the steps. Three bulls walked out with a black man, his hands cuffed behind him, his right eye swollen shut, with blood oozing all along the right side of his cheek. Al turned to Tucker and Robert as he started up the station steps.

"I think you boys should come inside with me."

Robert could see right away that bulls were gathered throughout the station. He followed close behind Al so there was no mistake they were with him. Al grabbed a train schedule, and signaled for Robert and Tucker to follow him out.

"Not a good time for you to hang around, I'd say. Let's get some breakfast."

After seeing the bloodied face of the black man at the station, all the signs for segregation on the buildings got Robert's attention as they walked to find a cafe. To the right was the Jackson Theatre for Colored People. To the left were signs above public restrooms pasted with "WHITES ONLY," and by the water fountains he noticed "NO COLORED PEOPLE ALLOWED" painted on the brick above.

It left him with a bad feeling about staying long in Jackson. Ever since he had crossed into the southern states, bulls had gotten meaner and people had gotten ruder to transients. But to black people the bulls were brutal and the locals looked down at them. He was looking forward to heading north again where communities seemed friendlier to people traveling through looking for work. He'd seen enough acts of brutality toward colored people in the South and didn't want to see more than he had to.

It was enough to see how differently black people were spoken to when they asked for a meal in trade for work, even if they were with whites. Most of the time they were turned away or told to get off the property. But if they did get a meal, they were told to eat by the barn or take the food and leave. That's what he saw traveling to Colorado too. He rolled his eyes at how poorly blacks must be treated in Jackson.

Reaching the center of town, they walked up the main street looking for a restaurant. Robert saw five men across the street headed in their direction. Just as the men neared the end of the block, a black couple turned the corner and were walking toward the men. The five of them spread out, side by side, taking up the entire sidewalk, not budging to make room for the couple as they came closer. The black couple turned to the side, pressing their backs against a store front to let the men by. When they got past the couple, the guy closest to them made a deliberate turn over his shoulder to spit chewing tobacco at their feet. As they crossed the street and approached the three of them, the five men shifted far enough over to the side of the walk to allow room to pass.

"How about Cora's Cafe across the street?" Al said. "Sounds like a friendly place, huh?"

"Looks good to me," Tucker said. "My stomach's been talking to me since daylight, so I sure appreciate you inviting me along."

The comfy atmosphere of the cafe was immediate as they walked through the door. Typical red and white checked cloths draped each table. A small high-glazed, deep pink pot, overstuffed with fresh pansies, sat in the center. Curtains across the front windows were a soft rose, pulled back with red and white checked ties. Robert felt his shoulders relax as they settled into chairs at a table directly in front of the windows.

"This is cozy, isn't it?" Tucker said. "I could sit in front of these windows, looking at people stroll by all morning, all day, if they'd let me. Beats the inside of those smelly trains, doesn't it?" Tucker looked over at Robert, then Al, waiting for one of them to reply.

"Yeah, that's an understatement," Al said.

Tucker's eyes were fixed on Al. "I've only eaten in a restaurant twice, so I sure appreciate that in the last two days, it's been two for two. You inviting us again this morning, that's sure kind."

Al grinned, nodding his head. "So what's your story, Tucker? Why are you joining thousands of kids riding the rails, spending time in the stinky boxcars you just mentioned?"

"Hi fellas, you must be looking for a good meal if you came to Cora's Cafe."

They looked up to see a young girl's spirited smile scanning each one of them, settling her eyes on Robert.

"I'm Mazie, Cora's daughter, so I'm a little prejudiced," she said, still smiling, and still looking at Robert. "Here are some menus. I'll be back in a few minutes, give you fellas some time to decide. Shall I bring some coffee, though?"

She shifted her eyes around the table, taking the order for three cups of coffee.

"Okay, be right back with them. Our skillet potatoes are the best in town."

Her short brown page flipped around her face, covering her cheeks as she looked over her shoulder, playfully walking away.

"Hmm, looks like someone's going to get a special touch on their order," Tucker said.

Robert glanced at Tucker, expecting his goofy grin. Ignoring it, he started reading the menu.

"It feels good to see a smiling face for a change, especially after last night," Al said. "I'll bet she has no idea how far-reaching that warm smile is to everyone who comes in here."

"Haven't seen a smile like that one for a while," Robert said.

"Here you go, fellas, three coffees."

Not realizing she had walked up behind him, Robert caught her smile. Her light blue eyes were settled directly on his. She slipped his coffee down next to him, and then reached across the table to hand Tucker and Al their coffee.

"Did I get you interested in the country potatoes?"

Tucker and Robert nodded in unison.

As she walked away from Robert's side with their orders, Robert lifted his head to take a sip of his coffee and saw Tucker grinning at him across the table. Feeling Al's eyes on him, too, he shifted in his chair to look out the window. It felt a little painful to sit in such a cozy setting, looking out between softly draped curtains giving an atmosphere much like inside a home, knowing he'd be out on the street in not long.

"So, Tucker, back to my question," Al said. "What are you doing roaming around the country, instead of being back home? Robert mentioned you're from Georgia?"

"Yeah, Georgia. I'm trying to find work like everyone else, someplace to sleep for a while. My dad told me to leave because he needed my bed for my younger brothers."

Tucker's short-lived playful spirit since walking into the cafe began to fade.

"How old are you, Tucker? And, tell it to me straight, okay?"

"Seventeen, be eighteen in another three months."

"You dropped out of school then?"

"Didn't want to. Told my dad that but he told me straight about needing my bed, saying he couldn't afford to feed me anymore. I'll find work, I will. Haven't figured it out yet, but I'm gonna."

Robert could feel Al's eyes on him now, but kept staring out the window, not wanting the questions to start flying. After a moment, he turned toward Al, knowing he wasn't going to get his own questions answered about work if he didn't open up to Al's questions.

"How about you, Robert, what's your story? Were you asked to leave home too? You never did answer my questions on the train the first time I saw you. Guess I can't blame you, not wanting to get into a conversation with a stranger. How about answering them now?"

Robert sat quiet for a moment trying to recapture the sense of comfort he felt coming into the cafe before he answered, but it was gone. Al waited.

"My buddy and I went looking for work to help out our families, just like everyone else was doing."

Al sat waiting for more. "So, what happened to your buddy?"

"He got fed up with not finding work and being hungry all the time. Said we shouldn't wait for something really bad to happen. He headed back home a month ago."

Al waited again. "Why didn't you go with him? Did he skip out on you?"

"I didn't go with him because I didn't want to give up yet, go home empty-handed after traveling for months. He didn't skip out on me either. He kept bugging me for a couple of weeks about heading home. Then he just got fed up with me for not agreeing to go back."

"That's it? That's the only reason you're not going back? Seems like if you left with a buddy, you'd go back with him rather than trying to fend for yourself on the road after experiencing, I'm not sure what. A lot, that I do know."

Al waited again for an answer. Robert turned his head back to the street trying to figure out what to say.

"Here you are, one country special, one biscuit and gravy with skillet potatoes, and two orders of scrambled eggs with skillet potatoes."

Maizie had slipped up behind Robert, stopping directly by his side again.

"I'll be back with more coffee in a minute, fellas."

She turned to smile at Robert as she walked away. The smile he shot back to Mazie seemed an automatic response, rather than one he meant to send.

"It hasn't been so long since my buddy left," Robert said, looking back at Al. "Not long enough to give up anyway."

"You sure it's not something else? Hate to see a good kid like you end up in some kind of trouble out here on the road. Lots of vagrants go to jail, spending months working labor."

Letting a sheepish grin slip out, Robert grabbed his fork and started eating intently.

Al put his arm on the table and leaned toward him.

"You've been lucky not ending up like those two boys on the train last night. The tally released by the government on people getting killed jumping trains last year was more than 6,000. Thousands more got injured."

"Well," Robert said, hesitating for a moment to get up his nerve. "Then maybe it's time to ask about the camps and the work you mentioned in Arkansas. We could use both."

Al put his fork down, shifting his body to the side to look directly at Robert.

"Look, I'd like to help you out, but you're too young for the camps. What, fifteen or so? If you had another year or so on you, you might pass for a little older, but I'm not here to fudge ages of kids on the road, which I couldn't do anyway because everyone who signs up for the camps needs a letter from their parents stating the date they were born. I'm out here trying to get some understanding of what really is going on with youth riding the rails. As I do that, I'm trying to get young men recruited for the camps by talking to local agencies so they can direct them to the camps as they pass through their town." Al paused to pick up a biscuit, hesitating before he took a bite. "Only so many boys are going to get in each camp. After that, they'll have to wait until someone leaves or a new camp opens up."

"What camps?" Tucker asked. "I've never been to camp. That's only for the rich kids, isn't it?"

Al and Robert's heads turned at the same moment toward Tucker, their eyes staring, stunned by his comment.

"What? Just askin, that's all."

"Well, I remember now you weren't around when we were talking about the camps before," Al said. "It's a new program President Roosevelt started to help get young men off the trains and put to work. In another three months, you'll qualify for the camps."

Tucker shifted his body forward, settling his elbows on the table. "What? For money, for a bed, something to eat, what?"

"For all three. The camps will put young men to work doing labor in public programs developing or rebuilding parks, roads, and bridges. They're meant to be training camps too, so young men come out with skills they can use."

"Another three months," Tucker said under his breath.

"Sorry, Tucker, but there are thousands of young men eighteen or older who are being signed up now. The good news is that more camps are opening across the country."

Robert shifted his attention out the window again. From time to time he could feel Al looking over at him, but he left him to his silence.

"Well, what about that work in Arkansas?" Robert said as he turned back toward Al.

"So you've made up your mind not to head straight north to Illinois?"

"Yep, I told you why."

Looking away, Al shook his head.

"Well, I'm relieved you're sticking around," Tucker said. "It's clear to me that I need more information on what the heck is going on around me seems like, if I'm going to stay alive, that is. Last night shot down my confidence."

Robert put his coffee cup down on the table, loud enough to get Al's attention again.

Releasing a sigh as he rolled his eyes, Al leaned forward and glanced at both of them. "Okay, boys. I overheard some guys yesterday say there's some work on farms in Arkansas, just outside of Marshall and Little Rock, harvesting. They were headed there. Probably not but a month's work left. They mentioned the Ferguson farm in Little Rock. Didn't say much about where the work is in Marshall. That's all I know about it, could be a long shot. Often is. There's probably thousands headed there from all different directions of the country right now."

A nod of agreement was immediate from Robert. Al pushed the empty dishes in front of him to the center of the table, spreading the train schedule out.

"Seems the only train going north to Little Rock this afternoon is a passenger train. There's a freight train coming through this evening. All the trains this afternoon are going south and west. I took two schedules so you can keep one. Not sure I'm heading out today. Depends on how many agencies I can meet with. I may buy a ticket on the passenger train, if I get things done by then. Are you two finished eating?"

"Well, like I said, I could sit here all day, but we've been here for a while, and the place is filling up," Tucker said.

Al turned to get the waitress's attention. Slipping a pen out of his pocket, he wrote something on a napkin. He tore it in half, then wrote on the other half.

"Here's where I'm based in Cincinnati, Ohio, Tucker. When you near eighteen, contact me if you haven't found work somewhere. I'll try my best to get you in a camp. Robert, hang on to it in case you need it for something. One more thing, since you're going to be here all day, you might want to stop by the Salvation Army or town mission. The town's large enough to have both. Between the two of them, you can probably get a shower and a meal before you leave, but you probably know that. Right, Robert?"

"You fellas leaving already?" Mazie was standing at Robert's side, looking at him. "Was I right about the skillet potatoes?"

He smiled. "Sure was."

"Well, you come back now."

Stepping out on to the street, Al put his hands on their shoulders. "Not sure I will see you two again. Good luck to you, boys."

He started walking up the street, turning to look back over his shoulder to give a quick wave when they yelled out another round of thanks.

7

———————

"So now what?" Tucker asked. "How we gonna kill a whole day?"

"I don't know about you, Tucker, but I want to take a quick nap. I didn't sleep much last night on the train. After that, let's check out the local mission or Salvation Army. I'm hoping to find a pair of trousers in better condition on one of the free tables, the hole at my knee keeps growing. Nobody's going to want to take me on for hire. You might get lucky too."

Tucker raised his eyebrows as if he was puzzled. "What does that mean?"

"Maybe you'll find a rucksack so you don't have to keep walking around dangling that pillow case from one hand. If you don't find one cheap and still usable, I'll show you how to bundle the pillow case. Watched some hoboes showing a guy how to do it once. Let's keep walking up the road and see what's around."

It didn't take long to identify the town mission. Lines of men and women were wrapped around the corner of the building, most wearing threadbare clothing and fraying shoes. Their withdrawn faces so distressed they turned away when people walked by them.

"Well, now we know where to come back to around supper time, since we have the whole day," Robert said.

Tucker stopped to scan a town map posted on a wooden stand next to the mission. "There's a park six blocks that way. Why don't we check it out?"

As they walked toward the park, they noticed a hobo camp alongside the railroad tracks.

"Think those girls are over there?" Tucker asked.

"Don't know, and I'm not going to try to find out, either."

The park was a block wide, clean-looking and with well-cut grass. It was heavily shaded by large maple and weeping-willow trees. They noticed some of the men from the train lying around the park. Robert stopped once he saw them. "I don't like the idea of both of us trying to sleep with so many people around. How about I sleep for an hour and then you sleep for an hour?"

"Sure. I did nod off for a bit last night. Can't believe it, but I did. You can go first. Sounds like you need it too."

Robert ducked under a huge weeping willow tree at the corner of the park. With the arms of the willow branches draped around him, he felt the first touch of privacy in days. Taking advantage of the setting, he fell straight back, resting his head on his rucksack so he could enjoy the thick maze of fern-like branches towering above that allowed only a few rays of the blue sky to peak through. He saw Mazie's warm smile for an instant before falling fast asleep.

Only minutes later Robert was jolted awake from Tucker's hands relentlessly shaking him from side to side. "What the heck you doing, Tucker? I just fell asleep."

"I think we should get out of here. Come and take a look for yourself."

Robert clutched his rucksack, jumped to his feet, and pulled aside the willow branches to look out.

"Over there," Tucker pointed to the corner of the park. "Looks scary and nothing good for sure. They've got that black man we saw earlier at the train station."

Dropping the curtain of willow branches, Robert moved cautiously toward the crowd. "Let's get closer so we can see what's happening."

Tucker lurched forward to catch up with him and yanked his arm backward so hard he began teetering back and forth trying to keep his balance.

"I don't think that's such a good idea. I've seen mobs like these in Georgia. They get out of control fast."

Several white men standing around the black man started yelling chants of theft, while dangling a rope over his head. Robert could see the horror on his face. Within minutes, others mulling around in the park joined the group and chanted with them. Many of the men were dressed in denim overalls, their faces lined with deep crevices from working outside. It was easy to assume they were local farmers. As the chants got louder, the crowd grew larger from people running into the park toward the commotion to see what was happening.

Tucker turned, walking away from the growing crowd. "Let's get out of here. The officers must have let that black man go this morning, and it looks like they're taking the law into their own hands. I've seen this before in Georgia, and it ain't pretty. Nothing you want to see, especially if you haven't seen it before."

Noticing Robert had stopped to watch the commotion, Tucker walked back and grabbed his arm. "If the sheriff doesn't hear about what's happening and come soon, they might hang the guy right there by that tree, instead of taking him out of town someplace. I've seen that before, too. Let's not wait around."

Robert's eyes were still on the crowd as Tucker pulled him forward. "Geez, I've heard hangings were still going on in the South, but didn't know people were still doing it outside of the law."

"Oh yeah, it's still going on, believe me. Seen two hangings myself in Georgia. I don't want to see another one. Left me sleepless for weeks."

Robert stopped at the edge of the park. "Yeah, they're getting worked up all right. Let's go back to the mission. Then we can figure out what to do until the train comes through. Let's hope we get on it. I don't like this town much either."

The chants got louder as more townspeople gathered around. Suddenly the crowd parted as men pushed their way through, shoving the powerless black man toward the street. They loaded him into the back of a beat-up red truck with side railings made from scraps of weathered boards. A flood of people ran to their cars, lining up behind the truck like a funeral procession. The crowd began dispersing out of the park in all directions.

"That doesn't look good, does it?" Tucker said. "But I guess we can stay here for a while after all. The park is almost empty now. Think you can fall asleep again?"

"Not sure after watching that, but I'm going to try. Sleep seems better than thinking about what just happened."

The sun was bearing down on him when Robert woke, beaming its way through an opening in a cluster of branches of the weeping-willow tree. Rolling flat on his back for a few minutes to enjoy the rustle of leaves and bits of sun on his face, he waited to get up, trying to hang on to precious moments of privacy that nestling underneath the willow tree provided.

"Hey, sorry, I slept so long, Tucker," Robert yelled from underneath the tree. "Tucker?"

Startled with no reply, Robert jumped up, swept back the willow curtain, and stepped out from underneath the tree. He scanned the park for Tucker. He wasn't anywhere around. It didn't take long to guess where Tucker might be, but he hoped a growling stomach sent him after food and not looking for the girls from the train. Worry about traveling with Tucker leading to trouble surfaced again, leaving him thinking he probably didn't go for food.

Robert wasn't sure what to do next. If Tucker was dumb enough to go after the girls in the hobo camp, then other trouble traveling with him was sure to come.

Irritated that he left him asleep in the park after all the commotion earlier, and annoyed at himself because he was contemplating going to the hobo camp to look for Tucker, Robert threw his rucksack on a park bench. He sat staring at nothing, hoping Tucker would appear with some lunch. If he didn't, it might be a good time to ditch him. He leaned forward, settling his elbows on his knees, and covered his face with his hands as he let out a sigh of frustration. *This is what you get for going against your instincts about traveling with someone you don't know. If he doesn't come back soon, then I'm not waiting around for him.*

When his stomach began to talk to him too loudly to ignore, he headed for the town mission. If the money the sheriff gave him was going to last, he would have to succumb to getting a free meal. But the feeling of being a bum crept into his mind, stopping him in his tracks. Anyone looking at him would probably think he was a bum, so why not get over it and save the money for a meal? He had to see about changing out his ripped trousers, maybe increasing the slim chance that the work in Arkansas might pan out.

Shrugging his shoulders at the idea, Robert set out toward the mission. Four blocks up he could see the hobo jungle along side the tracks. *Would Tucker really go into the camp after those girls?* The camps he had walked through with Johnny seemed harmless, yet they got enough warnings from guys on the trains to keep out of them if they didn't want trouble. It left them scared to stay too long when they walked through one, leaving them with little knowledge of what the warnings were about.

In every camp they passed by, a mirror tied to a tree branch dangled on a rope for men to shave, and a beat-up pan, or an old gallon size can to make stew hung above a fire pit. When younger kids came into the camps wanting something to eat, the hoboes gave them a specific ingredient for the stew to go bum in town. If they didn't come back with it, they didn't eat. Regulars lived in the camps permanently, usually men too old to travel or work much anymore.

Tucker knew the plan was to go back to the mission so Robert figured he'd bump into him there. *If I don't see him there, he knew the plan was to go to the Salvation Army from there. Maybe I underestimated Tucker's smarts.*

Almost past the camp, he stood at the curb waiting to cross, trying to rid himself of the urge to check it out any further, but his feet wouldn't move. Guess it wouldn't hurt to walk by a little closer to the camp to see if there was a sign or anything marked with a code on it. If there was a piece of old wood or rock some where outside the camp etched with an O X O and a half crescent line across the top, it signaled a safe camp. Three diagonal straight lines warned of an unsafe area. The slow stride he took around the camp trying to find a sign caught someone's attention half way around.

"Looking for something, kid? Whatcha need?"

Robert turned to see a guy just finishing a shave, dunking his shaver in a large rusted tin can. With his shirt off, a clean shave, and brown hair slicked back, he almost looked as if he didn't belong in the hobo camp. But his grey cotton trousers, part of the uniform of the road, gave him away.

"Nope, not looking for anything."

"Well, if you were, I'm sure we don't have it."

Robert slipped him a grin, waved, and kept walking. Finishing the trek around the park without seeing a code somewhere with either marking, he turned back toward the town mission.

"Hey Robert, stop."

Looking back over his shoulder, he saw Tucker crouched down behind a bush, waving him back toward the edge of the camp.

"What's up, Tucker? Looking for trouble?"

Tucker raised a finger to his mouth to quiet Robert. "Hope not, but I was thinking of talking to those girls one more time to try to knock some sense into them about going home or getting away from those old men."

Tucker motioned for Robert to come closer. "Look, they're set up in the far corner right over there. I've been listening to the way they're talking to the girls and it's creepy, calling them darling and sweetheart, acting like they're courting them or something. Disgusting, isn't it? They've got to be more than twenty years older than those girls. I just heard one of the guys say they were going into town to get something for the stew. I saw all three walk out of the camp and was just going in when you went by."

"Tucker, they didn't want your help, remember? I'm headed for the mission. You coming?"

"Not until I make sure they're all right. I'll meet you there."

Still in a crouching position, Tucker took off in a swift crawl along the edge of the camp. He stopped to look inside before slipping in through the thick maze of people. Frustrated, Robert kicked the grass, then stood with his hands on his hips, stumped about what to do next. Common sense told him to turn and walk to the mission. Instead, Robert walked to the spot where Tucker had slipped into the camp thinking he would give him a few minutes, and then leave if he didn't come back.

From where he was standing he could see Tucker hunched down on his knees by one of the girls, evidently talking in a low voice. He couldn't hear what Tucker was saying although he was only eight feet away. One of the girls was shaking her head from side to side. The other girl sat on the ground next to her, listening intently. It looked as if she was wiping tears away every few seconds. The smallness of their frames was noticeable without the wool caps and men's bulky jackets to hide in. To see them now in cotton shirts, neither looked more than sixteen. The haggardness on their faces was as intense as the mothers he'd seen on the trains with small kids.

Tucker stood up and began rapidly stuffing items in a cloth bag. He helped the other girl up and nudged them forward as he scurried toward the edge of the camp. Seeing how desperate they looked, Robert was excited the rescue might be pulled off.

"What the hell are you doing with our girls?" someone suddenly shouted.

One of the men had crept up behind Tucker. He had one arm around Tucker's neck, and the other arm around his waist, clutching him in a tight hold. In one swift movement, the guy dropped his hand down from Tucker's neck and slipped a knife tight against his throat. The other two men stood by the girls, trying to coax them back into the corner of the camp, rubbing their arms in gentle strokes.

Robert felt relieved to see Tucker wasn't trying to break the guy's hold or fight back. Blood was trickling down Tucker's neck from a few sharp movements he'd made before the man locked his body against his. The girls' eyes were fixated on the knife at his throat. The other men took hold of their arms, nudging them back to the corner. Tucker was steered out the back edge of the camp, still locked in a hold.

Robert followed along the side of the camp, keeping a distance between them as Tucker and the man disappeared into a cluster of trees across a gravel road. Increasing his pace, he turned his head to see if the other two men were following. Not seeing them, he crossed into the threshold of the trees, unsure what he could do, distraught that no one seemed nearby to help.

As he passed into the tree line, Robert couldn't see Tucker, but heard shuffling noises further ahead. Following the sounds, moving cautiously forward, he tried to think of what he could do to help Tucker once he got closer. A helplessness consumed him, but he kept up his pace.

He spotted them ahead and stopped. Seeing Tucker shoved against a tree and being punched in the gut relentlessly, Robert scanned his surroundings. Out of desperation, he grabbed a fallen tree branch still full of leaves. Creeping forward, he held the branch out in front of him. Hearing something from behind, the guy looked around. Robert whacked him in the face with the thickest part of the branch. As he swung the branch a second time, the man leaned out to reach for it, releasing the hold against Tucker's neck for just a moment, but long enough for Tucker to shove him and slip out of his grip. Catching his balance in a quick rebound, the guy raised his knife and stared at them with bloodshot eyes as if undecided who to lunge at first.

"You little bastards better run while you can because one of you is going to end up with this knife in your chest. You come back into the camp again, we'll be ready for you."

Robert and Tucker quickly backed away. At the first glimpse of the clearing, they turned and ran. Once their feet crossed the gravel path onto the sidewalk, they stopped to catch their breath and take a quick glance behind them.

"I don't know about you, Tucker, but I believe he meant what he said about the knife in the chest. Let's take the long way around to the mission so we avoid the camp, unless you want that knife in your chest."

Tucker shook his head, giving up any temptation of going back to the camp. Reaching up to feel the cut on his neck, he was startled to see his hand stained with blood. "Holy crap."

Robert pulled a handkerchief out of his back pocket. "Here. Follow me. There's a public bathroom across from the park we stopped at with a drinking fountain next to it. You can clean up before we go to the mission so no one asks questions about what happened to your neck. With the blood off, it might look like you just got sloppy shaving."

As they started to walk away, Tucker took a look back toward the camp. "I wonder what's going to happen to those girls. They know they've got themselves in a bad situation. They're scared too. They know no good will come to them staying with those men. They don't have any money either because they gave it to them boys to carry."

Tucker looked back one more time. "You think someone in the camp will see what's going on and help them?"

"I doubt it. From what I've seen, people stay to themselves, especially when there might be danger in getting involved. Those men have knives and who knows what else. If the girls want out, they're going to have to wait until they're left alone, then sneak out. That's what I'd do, but that moment might be a long way off now."

"Yeah, I know, but at least I tried."

Robert put his hand on Tucker's shoulder.

"You gave it your best shot. Almost pulled it off too. You should feel good about it since you're still alive."

Tucker looked over, letting a slight smile surface.

"Yeah, I tried. But, now I have this really bad feeling about what's going to happen to the girls."

8

Like most mornings, Lucille peered out the kitchen window to watch the freight train pass by the Elmhurst station, hoping Robert would be standing on the other side of the tracks when the last car went by. Kathleen's sudden shout startled her. Jumping back from the counter, she pulled her hands out of flour dough to look around for her daughter.

"Hey, Ma, did you hear me? Johnny Tominello is here. He wants to talk to you."

She caught a glimpse of Kathleen just as she pulled her head back from the open window. Her hands still caked with flour, Lucille walked over to it and leaned out. "Kathleen, come inside for a moment."

Kathleen swung through the door, turning to look back toward the porch. "What Ma? Didn't you hear me say Johnny's here?"

"Please don't shout that someone is here to see me. I need you to come in the house to see what I'm doing when someone stops by, and not shout at me through the window. I'm all full of flour. Let him know I'll be there in a minute."

Johnny hadn't come by since the first week after he got back from traveling with Robert. Lucille considered going to his home to ask his father if he'd heard anything from Robert. Still upset with him for making secret plans to run away with Robert and then coming home without him, Lucille wasn't sure how she would react to Johnny, or what he might have to say. She needed a moment to settle herself.

They were two foolish boys trying to be men. Yet Robert might be in serious danger traveling alone while Johnny was safe at home.

Taking her time, she shaped the dough into an oval mound, wiped her flour-coated hands onto her apron, and hung it next to the sink. Mustering up some calm, she walked to the door. "Johnny, come in."

Keeping his eyes toward the floor, Johnny's uneasiness was obvious as he stood inside the doorway.

"Please, come sit down."

Lucille looked behind her when the screen door opened again. Kathleen was standing next to him, smiling.

"I need you to stay outside to keep an eye on the kids while I visit with Johnny. You can talk with him later."

Lucille's tone was firm, not wanting Kathleen present to pick up her concerns for Robert's safety when she asked Johnny questions.

Kathleen started to speak but held back, disappointment showing on her face as she turned to leave.

Realizing she forgot to cover the dough, Lucille walked back to the corner of the room that made up the kitchen. Before she got more than a few feet away, Johnny began speaking, speeding through his words and starting over when he stumbled on them. He sounded as if he'd rehearsed what he would say. She turned to see Johnny still standing by the door, and held up her hand to stop him from rambling further.

"Wait. Let's sit down first." She walked over to the opposite corner of the room that made up the sitting area, filled by two rose-colored, over stuffed chairs, a round mahogany table, and a floor lamp, the only pieces of her prized living room furniture she was able to keep. Squeezed in the corner, the furniture looked out of place, the largeness of the pieces consuming the room.

Trying to show a calm presence to hide the angry emotions surging through her stomach, she motioned for Johnny to sit down. Feeling a warm blush surge across her cheeks, she stepped toward the chair across from him, taking her time to settle into it before looking over to him.

Johnny was Robert's closest friend and a family friend, too. She couldn't take her anger out on him for her son being gone when she knew both boys were naive about what was happening in the country.

"I meant to come back by to see you again, but I was afraid to. When I came by right after I got home, I knew you'd be disappointed that Robert wasn't with me."

He stayed sitting straight at the edge of the chair, keeping his hands clamped together tight. "I haven't been back because I can't tell you anything more about where Robert is than I did before. I kept asking my dad if he'd seen you and if Robert was home yet. I ask Kathleen whenever I see her around town. Fact is, I'm feeling really worried now."

Turning his eyes away from her, Johnny slipped back from the edge of the seat cushion, settling himself between the large, side-wings of the chair as if trying to find comfort from them. "That's not what you want to hear, I know. I've been thinking about going back, trying to find him, except I'm not sure where to go back to. Unless Robert stayed in St. Louis where we parted, I don't know where he would be. He wanted to keep going south to find work and not stay in St. Louis. Have you talked to the police? They could probably help."

Lucille took a deep breath, realizing she hoped he came by because he'd heard from Robert. The disappointment was crushing.

"Yes, I went to the police. They told me there were thousands of young boys from Illinois that took off like the two of you. It seems there's no way to track anyone since they're traveling by foot or on the freights so there's no paper trail to help them. The police took the information about Robert, but told me there wasn't much they could do other than send it on to the last place he stopped at in case his name came up on employment records or some other list."

Johnny rested his head against the back of the chair, closed his eyes and brought his hands up to his face for a moment. Lucille didn't know what more to say since Johnny had been home a month. It was difficult to understand why Robert hadn't come home by now. She was surprised he would take the risk of traveling this long by himself at such a young age.

"Do you think he found work or he's waiting until he's got money to bring home? You said that's why Robert didn't come back with you. He didn't want to come home without money. Is that right? But don't you think if he found work he'd try to call your father since you have a phone?"

Realizing she'd been rambling, Lucille sat back in her chair again, not expecting any answers.

Johnny shrugged, with a concerned look crossing his face. "I'm not sure, ma'am. Don't know why he was stubborn about coming home. It was exciting the first couple months, traveling west to Colorado, scenery so beautiful, something new everyday. I thought we would hop the freight trains for a long time."

Lucille put her hand to her forehead to think for a moment, trying to select the right words to say. "Then why did you come back without Robert?"

Johnny sat quiet for a moment as if formulating his thoughts. "It seemed like such an adventure but . . . then everywhere we went we got shooed away, the jobs going to the men traveling to find work. We were treated like bums, scum sometimes. Then we heard more and more stories about the railroad detectives hurting people, taking their money. Being on the road didn't seem so great anymore. That's why I came back."

Seeing Lucille's expression turn from concern to stark fear, he went silent. When he glanced over to her again, she noticed the look on his face was one of remorse.

"I should have stayed with him. I know that now, but I'd been telling Robert for weeks we should come home since we'd been drifting for months. Not finding work or any real work was getting harder to deal with. The farther south we went, the meaner people got. I was down right discouraged, ma'am. Finally told Robert if he wouldn't come, I was going home anyway."

"What did he say?"

Johnny scooted up to the edge of the cushion again and looked directly at her. "It was what he did. I thought he'd follow me when I walked down the tracks to catch the train to Illinois. I looked over my shoulder to see if he was coming, but he was just standing there. I thought if he saw me hop on the train he'd come with me, so I kept walking. When I turned around, he was way down the tracks going in the opposite direction."

"But you got on the train without him?"

"Yes, ma'am. Like I said, it seemed dangerous to stay out there, just wandering, having to mix with those strangers on the trains, seeing spooky-looking men in the camps along the tracks when we walked through. I was sure Robert wouldn't stay long behind me, that he'd come home, too. But he didn't ever show me he was getting scared like I was getting scared. He's probably all right because Robert has a way about him that people like. Keeps him out of trouble."

Far from being reassured, Lucille caught a glimpse of Robert's violin in the corner of the room. She shifted her eyes back to Johnny as he was finishing his last words. How naive this boy was, yet she had to believe that Robert was all right. Trying to recall anything that might help her understand why he would stay away and worry her so much rather than come home, she could hear the words Nicolas had said to Robert many times during his last months. *"You're going to be the man of the house son, so remember to be honest, be good, and look after your ma."*

Robert would stare at his dad each time, grinning with pride at his father's words. By then, he understood his dad was going to die soon. If she only knew then how important it was to assure her son that she would take care of everything, and not to worry, he might have stayed and not run off. But it was such a common thing for fathers to say to their oldest sons when they left for the military or to find work.

When Johnny finished speaking, they both sat silent, waiting for the other to say something more. Lucille had run out of words, and her emotions were stoked up.

"Well, ma'am, I guess I'd better be getting back home," Johnny said as he got up to leave. "You'll let me know right away if you hear something, won't you?"

"Yes, of course I will. It was good of you to come by."

Walking Johnny to the door, she caught sight of the violin once more, feeling a rush of sadness. She slipped back into a chair after he left to give herself a moment, going over the conversation with Johnny in her mind, trying to find some hope. But he had left her disappointed, offering nothing new to share. What he did say caused her even more worry about her son. Anger rose up again. Johnny was home; Robert was not.

It was too close to supper to sit long, but she needed more time to herself. Leaning forward to peek out the window to check on Kathleen and the kids, she saw her daughter standing at the edge of the yard talking to Johnny, turning her head back and forth from him to the kids. She seemed more of a young woman than a girl as she watched her chat with Johnny.

Clamping her eyes shut, Lucille pictured Robert coming through the door and seeing his violin. It had been a gift from his dad for his tenth birthday. For a while, it had been gone, but it was back where it belonged and waiting for Robert's return.

Left with only debt and no income from her husband's painting business, the struggle to manage from month to month overwhelmed her. All of their savings had been spent on travel for Nicolas to find a doctor who might have a cure for his cancer. It was during the frantic time after he died that Lucille sold most of their other possessions to pay bills and buy food.

When it came down to selling their piano, Robert insisted she sell his violin, too. She told him no, reminding him it was a gift from his father. Nicolas had spent many hours selecting a violin that would last his son forever. He would have wanted him to keep it. But he pressed her to sell it. "Ma, those people came by to say it might be better for the younger kids to live with other families. We need the money."

Several months later, William Hurst, a longtime family friend at their bank, stopped by to ask her to come by his office to discuss the mortgage on their home. When she arrived, she heard the words she'd been dreading for months.

He straightened his tie and adjusted his wired-rim glasses as he slipped into the chair behind his desk, clearing his throat before he began. "I know you're aware the mortgage on your home is months in arrears," Hurst said. "And, unfortunately, the bank will have to claim the house."

Lucille had prepared herself for the conversation for months, but it was still crushing to hear the words. She struggled to keep her composure.

"However, I've discussed with our bank president, Mr. Briggs, about your husband's long illness and the ages of your children."

He went on to tell her Briggs had recently mentioned a two-bedroom home belonging to a friend of his who had purchased it as an investment and planned to fix it up and then sell it. But with the economic downturn in the country, he was unable to do anything with it.

Noticing the puzzled expression on Lucille's face, Hurst paused a moment. "Briggs's friend is willing to let you live in the house for a nominal amount to cover the taxes."

A smile eased across her lips as she felt immediate relief knowing her family would have another home to live in.

Not long after Robert left with Johnny, Hurst came by again to talk to her about a new program President Roosevelt had created for widows with little or no income who were solely supporting their family.

"Without question you would qualify for this program. Why don't you stop by the bank this week, and I'll go through the paperwork with you?"

A few months later, the precious, small amount of monthly income started streaming in. By then, the money from the sale of their belongings had dwindled to the point it might cover only one more month of groceries, but only if she continued to be skillful by buying staples in bulk supply. The jobs she had been able to get doing laundry from her husband's past customers diminished to a rarity as the depression hit harder, affecting the lifestyle of more families.

But it was from another opportunity that Lucille was able to get Robert's violin back. Hurst came by to tell her an employee at the bank, Mr. Luft, was looking for someone to teach his two daughters his national language, German. Immigrants didn't speak their native language to their children. They knew it was critical for them to fit in to avoid the prejudices and cruelties that came with being a foreigner in America. At twelve and fourteen-years-old, Luft believed his daughters were established well enough in speaking fluent English, and he believed they could benefit from learning German.

It was the money Lucille earned teaching German that made it possible to buy Robert's violin back from the neighbor who had bought it. To ease the anxiety of putting aside part of her meager earnings for the violin, she invited her oldest children, Kathleen and Marty, to learn German at the same time. Her friend Elsa was delighted to have the younger children come over to play during the lessons.

Lucille found herself grinning as her thoughts drifted to Saturday morning German lessons. The girls' mother sent two homemade pies as a treat. The house was full of laughter as they all tried to pronounce the sharp-sounding German words. She couldn't help but smile when Marty began saying, "guten morgen" when he woke up in the mornings and "guten nacht" when he went to bed.

Finally having enough money put aside to offer the neighbor who bought the violin what he'd paid for it, anxiousness had consumed her as she knocked on his door. So fearful he wouldn't sell it back, she stumbled on her words as she explained why she'd come.

"Goodness Lucille, it gives me pleasure knowing the violin will be there when your son gets home. I'll find another violin for my daughter. She hasn't shown much interest in practicing as it is."

Putting away money for the violin was a luxury she couldn't afford. It was a decision that had left her constantly uneasy, knowing the money should go to assure they'd have enough for unexpected doctor bills and coal for the winter. Yet, it didn't seem like a choice to do anything else. She'd become distressed soon after the violin was sold. It was the last gift his father was able to give him, and Robert's only possession that would endure over the years, as the memory of his father's face faded away.

Lucille opened her eyes, realizing how much time had slipped by since Johnny left. Getting up to take care of the dough left on the counter, she felt the shift to a lighter mood, remembering what joy the German lessons had brought to her family. She wanted to hang on to it before the concerning conversation with Johnny started playing in her mind.

9

Standing across the street from the Jackson train station, Robert watched for railroad detectives mulling around. He tapped Tucker's shoulder to get his attention as he pointed to two bulls that walked out onto the loading platform.

Tucker nodded. "Do you think Al's gonna be on this train?"

Robert shrugged his shoulders. "Maybe, he said he might buy a ticket. I don't think we're going to find out unless we run into him in Little Rock because we're going to be yards down the track by the time he boards."

When they saw two more bulls walk outside and join the other two now standing at the far end of the platform looking down the tracks in the direction the train would arrive, they took the opportunity to slip behind the train station. Spotting another bull with his back to them as they passed by the other end of the depot, Robert grabbed Tucker's elbow, placed his hand across his mouth before he could speak, then signaled for him to follow. He headed for the high brush, stopping about twenty feet back. "We'll have to hustle to get far enough along the tracks if we're going to avoid the bulls coming after us. We can't get too far out though, or the train will be going too fast to jump on."

They bent down in the brush as they walked to avoid being seen in the last of the daylight. The discomfort in Robert's back became so intense, he had to straighten up a little after walking about fifty feet. Worried he was taking a risk of being seen, he rolled down into the brush.

Dropping down next to him, Tucker rolled onto his back. "Thank God, my back's killing me."

"I have to tell you, Tucker, I've never ridden on top a passenger train before because I hear it's tricky. The only way to ride it is to climb the ladder and lay down on top of the cars. Remember, we need to catch on a ladder at the front of the train where it's not as jerky."

Robert opened his rucksack. "Here, I got us these extra long belts at the mission so we can tie onto the rail on top the train. It's what I've heard you have to do in case you fall asleep on the ride."

Tucker leaned up on his elbows. His eyes widened when he saw the belts. "What?"

"We'll put the extra belts around our waist before loading. It's pushing our luck taking this train, but it's this one or waiting for the night freight train. Never tried hopping on after dark either, so we might be better to wait until tomorrow if we miss our chance with this one."

They got up, continuing to crouch in the brush as they walked farther out, stopping when they spotted the first bunch of guys waiting for the train. The blast of the whistle, signaling the train was pulling out from the station, sounded faint, but the bellowing engine noise was racing toward them.

"Okay, let's catch on the next car after these guys. I'll go up the ladder first, and you follow right behind me. No delay, got it, Tucker? You've got to climb up the ladder fast but without losing your footing."

"Yeah, got it. Just don't lose me, okay?"

The close roar of the engine and clouds of smoke nearly engulfing them left no time to reply. Robert took off behind the three men running for the ladder of the first car. He watched as they bounded up onto the top of the passenger train and out of sight.

Hearing Tucker's footsteps close behind him, Robert caught the ladder on the next car. Leaping up the rungs, Robert flung his body onto the top of the car in one swift motion. Tucker's head popped up seconds behind him, forcing Robert to move sideways before he slammed into him. Without time to ground his body against the jerking motions of the train as it increased in speed, Robert was startled by his loss of balance. He rolled onto his stomach and clutched the side rail running along the car with both hands. Tucker followed his lead and grabbed the rail.

With little time to get their bearings, a man's head peered up over the ladder, forcing another sideways crawl. In an instant, still another head surfaced. His body immediately heaved up and over, leaving no time for anyone to react. The last two riders ended up one on top of the other until Robert and Tucker were able to inch farther down.

Once they were out of the way, Robert scooted toward the front of the car, motioning Tucker to follow. Robert pointed to their belts. Sliding his body lengthwise, Robert hung onto the rail with one hand, unbuckled the extra belt with the other, and then slipped one end around the railing. He pulled the end of it back through a loop on his trousers to fasten the buckle, leaving enough slack to move around a bit. Nodding to Tucker, Robert watched as he looped his belt and anchored himself down. Tucker glanced over, giving him a thumbs-up, but the uneasiness on his face mirrored Robert's feelings about the decision to ride on top of a train for hours.

The loud rumbling across the steel tracks muffled the sound of Robert's chests heaving in and out as he lay trying to calm his body. Putting his arms under his head to cushion it from the metal beneath him, feelings of agitation surged through him, knowing he should have stuck with his instincts against hopping a passenger train.

From listening to guys traveling, Robert knew only two things about riding on top of a train. They could be more dangerous to ride because of the speed, and if you tried it, you should belt yourself down in case you fall asleep. The cinders blasting at his face and arms, one after the other, felt like being the bull's-eye in a dart game. The intake of smoke rolling off the engine and blasting up their noses left the two of them coughing in unison until they figured out how to position their faces at each bend in the tracks so the smoke didn't come straight at them.

Robert glanced over to the two guys who hopped on after them. Both looked to be in their thirties. Their bodies lay vertically, but on their backs. Tucker buried his head in his arms. Robert noticed the air flowing over Tucker's hair, starkly different from what Robert had ever seen riding in an open car. It was flattened against his head like slimy seaweed pressed up against a wet rock.

The shuddering of the train against the tracks as it continued to pick up speed was similar to being in an open car, but the intensity of the movement when the train entered into a turn caused the top of the car to brutally bump up and down against his chest and legs. Leaving one arm tucked under his head, Robert clutched the side rail to ease his nerves and guard against any unexpected movement. After shifting his right and left arm back and forth under his cheeks a dozen times, he finally managed turning on his back to stop the recurring numbness from setting into his arms, and ease the tension in his neck.

The soup and bread they had at the mission earlier in the day was wearing off. Robert estimated they had been on the train for over two hours with at least three more hours to ride. The thought was unbearable. *How the heck am I going to make it through the hours ahead?* Trying to get the long ride out of his mind he shut his eyes, hoping it would help him settle down.

When he woke out of his sleep, Robert was alarmed, not knowing how long he'd been out. He looked around to check on Tucker to see his long, lanky body spread catty-corner across the car. Still laying on his stomach with one arm under his head, Tucker's feet were hanging over the rail on the opposite side. The extra belt held his body from following his feet over the rail.

As the first light of dawn appeared, Robert looked back behind Tucker to see the guy's silhouette behind him apparently asleep, his body pressed against the side rails. Still groggy, he looked for the last guy who'd loaded. He rubbed his eyes when he didn't see him and kept staring at the spot where he should be. When he finally grasped what must have happened, Robert slid his arm up over his face. The moment was too surreal to comprehend as he tried to process whether there had been three of them on top of the train or four. Once the memory of the two guys piling on top of one another settled into his mind, he let the annoyingly loud roar of the engine drown out the unleashing of his yell.

The train finally started to slow, bringing Robert back to reality. He raised his head out of the shelter of his arms. Tucker now lay on his back. Robert reached over to tap his head. Shifting onto his side, Tucker didn't try to hide his stare at seeing the distressed expression on Robert's face.

When they felt the speed of the train notch down again, they unbuckled their belts, getting ready to unload before they got too close to the station. Tucker glanced over to his left, then back at Robert. Tucker's look of shock let him know he understood what happened. Robert pointed to the guy still asleep. Tucker shook him awake.

Turning to check how close they were to the station, Robert saw bulls farther up the tracks. They were easy to identify with rifles dangling from their arms. He turned back and looked past Tucker to the guy sitting to his left and motioned him to move over to the ladder on the opposite side of the train and away from the bulls.

But he kept staring to his left, obviously dazed at not seeing the man who boarded behind him. There was no time to let him get his bearings about what happened if they were going to avoid the bulls. Robert nudged Tucker to move. Tucker nudged the man toward the ladder. He responded, slipping his feet over the side, careful to hold on to the ladder until he had a firm footing before crawling down. With Tucker only a few steps behind, the guy didn't waste a second turning his body out from the train, allowing one foot to lightly touch the ground before stepping down and away from the ladder. Tucker carefully followed his model of exiting the train.

Once on solid ground, they ran at top speed for cover toward large boxes of freight sitting next to the tracks. Stopping for a quick look behind them to check if anyone was around, and seeing no one, they sprinted for the high brush ahead. Tucker was the first to fall to the ground, nestling himself down into the brush as he gulped in the air around him. Robert crashed next to him, waiting for the pounding in his chest to subside before turning his head toward Tucker.

"You doing okay, Tucker?"

"Yeah, luckily that guy knew how to exit the ladder. What the heck are you grinning about? That whole thing was nuts."

"It's your face. It's covered with soot."

Tucker rolled over to take a closer look at Robert, and then brought his arm up over his face to cover a smirk. Robert saw it. Rubbing his fingers against his chin, he lowered them to see black soot and couldn't help but grin.

It was quite awhile before they heard the train pull out of the station. The guy with them propped himself up on his elbows to peek up over the brush, signaling a thumbs-up that it was safe to sit up. Robert poked his head out to check for himself, taking no chances of risking a bout with the bulls. Not seeing any walking along the tracks, he sat up.

"I'm Robert, this is Tucker."

"Yeah, I'm Finn. Where're you headed?"

"We're stopping here," Robert said, trying to cut Tucker off before they ended up traveling in a pack. "Were you with the guy that hopped on behind you?"

"No," Finn said, turning his head in the opposite direction so fast it sparked a silence among them.

Robert glanced at Tucker. "I'm ready to head into town. My stomach is talking to me."

Robert peeked around one more time before getting up out of the brush. Remembering the soot on his face, he pulled the handkerchief from his rucksack, rubbed it across his face, brushed off the debris stuck to the right side of his shirt and trousers, and then passed the handkerchief over to Tucker.

Robert looked down at Finn, still sitting in the brush, his body now completely turned away from them. It was obvious Finn was avoiding traveling with others, too. Tucker kept looking back at him and then over to Robert as if uneasy about not offering an invitation to join them. Robert nudged Tucker along toward the town. Tucker shuffled his feet forward but turned his head back toward Finn.

"If he wanted to come, Tucker, he'd stand up and join us."

The entrance into Little Rock looked the same as Jackson, and like all the other towns Robert had entered from the track side of town over the months. A hobo camp was perched thirty feet from the tracks at the outskirts of town.

Passing into the first few blocks of Little Rock, Robert noticed a huge difference in the tone of the "whites only" signs posted on restrooms and restaurants. They didn't seem to shout the words like the signs in Jackson. It was the absence of *"!!!"* and *"we mean it"* after the words that gave the signs a little decency about them, instead of seeming downright repugnant. Even so, the signs left him unsettled. Just a few blocks up the main street they walked by a small cafe. "Nellie's Good Eats" was posted in black and white above the door. Robert stopped in front of it.

"Let's see if we can wash dishes or something. I don't want to use the little money I have left. We might get lucky. Is all that soot off my face?"

"Yeah, how about mine?"

Robert gave a slight nod, pulled the screen door open, and then walked in. Sizing up the counter as he usually did, he waited near the door for a moment. Three seats were open straight ahead. He signaled Tucker to follow him in.

The waitress gave them the same "sizing up" look when they came forward. As they slipped onto the stools, she turned away from them to reach for a couple of platters sitting on the ledge of a window into the kitchen, and then walked away to another customer without acknowledging them. Robert didn't get a good feeling from her but was hungry, so he decided to stick it out. The eyes of the person sitting next to Robert seemed to be peering at him. He gave a quick glance over to see a gray-haired man, caught his eyes for a second, then looked straight ahead.

The waitress walked to the window again. Hesitating, she let out a sigh as she turned to ask if she could get something for them. Robert took a deep breath, hearing his own sigh as he began to speak.

"Uh, ma'am, we're real good workers. We were wondering if we could wash some dishes or sweep things out for you in trade for something to eat?"

The pounding of his heart surprised him since he and Johnny had done this routine a number of times. It took just a second before the image of carrying his food out to the back of the restaurant in Georgia smacked him in the face.

"We don't need no help," she said curtly as she turned her back on them and walked to the other end of the counter.

They turned toward each other, shrugging their shoulders at the same time. Tucker spun around on his stool to leave, the red blush behind his freckles showing his embarrassment. The man next to Robert caught the waitress's attention.

"Why don't you fix up the breakfast special for these boys?" He pulled out a dollar and coins from his pocket, laying it in front of his plate. "This should take care of all of us."

She turned to look at him with expressionless eyes, nodding as she wrote up a ticket and slapped it on the window ledge to the kitchen.

Robert smiled, stunned by the man's kindness.

"Why, that's really appreciated, mister," Tucker said, leaning his body around Robert's back. "Really appreciated."

Swiveling on his stool to get a better look at him, Robert was surprised to see the weathered face of a farmer.

"Thank you, mister. That's very kind of you. Is there any work we can do for you to repay your being so generous?"

Turning away to take a sip of coffee, he slipped on his hat and stood up. "Nope, I've got plenty of help. Enjoy your breakfast and you boys be careful now, you hear?"

The waitress didn't say a word or share a smile when she set the food down. The platters were loaded with scrambled eggs and ham, a heap of potatoes, and two biscuits piled on top. Then her expression changed as she set down a bag in front of the platters.

"You boys might need these, if you have extra left."

She gave them a quick wink, and walked away.

10

The clock on the Bank of Little Rock showed three-forty. They'd been scouting out the town most of the day, ending up on the main street again with no more information about harvesting work than they started out with. The city sprawled in all directions, and finding an opportunity to start up a conversation with locals about harvesting in the area hadn't happened. The lines at the local mission when they passed by wrapped around the entire block, giving them a good indication of their chances of getting anything to eat for supper, let alone getting a job before the men in line.

After walking around all day, Robert needed to get off his feet for a while. Spotting a wooden bench across from a newsstand, he headed for it, eager to get a peek at the latest headlines.

"SCHOOLS CLOSING IN SOUTH DUE TO LACK OF FUNDS" was the headline in big black letters on the front page of the Little Rock Gazette.

"Look at that headline, Tucker."

"Wow, I guess my wanting to stick around home to finish school doesn't much matter now. My dad said they might close, come fall."

"Makes me wonder if the schools will close up north, too."

Robert took a closer look at the rest of the headlines. Except for "Roosevelt Starts New Program to Aid Families" on the front page, the rest of the headlines gave the same desperate picture of the country he'd been reading about for months. He tried to process what it meant if the schools closed in Illinois. Kathleen was supposed to graduate next year. *There's not going to be anything for me to do at home, just be more of a burden to ma. That's for sure. The senior kids are sure to grab the jobs, if there are any.* He leaned forward, sinking his face into his hands.

"That bad?" Tucker asked.

"Yeah, that bad."

It was the ongoing loud chatter of men nearby that brought him back from worries about home. Five old farmers sat in tall-back, wooden rockers outside the general store, less than a half block away. He'd noticed locals sitting in rockers set out in front of general stores in other towns, looking so relaxed in them you'd think they were sitting on a neighbor's porch, instead of rockers that were for sale. Most of the time, the men appeared to be too old to do hard labor anymore, so they sat in the heart of town much of the day.

Robert jumped up. "I'll be back, Tuck."

Settling himself on the edge of the porch, Robert sat right in front of the men. Sitting by locals was always a gold mine opportunity to hear what they knew about what was going on across the country and the most reliable place to find out what was happening in their community. It seemed like his best bet all day to get information about the harvesting Al had told them about. Robert could sit, listen and wait for his chance to ask questions.

"The God damn country is gone to hell, and we're all sinking to hell with it," one of the locals said. "Roosevelt's putting out new programs to help people survive and create jobs, but I haven't seen any of it come this way."

"No, me neither," another grizzled old man added. "Did you listen to Roosevelt's radio program last night? He says help is coming for everyone. They're going to turn things around program by program, new job by new job, one day at a time. Guess you gotta like the man for doing something. Not like that do-nothing bum Hoover, huh?"

"Yeah, I sure agree with that. Seen another article in the paper this morning about farmers in the states affected by dust storms that can't plant nothing no more. Looks like they're getting a subsidy from the government. Doesn't help us though, does it?"

"No, but it lets you know things could be worse for farming families."

There was a sudden pause in their conversation. Robert wanted to turn his head to look behind him, but he was trying not to be noticed.

"Hey, kid. You're not from around here, are you? Whatcha sitting there listening in for?"

Wanting to get a look at the guy before answering, Robert turned his back against the timber holding up one side of the lean-to porch framing the entrance to the store. Just as he settled against it, the man sitting closer to him suddenly leaned forward in the rocker, as if to get his attention. Startled, Robert glanced up. The guy grinned, and held out the soda in his hand.

"Name's Frank. You thirsty, kid? Don't let that old goat scare you now."

Reaching out for the soda, Robert smiled back. "Hey thanks, that's real nice of you."

He took a small sip of the soda feeling like he had to. "I heard there was some harvesting going on here in Little Rock at the Ferguson Farm. Was hoping to find out about it. Do you know if they're still looking for workers?"

"You're a little late I'm sorry to tell you. Ferguson Farm finished string bean harvesting end of last week. The other farms around here finished the week before. Don't know of any more harvesting until next season."

Robert pushed his head back to rest against the timber again, trying to hide his disappointment. Thinking of what to ask next, he remembered Al telling him if the Ferguson Farm didn't pan out there might be work in Marshall, Arkansas. But, he didn't know if Marshall was even close enough to Little Rock to ask about.

"Heard there was some harvesting in Marshall, too."

Frank moved his head back as if surprised by the comment. "Don't know anything about Marshall." He looked around at his friends. "Does anyone know about the harvesting up in Marshall?"

There was a long silence.

Robert wasn't going to lose out on the chance to get more information and figured his best bet was to talk directly to Frank, since he wasn't getting much from anyone else.

"How far is Marshall from here?"

"About a half day driving. Chances are the harvesting in Marshall is done for the season, too. Any of you got work for this kid?"

Robert looked around to see their heads turning back and forth, and then almost in unison they shrugged their shoulders. Pushing his straw hat back on his forehead, Frank gave him a "tough luck" grin.

"Well, I'll tell you what. I've got some work on my farm cleaning out the barn and splitting logs that have been stacked up for a while. Are you with that kid who was sittin' next to you on the bench over there?"

Robert nodded, surprised he would've noticed him sitting next to Tucker, or noticed them at all.

"Then it would be a day's work. It's worth two dollars a piece, and a couple of meals. Seems like you and your friend can handle it. You interested?"

"Yeah, you bet. Thanks mister."

Not sure if they should take it or head straight for Marshall, Robert wasn't passing on the offer until he had time to think it over. And he needed to talk it over with Tucker.

Frank stood up to leave, groaning as he stretched out his back.

"My wife will be waiting on me for supper. The farm is an hour out of town, walking. Take County Road 15, just to the west of town. Look for the sign for Parson's farm on the right. I'll look for you in the morning. If you come up tonight, you can sleep in the prairie on the edge of our property, but be sure to knock twice on our screen door to let me know. There's a pump out by the barn, if you want to wash up."

Robert walked back to Tucker, glad he was traveling with him now even though Frank seemed honest enough. Tucker wasn't happy with the news about the harvesting work, or working all day for two dollars.

"Well, what do you want to do? We could just head up to Marshall instead."

"I guess we should take the job since we're getting a couple of meals and a place to sleep. No telling when we'll get another offer for work or a meal."

"Okay, then let's head for his farm. I'm tired of walking around." Robert motioned for Tucker to follow him. "I want to get there while I can still stand up. I'm beat, and stretching out in that prairie sounds good to me."

They found the county road and walked without saying much. Robert broke the silence. "Hey, I've been thinking about the train ride last night."

Tucker cut him off before Robert could say anything else. "You're kidding me. Right? I've been trying to get that ride out of my mind."

"I know, but I was thinking being shook around on the top of that train all night was like being one of those lightning bugs I used to catch when I was a kid. I'd catch a few, then stick them in a jar and shake it so they would fly around and light up. I'd watch them slam into the sides of the jar, trying to find a way out. Guess I won't be doing that anymore now that I know how it feels."

Robert heard Tucker laugh, glad he got the frown off his face.

It seemed like much longer than an hour before they saw the sign for Parson's farm. Robert hoped the rest of what Frank told him about the job was what he'd said it would be. After knocking on the door twice to let Parson know they'd arrived, they walked out by the barn to wash up and then headed out to the prairie.

Exhausted, they sat not saying anything, enjoying the quiet place to rest and safety of the prairie. It wasn't a bed or even a bedroll, but Robert learned to appreciate the opportunity to rest in a place where he didn't have to worry about someone running him off or trying to nab what little he had.

He began wondering about the work in Marshall. Maybe it wouldn't pan out, but at least it was north of Little Rock and on his way home. There wouldn't be much to lose in checking it out. At least there was work for the next day to think about.

He nestled down into the grass around him, resting his head against his rucksack. The stillness of the prairie allowed the star-filled night to illuminate into a breathtaking magnificence. His experience bedding in open prairies with Johnny over the months had turned from lonely and frightening to familiar. It became an opportunity to embrace the sounds of nature, sounds that were distinct yet similar as he traveled across the country.

Lying on his back, mesmerized by the sky and tuning into the sounds of the night, Robert was grateful for the moment.

"Hey Robert, if all this ended tomorrow and we could go home, that'd be great, huh?"

Robert started to answer Tucker, but hesitated.

"I don't know, I'm starting to like the freedom and adventure we have traveling."

"Well, you can have it. I want my bed back."

Tucker's blunt comment pulled him back to the real world surrounding them. The dangers and tragedies happening around him every day he traveled crept into his mind. Yet as he lay gazing at the moonlit sky looming above, he felt torn between the two worlds of danger and freedom. But then thoughts of his family, waiting for his return, brought a pang of guilt just as he fell asleep.

11

Tucker had been standing on the side of the road with his thumb out for over an hour. They had walked from the Parson's farm to the highway in their beat-up shoes to thumb a ride to Marshall. Still exhausted from the ten hours of hard work the day before, their clothes smelled of live stock from working in the filthy barn and their backs ached from chopping wood. Two dollars is what they got for working from morning until dusk.

Frank came out every few hours to remind them of what was left to be done. At least their stomachs were full from three good meals yesterday and a homestyle breakfast today of eggs and fresh bread Frank's wife made before they left. They could appreciate the chickens that laid the eggs after cleaning out the chicken coop, which hadn't been cleaned for months.

Tucker whistled to Robert.

"This is the shits. Maybe you should try for a while."

Robert shrugged, pulled himself up off the side of the road, walked in front of Tucker, and stuck out his thumb. "Haven't had luck getting a ride since we got to Little Rock."

Just as Tucker got settled in the brush to relax, a vehicle heading in their direction skidded to a stop. He jumped back up and stood next to Robert, giving him a slight smirk. "Oh, wouldn't you know."

Tucker leaned his head down by the side window. "Thanks for stopping, mister."

"Where you boys headed?"

"We're trying to get to Marshall," Robert replied, slipping in front of Tucker.

"Name's Owen. I'm turning ten miles before Marshall, but you can ride that far."

Tucker walked to the front of the truck to take a look, and then leaned down into the window again. "Thought this was a car when I first saw it coming with the bronze grill across the front. Never seen a truck like this one before."

"Yeah, we rolled our '26 Ford sedan last year but got lucky. The front grill was dented only a little. It was my idea to put the grill on the truck. It took some doing, but it fits like a glove. A beauty, isn't it?"

They both stood back to look at the faded dark green truck. The spoked hub caps accented with chipped gold paint finished off the look of a unique ride.

Tucker walked around the truck. "Yep, it's a beauty all right. The hubcaps add a touch, too. Where'd you find them?"

"Traded some wheat with a metal worker needing some feed for his horses last winter. He'd picked them up from the owner of a scrap yard. I gave him a fair trade for them though. Hey, hop in the back if you want a ride. I'm running late to take some feed to my brother's place. There should be enough room, just don't sit on the feed bags."

Two feet of empty space was left between the feed and the tailgate. Tucker hopped in first, stretching his long legs across the rusted-out floor bed. Robert stood trying to process his options, realizing he had only one as he hoisted himself over the gate, then stretched out his legs in between Tucker's.

"You think it's going be a long ride to Marshall?" Robert said, letting the first grin in a few days slip out.

They were asleep against the bags of feed when the truck stopped abruptly. By the time they shook off their sleep and stood up to hop out, Owen was standing at the back of the truck.

"This is the end of the road with me."

Robert reached out to shake Owen's hand.

"Thanks for the ride. We heard there might be some harvesting in Marshall."

The laugh from Owen left them speechless, but his face was quick to read the discomfort on Robert's face.

"Hey, sorry, I'm not laughing at you. I figured you were kids looking for work. It's just that we only have a couple of hundred come through a week, not counting all the men searching for work, too. Most of them are usually looking in Little Rock though, not this far north. What makes you think there'd be something in a town the size of Marshall this time of year?"

"Just had a tip about work harvesting. Maybe a bum one?"

Owen walked back to hop in his truck but turned, standing with his thumbs resting at the edge of his overall pockets.

"This is the end of the season, so good luck. Only harvesting left might be the strawberry fields. Watch out though, the town has been in the news for some outlaws on the loose up there. Some gang broke into the bank and stole several thousand dollars from the safe in Alma. They've alerted towns people they might still be in the area. Sure you want to go up there?"

They stood staring at him, trying to process what Owen had just said. Robert shrugged his shoulders. "We need work."

"Yeah, everyone does. At least I warned you."

He hopped in his truck and waved out the window as he headed west.

Tucker threw his arms up in the air. "Well, that's swell, huh? But we're here now. Might as well follow up. Beats standing in the middle of the road, huh?"

Shaking his head in agreement, still speechless, Robert started walking.

Marshall was a barren looking town. The only building with merit was the two-story, faded red brick court house positioned on a small knoll of grass in the center of the town square. It was surrounded by typical small town businesses. Robert scanned the block—-Woodpecker's General Store, Bob's Pharmacy, E. Daniel's Hardware.

Two blocks up he saw what he was looking for. Several men sitting in chairs perched outside the general dry goods store. There it was, the most likely place to find out information about harvesting. Trying his usual approach, Robert settled on the steps right in front of the men, and waited for someone to strike up a conversation. It didn't take long before one of them asked what they were doing in Marshall.

Robert was quick to turn around to answer. "We heard there was work harvesting here. Maybe in the strawberry fields."

It was more of men choking than muffled laughs that followed, and then it quit as suddenly as it started. Robert glanced over his shoulder to see the men looking straight at him, staring blankly as if any word would set them off again. He put his hand to his forehead for a second, trying to come up with what to say.

"There's no harvesting left?"

"The strawberry harvesting is five miles out of town off County Road 9, at the Burkett farm. I'm Sam Burkett's neighbor," the man sitting closest to him said.

Robert turned to see him reach his weather-beaten hand out.

"The names Jack Carter. Didn't mean no harm, but Burkett probably picked his men for the season. If you still go up there, tell Sam that Jack Carter told you how to get to his farm."

Robert caught the strong emphasis on "picked his men for the season" along with its meaning.

"I will. That's mighty good of you."

Robert gave Tucker a nudge to leave.

A newsstand was at the end of the block. Robert headed toward it, stopping to grab part of a newspaper laying on top of the trash in front of the barber shop. The headline read "BARROWS GANG STILL LOOSE."

Robert looked over at the grassy knoll surrounding the court house. It was all couched up with people lounging around. Eager to read the article, he figured it was okay to join them without being chased away. He headed to it, unfolding the Marshall Evening Chronicle as soon as he sat down.

"Hey, catch this. It's about those outlaws."

BARROWS GANG STILL LOOSE

Marshal Henry Humphrey was shot and killed by the notorious outlaw gang led by Bonnie and Clyde.

Humphrey was working the night shift, and in the early morning of June 22, 1933, two men captured Humphrey as he was making his rounds outside the Commercial Bank building in downtown Alma. They bound Humphrey with baling wire, stole his flashlight and pistol, and broke into the bank where they went to work securing the bank safe.

The next day, June 23, 1933 Humphrey got a call from his office alerting him there had been an accident on the old highway going through Alma. He was given the license number and was notified of another robbery in Fort Smith at Brown's Grocery, a car theft. Crawford County Deputy Sheriff Ansel and "Red" Salyers, a friend of Humphrey's, offered to go with him. Due to the urgency, they took Deputy Salyers' car.

As the Marshal and Deputy Salyers drove north on Highway 71, they passed a slower-moving blue Chevy truck driving south; seconds later a Ford Sedan sped by them, also going south. The Sedan disappeared over a hill and the officers heard a loud crash as the Sedan rammed into the back of the Chevy truck. Humphrey quickly turned around and rushed to the accident. He then realized the Sedan was the car they were looking for - it was Buck Barrow and W.D. Jones, who had robbed the store and stolen the Sedan. The gang quickly recovered from their crash and grabbed their guns as Deputy Salyers' car approached and blocked the road. Humphrey drew the Smith & Wesson .38 revolver he had borrowed from his brother-in-law, as his weapon had been stolen the day before, and as he appeared out the door of the vehicle, Buck Barrow shot him full in the chest with buckshot and he fell into the ditch. Two or three minutes of gunfire erupted between Salyers and the suspects before Buck's shotgun jammed or was empty. Salyers ran to find cover and ran toward a house nearly one hundred yards to the west of the scene. The second suspect fired at him but missed, although bullets passed through the house and barn and nearly hit a man working in a nearby strawberry field. As Salyers reloaded, Buck and W.D. ran to the Deputy's car where Humphrey was still laying, grabbed the wounded Marshal's gun and drove away. The Marshal was taken to the hospital and on June 26, 1933, he died after having only been with the agency two months.

The two gang members are still on the move but they are thought to be headed south toward Fort Smith.

"That last part doesn't sound good," Tucker said. "But then, no one else seems interested in us, so the Barrows gang probably wouldn't be either."

Tucker was so somber when he replied it made Robert break a smile. "You're right. Let's head to the Burkett farm. It didn't sound like there's much chance of getting on with him, but let's find out. We'll have to come back to Marshall to catch a train north though."

It was late afternoon when they found the sign for the Burkett Strawberry Farm. The sun sat high above, generating a shimmer effect on the strawberry fields, which extended far into the horizon. The men were working on nearby fields. They could see them hunched over with bags hanging from their side.

When no one answered the knocking at the farmhouse, Robert yanked the bell hanging on a chain next to the door. "Let's sit here for a while. Maybe Burkett is out in the field."

"Sittin' sounds good. I'm starting to get a blister on my foot from walking. Guess I should of taken your advice and bought boots when I was at that mission in Little Rock. Not sure though. Hated to let go of forty cents. Thought it would be better spent on meals."

The soles in the front of Tucker's shoes were breaking loose. He shook out small stones collected under his dirt-crusted socks. "How about you, did you take my advice? Write a letter to your ma to let her know you're okay? They were supplying paper and the post for free. Couldn't make it much easier."

Robert turned away, then lifted his arm to point at someone coming up a trail from the strawberry fields. As the guy got closer, Robert saw the shot gun hanging from his arm, tipped down but still facing toward them. The man's expression didn't look friendly as he got closer to them.

"What can I do for you boys?"

Robert stood up. "Are you Mr. Burkett?"

"No, the Burketts went over to the auction at the Johnson ranch. Should be back soon. I'm sure I can help you though. If you're looking for work, we don't need no one. If you're looking for a meal, I'd try someplace else."

He turned his back on them, and headed toward the field. His gait sped up as he walked away, leaving no chance for more conversation.

Robert turned to Tucker, still sitting on the porch stoop. "Let's go." He hopped off the porch and started walking but turned around when he didn't hear Tucker following behind. "Come on, Tuck."

"Where we going this time of day? It's more than an hour back to Marshall walking. My feet are aching. It's not going to hurt nothing sitting here for a bit."

"Do you want to go ask the guy with the shot gun if we can stay awhile and rest? I don't. Let's go."

"Okay. I'm coming."

Dust spun up like the tail of a tornado when a truck turned into the farm. As it passed, Robert and Tucker waved. The woman on the passenger side kept her gaze on them as they drove by. The squeaky brakes on the truck signaled its stop. The gravel spitting up from the road as the truck backed up, made Robert and Tucker stop and pause to cover their eyes while more dirt swirled around.

"What are you boys doing here?"

Robert stepped up to the side window to get a better look at the driver. "Hello. I'm Robert. Are you Mr. Burkett?"

"Yeah, why do you ask?"

"We were asking in town about the strawberry harvesting around here. Jack Carter told us how to get to your place."

"Oh he did, did he?" Burkett replied as he let out a quiet laugh.

Robert noticed his wife nudging her husband's shoulder, leaning into him to whisper something.

"Come back up to the house if you want. You're welcome to have supper with the help."

They stood watching the truck head up the road. Tucker prodded Robert forward. "Come on! Looks like this is our lucky day. I'm starving."

"Yeah, how about that. We're not even going to have to work for our supper seems like."

Still thirty feet from the house, they could see the guy with the rifle walking back up to the porch. He met the Burketts at the top of the driveway just as they were getting out of the truck. After the encounter with the rifle a few minutes earlier, Robert suddenly felt uneasy as he and Tucker finished the walk back to where they stood. The three of them turned in unison as they came up. Burkett stepped forward.

"Meet my overseer, Dexter Black."

"I already told them we didn't have any work," Dexter said in a gruff tone.

Mrs. Burkett moved forward to stand next to her husband. "Now Dexter, we offered them supper."

Dexter shifted his eyes over to her, then to Burkett. He started to say something but she began talking at the same time.

"They'll wait for the bell and then come down to eat, Dexter." Mrs. Burkett smiled as she spoke, but her voice was firm.

"Yes, ma'am." Dexter glanced over at Burkett, letting his irritation show before turning back toward the fields.

After watching and listening to the conversation, Robert's uneasiness about what was happening increased a level.

Mrs. Burkett smiled as she turned to look at them. "You boys can wait on the porch until supper if you like. Shouldn't be more than an hour before supper is served. How about some lemonade?"

Tucker nodded and stepped toward her. "That's right kind of you, ma'am. Haven't had anything to drink all day."

They sat on the porch, feeling the cool sweat from the ice-cold lemonade against their hands, watching the sun moving west lift the glimmer off the strawberry fields. They knew they were lucky just to get off their feet for a while and enjoy a cold drink and supper before taking the walk back to Marshall. The rest eased the disappointment a little of failing to find work again.

They sat with elbows leaning back against the porch landing as if all were well, watching the sun descend farther west. The screen door opening and closing got their attention. They both stood up to see Mrs. Burkett standing with a pitcher in her hand.

"More lemonade, boys? Need to use the bathroom?"

"Yes, to both, ma'am," Tucker replied without hesitating. "That's good of you to offer."

She held the screen door open through a long pause, before they realized it was her invitation to come inside. "The bathroom is just down the hall on the right," she said as she glanced at Tucker. Extending her arm toward the dining room table, she motioned for Robert to sit down. Just as he settled in the chair, Burkett came into the room and glanced at his wife with an expression of concern. When Robert didn't get an invitation to leave, he stayed seated.

Burkett brushed away his thick graying hair from his forehead as he slipped into the seat across from him. "You look quite young to be on the road. You're probably not having much luck finding work, are you?"

He didn't wait for an answer. "Dexter's my overseer. He doesn't like kids working for him. He wants to leave the work on the farm to men needing to feed their families. Likes to do the hiring himself. Gets mighty upset if we hire anyone he hasn't approved."

He glanced at his wife. "Can't blame him, I guess, given he's responsible for the work that gets done. He runs a tight operation."

Robert didn't know what to say to the frank comments.

Mrs. Burkett slid into the chair across from her husband.

Not willing to pass up a chance to at least try to get work, Robert mustered up his nerve. "We're good workers though.

We'd give you as much hard work as those men. I have experience picking green beens. I'm very fast."

Tucker came into the dining room just as Robert finished, and stood next to him, waiting for an invitation before sitting down. "If you're talking about work, I'm real good in the fields."

Robert turned his head away, his eyes fixed on a violin leaning upright near the fireplace. He could hear Burkett talking but tuned out the conversation. Gripped by an overwhelming sense of melancholy, he couldn't take his eyes off the violin or his mind off of what it represented. His father's smile loomed in to his thoughts and the times he had played for his entire family. He could almost hear the notes and feel the bow against the strings.

Brought back to the Burketts' dining room by Tucker's hand nudging his shoulder, Robert didn't know how long he'd taken himself out of the conversation, or if he had blown their chance to sell themselves to Burkett. He hadn't even noticed Tucker sitting down next to him.

"You play, son?" Mrs. Burkett asked.

"Yes. I haven't played in quite a while though."

"Our son Collin used to play. That's his violin. He . . . he was in a tractor accident out in the field last fall." She paused and swallowed hard. "He died in the hospital a few weeks later."

Burkett got up, stood behind his wife and gently put his hand on her shoulder. "Now, we don't need to bother these boys with our sadness. They should head toward the field house. Supper's served right at six o'clock. It'll give them time to wash up."

Getting the hint to leave, they stood up and both turned when they got to the door to give a slight bow to Mrs. Burkett. "Sure was generous of you to let us rest on the porch," Robert said. "We were mighty bushed."

"Yes, ma'am," Tucker said. "And the lemonade hit the spot given it got so hot today."

Dexter's welcome was non existent when they walked in. So was any acknowledgement that they were standing in front of him. Waiting for a sign that it was okay to get some food, they got nothing other than a quick glance, remiss of making eye contact. It seemed they were on their own about getting supper from the cook.

Tucker elbowed Robert in the side and pointed toward the food as they got in the back of the line. "Warm stew with beef and corn bread, too. Not salt pork. That's something."

Looking for an opening at one of the four long wooden tables in the dining hall, all heads turned as they approached the only bench with room for the two of them. Robert sat next to a large, muscular man who looked in his thirties. His face was deep red from the sun, and his lips so swollen with blisters they looked like shriveled plums. It was hard to act as if he didn't notice his lips, but he made sure he didn't stare.

"Name's Carlton. You starting work here? Not seen any kids working in the fields here before."

"No. Just getting supper. How much work is left, do you know?"

"Two weeks, maybe three."

No more conversation was directed at them, just heads tipping down in acknowledgement of their arrival at the table. They listened to the exchanges between the men. The conversation staying with the day's heat, aching bodies, what time the poker game started for the night, and who was in.

Robert noticed Burkett's tall frame enter the food hall. He walked over to Dexter, pulling him to the side. Dexter seemed irritated almost immediately, talking with his hands, then throwing them up in the air as his boss walked away. Burkett looked over to Robert and Tucker, nodding at them as he left.

One by one the men at the table finished their meals, picked up their plates, and left. The two of them were finishing the last of their stew and corn bread when Dexter slid into the bench across from them.

"Looks like you two got on the good side of Mr. Burkett or maybe Mrs. Burkett, didn't you?" It sounded like more of an accusation than a question. "You got a job as long as you do the work. If you don't, you leave. Got it?"

Robert jumped in to reply. "Yes, Mister. We're going to give you good work. We will, won't we Tucker?" Turning away from Dexter so he didn't have to keep staring at the obvious anger on his face, Robert waited for Tucker to say something.

"You bet mister; you bet we will."

"Ask any of the guys in the bunk area about how things work. We start in the fields at 6:00 a.m. The first time you're late, you're out."

Dexter stood up, placed both hands in the center of the table, and stared at them like a couple of insects he wanted to swat. As he turned to leave, he looked back with an expression of disdain.

When he left, Tucker shifted forward, putting his hands over his face for a moment. "Geez, what was that about? I didn't think we were that charming for Burkett to hire us. Dexter sure doesn't think so. I'm thinking he's already figuring out how to get rid of us."

12

In the bunk house they were met with stares and silence, everyone begging the question of why they were there. As Robert and Tucker walked down the row of bunks, the men shuffled around, turning their backs away like pigeons scattering in a park. Some of the men looked to be in their thirties, but most seemed in their forties and older. Spotting Carlton sitting on a bunk pulling off his boots, Robert headed straight for him. When the bodies standing around him didn't take the normal course of men winding down for the evening, he looked up. He seemed startled when he saw the two of them again. "What? You get to sleep inside for the night too?"

"Well, seems we got hired on. Dexter told us to ask someone in the bunk house about how things work," Robert said.

Carlton's expression showed disbelief, but he refrained from expressing it.

"How things work, huh? Okay, breakfast is at five. Work starts at six. Just follow the men to the picking sacks after breakfast, then out to the field. Remember to fill the sacks full before heading up to empty them in a crate. Be gentle with the berries, like they're precious glass that can break. But don't take too long picking them, or emptying them out of the sack. Got it?"

Tucker and Robert glanced at each other, trying to digest the curt instructions, and then nodded.

"Where do we bunk?" Robert asked.

"Good luck finding a bunk. We were full up last time I noticed. Might be an extra straw mattress or blanket laying around by the back door you could toss down somewhere." Carlton started to slip a sock off, but looked back up. "Be smart, boys. Be the last to wash up, the last to use the outhouses, and stay out of the way of the men. They might be looking for a reason to pick a fight with boys taking on some of their work and wages."

"Sure will," Tucker said. "Thanks for letting us know."

Robert stepped up to shake his hand. "We got it," Robert said with enthusiasm. "We're going to work hard for our wages. Don't need to worry about that."

Carlton gave them a brusque look but said nothing.

They looked around and found a short pile of straw-filled mattresses stacked in the corner by the back entrance of the bunk house. Tucker slid a mattress on either side of the door. "Like finding a gold mine, ain't it? Look there, some blankets on the top shelf behind you." Grabbing one, he dramatically plopped down onto the mattress and stretched out.

"Yeah, you got that right. Having a mattress and a blanket, it's too good to be true."

Four o'clock came fast. Heeding Carlton's advice, they were the last to head for the dining hall to get breakfast and last to use the can before following the men to the fields.

During the first hour picking strawberries, they watched how the men hung the sacks over their bodies, saw the way they leaned into the strawberry plants, gauged how many berries were grabbed before placing them into the sacks and noted the height to which they loaded the bags with berries before emptying them into crates. By late morning their techniques were smoothing out, and their swiftness in keeping up with the other men's pace improved.

Tucker's face was tomato red by midday. By late afternoon their backs ached, but they were thankful to have kerchiefs to shield their necks from the powerful sun that beat down on them. Dropping onto the mattresses at the bunk house after dinner gave them relief from the unfriendly looks of the men. Carlton didn't have any comments about their first day's work either.

The next morning, still exhausted and half asleep, they jumped up when they heard the shuffling of boots against the planked floor. Throwing on their clothes, they watched as the last few men headed out the door for breakfast.

Robert raced to zip his trousers and to buckle his belt. "We'd better forget the morning wash-up. Let's get over there. Hey, wait, I don't see my neck kerchief anywhere. I left it on top of my clothes."

"Don't see mine either. Rats."

At the breakfast line it didn't take long to spot their neck kerchiefs on the necks of two men who had worked in front of them the day before. Tucker poked Robert and nodded toward the men. He just shrugged his shoulders, knowing they couldn't take the risk of making a flap about the kerchiefs that might end in a quarrel.

The larger of the two guys stood in the line in front of Robert. He turned around and settled his eyes on him. The subtle smile on his face and lingering look caused an eerie feeling in Robert's gut. The man, burly and with arms as thick as the boughs of trees held out his hand to him. "I'm Arlie."

Robert shook hands with Arlie, whose grip was so strong he felt the sensation for several moments. But he wasn't unfriendly other than his uncertain smile.

The next four days were about blisters, deep pain in their backs, aching feet, and Tucker's face turning from tomato red to a deep ruddy red. Pulling their shirt collars over their necks as they picked strawberries did little to shield them from the sun.

On the fifth day, Saturday, they found out why they were hired. They saw Burkett for the first time since they had started working. He walked into the dining hall and stood at the entrance looking around until he spotted them at the end of the long food line. He headed toward them.

"So you made it through your first week?"

They stood bobbing their heads up and down like a couple of prairie dogs poking their heads out of the ground trying to figure out if it was safe to make a move. Hearing noise from boots shuffling on the wood floor, Robert glanced over to see the men sitting at the table next to the food line shift themselves around to listen. He turned his attention quickly back to Burkett as he continued speaking.

"The Mrs. wants you to come for supper tonight since it's Saturday and you don't have to worry about getting up early tomorrow. You can walk up to the house with me."

Burkett started walking to the door, stopping when he didn't hear their boots moving behind him. They stood frozen in place, still trying to think of what to say or do.

"Oh, hey, Mr. Burkett. Why, we're mighty glad to have supper here in the dining hall," Tucker blurted out. "No fuss necessary for us, sir."

"Follow me, boys, the Mrs. is waiting for us," Burkett replied firmly, turning again toward the door.

This time they followed. Robert looked back at Tucker to see the same bewilderment on his face that he felt. He was sure Tucker was just as afraid as he was that the other men would be resentful of any special treatment they got.

On the way up to the house, Burkett began chatting about the report on the progress made in the fields the past week, seeming very pleased that the work would wrap up as scheduled. Mrs. Burkett came out the door as they stepped onto the porch. Holding the screen door open, she waved for them to come in. "Good to see you boys."

The fragrant aroma of a home-cooked meal was immediate as they entered the house. A rump roast sat in the middle of the table surrounded by golden, roasted potatoes and cut carrots. Mrs. Burkett slipped off her apron as she went into the kitchen. She came back with a basket of rolls baked so recently the scent somehow drew attention from the strong scent of spices in the roast. Robert noticed Tucker's eyes fixed on the food, an expression of disbelief on his face.

They ate with a hearty appetite after the Burketts urged them to feel at home and to dig in. It was after a dessert of warm apple pie when they found out why they were there and why the other men were in the dining hall.

"You boys probably think being invited up here, special like, is unusual," Mrs. Burkett said. "We know it is, but we just want you to think of it as a bribe."

Surprised by what she said, Robert spoke up.

"A bribe? Why, ma'am, we don't have any way to repay you for this fine supper. We're mighty appreciative though for the work and meals over this past week. Haven't eaten like that in a long time."

She got up suddenly, motioning for them to follow her into the living room. Picking up the violin resting against the fire place, she turned to Robert and placed it before him.

"I'm bribing you," she said with a playful smile, brushing strands of her dark hair back. "I've missed hearing my son's music, so much it hurts inside at times. Collin's playing was part of every Saturday evening after supper. Would you play for me . . . for us? It would mean so much. It'd be like having my son back to play for me for a while, just a little while." She clasped her hands together. "Would you . . . please?"

Robert saw the pain etched in her blue eyes. She had a quizzical look but he knew he wasn't being offered a choice. *Geez . . . like having her son back. There's no getting out of this.*

Mrs. Burkett motioned to her husband and walked to the door. She waited for Robert to follow them before stepping onto the porch. Giving a quick glance of surprise to Tucker, he followed them as he tried to think of which piece of music he would play. *"I sure hope I don't sound rusty and disappoint her."*

Settling into a straight-back, cane chair, likely placed there for him, he took a few deep breaths to calm the nervousness he felt from having to play for someone other than his family. Taking a moment, he closed his eyes and waited for the right piece to come to mind. When it did, he took an extended amount of time before he raised his arm to place the violin under his chin and the bow against it. He let the entire piece flow through his mind until he was confident all the notes would be there.

Robert began to play his father's favorite, a sonata by an Italian composer, Niccolo Paganini. He knew instantly the sound coming from the violin and the movement of the bow across it was flowing as freely as the last time he'd played it.

Emotions welling up at the chance to hold a violin again, and the connection he felt to the sonata, he gently shut his eyes. His mind was quick to slip away from the porch, back to when he played for his family on the Italian-made violin his father gave him. For a moment he imagined he was holding his magnificent violin, with the top carved from a solid piece of spruce, and the sides and bottom carved from sycamore. Keeping his eyes closed for a moment longer as the sonata came to its end, Burkett, Mrs. Burkett, and Tucker sat without stirring.

Robert slowly opened his eyes to see Tucker sitting directly across from him with eyes wide open, his chest leaning forward in the chair. He appeared stunned but moved deeply, it seemed. He glanced at Mr. Burkett reclining against the back of the wooden porch swing with a hand over his forehead, concealing his eyes. Mrs. Burkett sat next to her husband. Her fingertips were slowly moving along the bottom edges of her calico dress. "That was so beautiful," she said, with her face shining with emotion. "It seems as if anything beautiful has been stripped away each year of this horrible depression. It's left people bereft, going through one month to the next with less and less hope. Your music helped pierce through the bareness of life. It gave me something to remember and hang on to for a while."

Her blue eyes were moist, the grief of enormous loss sitting boldly on her face.

Not knowing how to respond, Robert sat still for a minute before standing up. "I was glad to play for you, but if you don't mind, ma'am, we'll be getting back to the bunk house." He rose straight up from the chair with Tucker doing the same an instant later. "Thank you for the delicious supper. It was kind of you to let me play your son's violin."

The Burketts stood at the same time, seeming surprised by his abrupt departure. "Oh, I thought you might want to play another piece," Mrs. Burkett said. "But we are so grateful you played for us tonight."

She glanced at her husband. "Thank you," he said. "It was very special to hear music again."

Feeling overwhelmed after holding a violin again and unsettled at seeing Mrs. Burkett's grief after he finished his sonata, he didn't know what else to say. A nod and bow was all he could muster up. Laying the violin gently across the chair, he settled the bow next to it, and then jumped off the porch, not waiting for Tucker. He could see men clustered outside the bunk house and watched as they shuffled back inside when they saw him get closer. With the sound of Tucker's footsteps walking at a fast pace behind him, Robert sped up his steps, noticing at once when the footsteps behind him stopped.

Entering the bunk house without looking around, he headed for his mattress and laid face down without undressing or taking off his shoes. The rush of melancholy hit so fast, he needed time to sort it out and get rid of it before he gave Tucker any opportunity to ask him about the music he just played.

The morning light was just streaming through the windows when he woke. Tucker was still out cold, face down on the mattress. He hadn't heard him come in the night before. When Robert stood up, his neck kerchief fell off his body onto the floor. Tucker's scarf was laying at the end of his mattress. The men had cleared out of the bunk house, but he wasn't sure where they went. It was Sunday, so he figured they probably headed for town.

Stepping outside, he saw a small group of men standing in their underwear next to the pump. They were dunking their clothes in sudsy water in a horses' trough and rinsing them in a huge metal tub used for feeding oats to horses. Never during his months on the road did he see a scene like it, but once the opportunity registered, he wasn't going to let it pass by.

Bolting inside, he grabbed his rucksack so he wouldn't miss the chance to be next in line to wash his extra pair of socks, underwear, shirt, and the neck scarf he just got back. The lingering smell of live stock on his clothes from sweeping out Parson's filthy barn the week before had trailed him for long enough. Although he'd noticed it had become tough to distinguish that stink from the drenching smell of body odor in the bunk house. He gave Tucker a slight jab in his side. He opened his eyes a sliver, shaking off sleep as he rolled on to his back.

"Don't miss this chance to wash your clothes, buddy; it might not come around very soon again."

Rolling onto his side, Tucker lifted himself onto his elbow. "What are you talkin' about?"

"There's a place to wash your clothes rigged up outside."

Robert came back into the bunk house after tossing his clothes over the fence to dry, figuring they wouldn't take long. It was only eight o'clock and seventy-five degrees was already registered on the temperature gauge outside. Tucker was just starting out the door with his dirty clothes bunched together. "I see we got our neck kerchiefs back."

"Yeah, I wonder what that's about. I'm heading out for breakfast. When I get back I'm going to wash my trousers and the shirt I have on."

Tucker shoved something into his mouth. "Mrs. Burkett sent cinnamon buns with me last night after you ran off. I left them out on your mattress. Ate my share already."

"We'll, I'm eating mine before some of the men still lingering outside walk by and see them. Won't make this next week any easier if they do after eating supper with the Burketts."

"Hey, I say we've got a good situation with you making the Burketts happy with your music. Don't worry about the men. We got our neck kerchiefs back, didn't we?"

13

The work in the strawberry fields would end two days earlier than expected. Just after supper ended on Monday, Dexter announced the last meal in the field house would be Thursday night, and they could all clear out Friday morning after they picked up their pay. When he finished the announcement, it felt as if all the men turned toward the two of them. Robert glanced across the table to Tucker to catch his eyes staring back at him with concern.

It didn't take much to know the work week and the men's earnings were decreased by the two of them being hired on. The tense mood in the room was heightened when Burkett entered the field house. He scanned the room and walked directly over to them.

"You boys had a good week?" he asked, not waiting for an answer. "Mrs. Burkett has this idea. She'd like it if you boys would come up to talk about it?"

"Why sure," Tucker said, when Robert stayed silent.

"Good, we'll see you after you finish your supper then."

They stood staring at each other after he walked away.

"Geez, I wonder what that's about," Robert said. "Let's eat and get it over with."

Surprised by his reaction, Tucker shrugged slightly and finished his supper without saying anything more.

On the way up to the Burketts' place, Robert was curious if they wanted him to play the violin again.

"Well, what do you think this is about?" Tucker asked.

"Not sure but if they want me to play a piece for them tonight, I will."

"That'd be swell. I'd sure like it if you did. It was really something to hear you play."

The Burketts were sitting outside on the porch, waiting for them.

"Evening ma'am, Mr. Burkett," Robert said, bowing a bit.

Tucker came up along side of him, grinning as he nodded in acknowledgement. "Mr. Burkett said you had something you wanted to discuss, ma'am. Be glad to help out any way we can."

Smiling in reply to Tucker's comment, she motioned to sit down. The lemonade pitcher was full, also waiting for their arrival. She slipped a glassful into each of their hands. Feeling the ice cold drink against his fingers, Robert raised the glass to his cheek for just a second, appreciative of a cold drink in the ninety degree heat. The lemonade was comforting, allowing him to relax for a moment, but his thoughts of why they were there took over. He was now a bit worried about being invited to their house again after the announcement that the workweek was being cut short. Going back to the bunk house later would be tough enough.

Mrs. Burkett began speaking, keeping her eyes fixed on Robert, cutting his moments of relaxation short. "It seems Dexter and the men are irritated because we gave you a few weeks' work and now the harvesting is ending early. We know you must be feeling it, so we were wondering if maybe you could play a few pieces of music for the men on the last day of picking."

There was a long, awkward silence. The expression on Mrs. Burkett's face turned to a questioning look. Robert was sure it was a reaction to his stunned look. He wanted to decline politely, but he fell silent when the words didn't come.

"I thought . . . we thought, playing for the men might make it easier on you, working with them through this week." Pausing as if she was struggling to come up with the right words created more uneasiness in the moment. "And I . . . we wouldn't feel selfish asking you to play just for the two of us again before you leave."

Waiting for a reply, her eyes stayed fixed on him. "Would you play for the men?"

The image of performing in front of strangers, most of whom had shown their resentment every day they'd been on the farm, set off a slight trembling in Robert's knees. Desperately trying to piece together a respectable reply, a wave of anxiousness surged through him when he thought about performing in front of an audience. It was one thing to play for the Burketts, who needed to hear violin music again, but another to play for field workers who resented him for being around at all. He doubted any of them had any hankering to hear classical music.

Mrs. Burkett tilted her head slightly and smiled, letting him know she was waiting for his answer.

Keeping his eyes frozen on hers, Robert slid forward in the chair to ease himself up. Standing at attention like a soldier, throat dry, sweat seeping its way onto his eyebrows, the discomfort from his silence grew as each moment passed. Conflicted, he watched Mrs. Burkett raise her eyebrows, revealing she was disquieted by his lack of response. Moving forward in her chair, she capped her hands over the front of the cane rocker as if prompting him to say something.

Swallowing a few times to get some fluid in his throat so he could speak, he was afraid his voice might be shaky. At the same time, he tried to force away the sporadic images flashing through his mind about turning and running back to the bunk house. Taking a deep breath, he began racing through his words. "Ma'am, it's kind of you to think of Tucker and me like that, but I don't perform in front of people, never have, only played for my family until I played for you. I don't feel comfortable, and haven't played much over the past year or so. Sorry."

He edged backwards to steady himself against the porch rail, afraid he'd made a mistake in being so frank.

She didn't hide her disappointment. "It didn't sound like you haven't played for a while. Your music is so beautiful. Think what a gift it would be for everyone. I'm sure the men haven't heard such music for quite some time, some maybe ever. Could you do it for them, for us?"

Burkett glanced over to his wife and smiled slightly as he stood up. "Now, the boy said how he feels. Let's not press him."

"Thank you, sir. Sorry, ma'am." Robert turned toward the steps, looking over his shoulder to say good night as he headed toward the bunk house. Tucker was quick to say goodnight and scurried to catch up with him.

"Hey, you dope, your music is great, don't you know it? Why can't you do it for swell folks like them?"

When Robert didn't answer, Tucker began again. "Kind of selfish not to, isn't it? What the heck's wrong with you?" Tucker kept walking alongside him, turning his head to look at Robert every few steps, waiting for an answer to any of his questions.

"I'm going for a walk, alone. I'll catch you later, Tuck."

Turning on the dirt road behind the bunks, he kept a swift gait for a while, trying to calm himself from the anxiety erupting through his body that felt like firecrackers gone wild. He plopped down on his back on a patch of wild grass separating two strawberry fields.

A small crescent moon left a dark, vast blanket of stars hanging above him. Robert hoped the stars would settle him as they had always done before. They seemed like glorious diamonds locked in their place in the world, families of stars, safe and secure of ever being ripped apart. Without any notice, a tear slipped down the side of his cheek as his family came into his thoughts. He squeezed his eyes shut to keep any more tears from seeping out and tried to calm himself.

Lying quietly for a while, Robert opened his eyes again to take in the net of stars hanging above once more. Fixing his mind on the beauty of this simple gift, his thoughts suddenly jolted him. *Life's becoming a series of fading memories, of dad, of life before everything changed.*

Tucker was sitting hunched up behind the bunk house, waiting like a guard dog when he came back. "You okay?"

"Yeah, better anyway."

"Come to your senses about playing on Thursday?" Tucker asked, timidly.

"Yeah, I did. I'm going to play. I'm walking up to tell them before I change my mind. It's the least I can do for them." He brushed past Tucker, letting him know he wasn't invited to tag along.

The next morning, Robert's body was soaked with sweat from a terrible dream still troubling him as he tried to pull himself out of his sleep. He remembered being helpless against a violent force keeping him cowering behind a leaky wooden rain barrel that sat next to the Burketts' porch. Its withered-wood, transparent from the years of rain pellets shooting down on it from all sides, began to expose him inch by inch as the rain poured out from the gaps in the walls of the splintered wood.

Alarm electrified throughout his body as the water level lowered enough to reveal an audience, waiting for him to play his violin.

Robert ignored Tucker's shoe nudging at his side. "Hey, wake up or you're gonna miss breakfast. I'm starving, so I ain't waitin'. See you over there."

The week was long with snubs and backs turning away from them as they sat down for meals, reigniting Robert's nerves about performing in front of these men. The Burketts had been very pleased when he came over to tell them he had changed his mind and would play for the workers. But the announcement of the Thursday music gathering did nothing to ease the tension with the workers. Instead, it had escalated with the knowledge that work was finishing two days early. Quips by the men about his practicing the violin at the Burketts' house were pointed and nasty.

"Daddy give you a raise today, boy?" one of the men going through the supper line mumbled.

"Yeah, maybe even a bonus, huh," the guy directly across from Robert blurted out.

The remarks were followed by barely muffled laughs.

Thursday night didn't come fast enough for Robert. He was ready to get his performance over with. For all the snubs and crummy remarks, there had been a bit of encouragement about his performance from a few pockets of men, easing his fright about being heckled, but it was still worrisome.

Dexter asked the men to carry the weighty benches made out of six-foot split logs from the meal hall to the Burketts' front yard. Robert watched them put the benches down and then sit on them, noticing they seemed as uneasy as he was about not knowing what to expect for the evening.

Robert picked out two more sonata solos for the violin by Austrian composer, Wolfgang Amadeus Mozart. They were two pieces he played for his family, and selections he continued to play by his father's bedside until the afternoon he passed away.

Burkett stood in front of the men, rambling on and on about the special treat prepared for them on their last night at the farm. "His music sure won't disappoint you."

After Mr. Burkett's long and enthusiastic introduction, Robert hurried into the start of the sonata he'd played earlier for the Burketts. Not feeling any less nervous after playing the first sonata, he rushed into the second and third, purposely not leaving much of a pause between the pieces to avoid the slight of no one applauding. He was careful though to take as much time as needed to move his fingers for each note, sliding the bow with instinctive elegance to capture the possibilities of each sound vibrating out from the violin. Still, at the end of the third piece there was an uncomfortable moment. The silence was long enough to ignite a warm blush across his face. Then came a restrained applause.

Mr. Burkett stepped forward, putting his hand on Robert's shoulder. "I told you he wouldn't disappoint you. We're lucky to have the opportunity to gather together to hear such special music before you leave. Thank you all for another great season of harvesting. The Mrs. and I appreciate your steadfast work."

Robert laid the violin down gently on the chair, slipped past the men, and walked past the bunk to the trail he'd come to rely on to settle his mind. He could hear Tucker's footsteps following behind him again, but they had stopped at the bunk house.

With his stomach in knots, he rolled down onto the ground, slipped his arms underneath his head, and let the music flow through his mind, knowing he had played every note as it was written to be played. It was sunset. By nightfall his nerves had calmed down.

The sound of footsteps walking toward him was unexpected. He was sure Tucker understood when to leave him alone. "I'll be there in a few minutes," Robert shouted. He wasn't ready to talk just yet.

Leaving his eyes closed a moment, waiting to hear Tucker's footsteps move away, his eyes shot open when he felt someone close by. He tried to raise himself up to see who it was, but his upper body was slammed back down with such force his head knocked hard against the dirt. A hand held his jaw cocked to the side. His body was pinned down by the weight of a much heavier person's body on top of him.

"So you play the violin, sonny. Real sweet."

Robert shifted his eyes to see Arlie, the guy who had taken his neck scarf the first day he arrived. Robert tried to yell, but Arlie was quick to slip his hand over his mouth with a forceful grip. Using his other hand, he yanked open Robert's belt, crushing his weight back down on top of his ribs and stomach. Robert stiffened and stilled for a moment, his heart palpitating as if it were going to leap out of his chest. Frantically, he tried to wiggle out from under the heaviness of the large frame suffocating him with weight, but in one fast motion Arlie flipped him over. With one hand still tight across his mouth and a thumb and index finger now pinching his nose closed, Robert was losing the strength to respond to the fight as his breath began to slip away, weakening any ability to move.

In an instant his rough grip was gone. Robert rolled over to see Arlie hanging close above him, looking as if he was hooked to the end of a bailing lift. Carlton swung him off to the side, thrashing his body against the ground like a bail of bound hay. In one quick movement, Carlton knelt down, pressed his knees against Arlie's lower back, secured his hands behind him with rope, and pulled him off the ground.

"You're out of here," Carlton said, as he shoved him toward the field house.

Tucker hurried past them. "You okay?"

Robert was too breathless to answer.

"I saw that guy follow you out here and knew no good was coming. Come on, buddy," Tucker urged. Reaching his hand out to pull him off the ground. Robert staggered, dizzy, trying to stand up. Tucker steadied him as he lowered himself back down to the ground. Robert kept his head buried in his hands as he tried to overcome the lightheadedness.

"That was one of the guys that took our neck scarfs."

Arlie's eerie stare in the breakfast line their first day flashed through Robert's mind. "Yeah, I know."

It wasn't long before Dexter walked up. "You okay, boy?"

Unable to say anything, he gave Dexter a nod.

"Carlton is hauling him off the property right now. Why don't you come back to the bunk house and get some rest before you check out tomorrow?"

Dexter turned to leave, but paused to look back at Robert. "And we won't worry the Burketts with this."

Robert gave a nod of agreement as he sucked in a deep breath. "I think I'll just sit here right now, sir. I'll be okay." He understood Dexter wanted the incident kept quiet. Maybe Burkett, if he already knew, felt the same way.

"Your music was something good for us all, kid, especially for Mrs. Burkett. She was hoping you'd come back by tonight so she could thank you, but I'll tell her you'll stop to see her before leaving in the morning. You will, won't you, boy?"

"I sure will, sir."

Robert waited until Dexter turned to walk away before covering his face again with his hands to hide his shame, still queasy from Arlie's weight bearing down on him.

"Tuck, you can go back. Please go back. I'll be there in a bit."

"You sure you're all right?"

"I just need to sit here awhile."

Hearing Tucker move away, he strained to control the shuddering going through him until he couldn't hear his footsteps any longer. Collapsing into a ball, he tried to get the image of what had just happened out of his mind, but the emotions he'd forced back for all the months he'd been on the road overcame him. The memories of his father that always brought him joy instead brought back all the grief of losing him. Emotions he'd stored up while playing a borrowed violin over the past weeks suddenly surfaced in a flow of unstoppable tears. In wanting to help his mother and siblings by selling his violin, he'd never really acknowledged the loss of it. He had to get over it. But how?

———

Tucker shook Robert's shoulders at six-thirty the next morning, thirty minutes before breakfast closed. It took tossing around all night for him to shake off what had happened. He had only fallen into a deep sleep as dawn broke, thankful he slept at all.

"Hey," Tucker said, "the line for getting our pay started forming about a half an hour ago. You'd better get up so you can eat and get in line."

The guys lined up to get paid was solid when they walked to the field house for breakfast. Robert was glad he might avoid looks from most of the men by being the last to eat and last to join the line outside.

A numbness had settled over him about what happened the night before. He refused to allow Arlie's face to surface. It was the sheer physicality of being crushed and helpless that stuck with him as he moved through the morning.

Robert saw Dexter approaching them as they waited for their pay. "Glad you boys were last in line. It gives me a chance to let you know you did good work, keeping up with the other men and all. You took lots of crap from them, don't think I don't know it."

Dexter put his hand on Robert's shoulder. "Last night was an unfortunate way to end your stay. Your bringing back music for Mrs. Burkett has made her very happy. The Burketts would like you boys to stop by before you leave. Don't forget now, and good luck to you."

Minus a smile, Robert reached out to shake his hand. "We appreciate the kind words. Glad we did a good job for you."

Mrs. Burkett was out on the porch when they walked up later in the morning. She stood to greet them, and then opened the screen door slightly to let her husband know they were outside.

"Hate to see you boys leave," Mrs. Burkett said. "Everyone was thankful for the music last night. Many of the men mentioned it on their way out this morning. I wanted you to know what they said."

She walked closer to Robert, stopping directly in front of him. "Robert, Mr. Burkett and I would like you to come in the house for a minute. Do you mind?"

Robert was silent, feeling odd about Tucker not being invited in, and alarmed about why they would want to speak with him alone. His body went clammy. *They must of heard about what happened last night. It's not right to bring something like that up.* Taking a glance down the road, he felt the urge to bolt.

Mrs. Burkett stepped to the door and held it open, an affectionate smile urged him inside. Her husband's uneasiness showed as he stood inside the doorway, keeping his head down as he waited for him to come in. Robert paused as he turned back to give Tucker a questioning look before moving inside.

Mrs. Burkett raised her arm toward the dining room table. After settling into the chair, he watched as the Burketts looked back and forth to each other, waiting for the other to start the conversation. Burkett turned toward the wall, studying it as if he were analyzing the pattern on the wallpaper. Mrs. Burkett glanced back to Robert, seeming to give up on her husband starting the conversation.

"We know you like to play the violin," she said at last, "and . . . you need work being out on the road like you've been for some months now."

She stopped, bent her head toward her lap, gulping in a large breath of air before speaking again. "We . . ." Hesitating a moment, she turned toward her husband, who continued to look at the wallpaper. When he didn't glance over, she went on. "We thought you'd like the idea of living here, having the violin to play whenever you wanted to, and, uh, we'd enjoy listening to your beautiful music, of course."

Pausing again, she added, "You could work in the strawberry fields next season, help Dexter out between seasons, and do some work around the house and barn in the meantime. There's always something that needs fixing."

Looking down to her lap once more, she took another deep breath of air before raising her head. Robert wasn't sure if she was nervous or holding back bursting into tears by the way her voice crackled when she spoke. Either way, he wanted to get up and run.

"So you see, we would like to invite you to live with us, not stay out in the bunks, of course, but here with us and become part of our family in time." She turned again to her husband, leaving a long, uncomfortable silence in the room, while waiting for him to speak. Feeling her stare, he turned to Robert.

"It would be mighty nice for us to have you stay, son, and it seems you need a home. I hear it's dangerous out on the road these days with kids getting hurt hopping the trains, even getting arrested." Burkett paused and glanced at his wife before continuing. "You could send the money you earn home to help your family out. We'd really like it if you stayed."

Shifting his eyes back and forth between them for a moment, Robert was stunned speechless by their offer, surprised by the sadness he felt for them, and edgy about what Mrs. Burkett said about becoming part of their family. He had a mother to go back to, sisters, brothers, and a home, maybe not much of one anymore, but he wouldn't ever consider giving it up for a better one or to be someone else's son. Staying with strangers, good people as they are, he didn't want someone else's violin to play. His mind raced back to the grief he felt the night of the concert over selling his violin. *No, the violin Dad gave me can't be replaced, but the memories of playing it for him will always be there.*

Yet, he continued in silence, grappling with an answer as he considered the money he'd earn if he stayed. It was what he had left home for but leaving home to become a stranger to his family was not. They'd made it clear they wanted him to stay permanently, live with them, be part of their family. *I need to get home. I've been gone too long.*

Wanting to break the silence in the room, he struggled to find the right words to say to such kind people. They waited patiently, both seeming uneasy about what he might say. Unable to hide the rise and fall of his chest as he inhaled a deep breath so he could speak, he realized the only way to answer was just to blurt it out, straight and firm, leaving no chance for Mrs. Burkett to offer again, or release the tears misting around her eyes as she waited for his answer.

"Ma'am, Mr. Burkett, your offer to help me out with work, live here in your home, the chance to play the violin again, that's so kindhearted." Feeling shaky at having to say the rest, he stopped again to catch a breath. "I can't stay though. I just can't. I'm heading north, home to my family. Just been gone too long, but thank you both. You're such good people."

Mrs. Burkett's eyes were tearing, unable to hide her disappointment. She leaned toward him, touching his arm.

"But . . . " She was interrupted when her husband rose out of his seat with a pinched but determined expression. "My wife packed a big lunch for Tucker. Just give her a chance to pack one for you, too." He walked over to her, resting his hand on her shoulder. Her head slumped against his side.

When Robert stepped onto the porch, Tucker jumped up from the porch swing so fast it hit the rail behind him.

"You done already?"

"Well, Mrs. Burkett is making lunches for us to take. She'll be out in a minute. We can head out then."

Tucker kept his eyes on Robert, waiting for him to say something else. Instead, he pointed to a worker coming from the field house. "I guess we're not the last to leave after all." They waived as he passed by.

"Hey kid, keep playing your music," he yelled.

Burkett came outside, holding the door for his wife. She held out a bulging lunch to each of them. "This should get you through until later," she said, managing a smile.

"Thank you ma'am," Tucker said. "I know it'll be good."

Robert took his lunch. "Thank you, and thank you for all the kindness you've both shown us."

"We'd better get, Tuck." Robert stepped down the porch steps, swiftly turning to face the Burketts. "Thank you again for the work," he said, sending a huge smile to them. "Really do appreciate everything. I won't ever forget it, or the two of you either. I won't."

Mrs. Burkett walked to the edge of the porch staring down at him, her mouth tight, her eyes appearing as if she had something urgent to say. Instead she smiled back, then stood fidgeting with the front of her apron, finally saying goodbye.

Continuing to walk backwards, the two of them waved. Tucker raised the lunch she packed. He pulled it toward his chest as if hugging it, bringing a grin to Mrs. Burkett's face. Robert was too uncomfortable to turn his back on them, and kept walking backward until they went inside.

It was a quarter of a mile up the road when Tucker broke his silence. "Okay, what was that about? Did you think I wasn't gonna ask? Did they give you a bonus for the violin playing or what?"

"They wanted me to stay, live with them, give me the chance to play the violin and work for Dexter."

"Kinda thought it might be something like that."

"Well, I sure wasn't expecting it."

"Really, what did you tell them? Hope it was gentle being they're really fine people and all."

"I told them I had to look out for my buddy," Robert said, keeping a straight face.

"Ah, you didn't. Did you?"

"No, of course not."

Robert pulled out his pay envelope, trying to avoid saying anything else about it. "Let's take a peek."

"Fifty bucks, does that seem right?" Tucker asked. "Don't seem like much for almost two weeks' work, ten hours a day. Is it?"

"I don't know, but it's the most money I've ever seen. I wonder if I'll ever see this much again."

"That's a dismal thought. I sure hope we get a ride back to Marshall so we can get off our feet for a day. You thinking about heading north today?"

Robert started to say something, but pulled back realizing he didn't have the answer. "Guess that depends on what we find when we get to Marshall. You've got to figure all the men who left the ranch before us are going to be scouting around for some kind of work before we get there. And, heading north today depends on what the train schedule looks like."

14

Lucille was about to open the screen door to sweep out the dust from the plank floor for the second time that day when she looked up to see Mr. Tominello standing on the porch.

"Hello, ma'am."

She was taken aback to see him at her door. Not once had he visited their home since they moved into it, not before or after Johnny and Robert ran off, or even after Johnny came back. It was always her efforts or Kathleen's to get information from him about the boys.

"Goodness, I didn't know anyone was at the door. Please, come in. Please."

Very seldom had she seen anyone in a suit outside of church anymore. His worn twill suit seemed out of place on such a warm day. Slipping his hat off as he entered, he stood spinning it in circles as he glanced around taking in their small living quarters, showing a stunned expression Lucille read as surprise. He seemed nervous as he stood without speaking. The somber look on his face sent worrisome thoughts about Robert racing through her mind. Her heart began beating so fast, she felt like it would pop out of her chest, leaving an immediate need to sit down to steady herself.

"Please sit down, Mr. Tominello. Can I get you some water?"

"No, ma'am."

He sat quietly. The immediate tapping up and down of his boot heel against the wood floor was so rhythmic, it sounded like a woodpecker tapping on a tree. Trying to maintain a calmness for what might come was lost to the noise from his heel continuing to thump up and down, intensifying the anxiousness she felt from the sound as it increasingly pierced through her.

"Johnny's run off again. Left a note he was going after Robert. Didn't say anything else, except he was sorry for leaving again."

"Oh, no." Stunned by Mr. Tominello's words, Lucille tried to make sense of them. "Did Johnny say where Robert might be? Johnny told me when he came by that he didn't know where to look for Robert. Did Robert write him?"

"Not that I know about. Johnny never said he got a letter." Seeming reluctant to look at her, he continued to tap the heel of his boot and to keep his eyes focused on the floor. The sound from his heel filled the small room with such volume that when the tapping suddenly stopped, her thoughts shifted away from how to reply to what he had just told her. She waited for him to look at her and say something. When he glanced up, a noticeable mist sat in the corner of his eyes.

Thrown off by the news about Johnny leaving and seeing the disheartened look on the face of someone whom she'd known for years, any reply was stunted for a moment. Their children grew up together and were best friends. Johnny was at her house almost everyday over the years. Hearing he left again concerned her too, and she understood his father's pain.

"He's all I got now, ma'am. Have you heard my girls moved to California with their mother to live with her parents?" He didn't wait for an answer. "I just came by to tell you Johnny went after Robert. Seems unlikely Johnny will run into him though, doesn't it? Seems like he's putting himself in harm's way for nothing."

Taken aback again by the insensitivity of his last comment, Lucille felt her anger well up as she struggled to hold back her reaction to his words. She had other children, so her loss would be less than his if something happened to Robert. That's what he thinks? What was the point of saying Johnny was putting himself in harm's way for nothing? Robert's nothing to this man?

Silence sat between them. If he was waiting for her to say something, she couldn't reply. What would it accomplish after all to tell him her feelings about Johnny taking her young son with him on the road to begin with? Yet, wasn't her resentment toward Johnny being safe at home the past months just as small and petty as his father's insensitive rambling? There's so much loss, so much pain and fear affecting everyone. Did she need to add to it by deflating this man more?

From what she'd been hearing on the radio the country was declining in every way possible. The months and months of it having gone into years was wearing down everyone, leaving only a growing sense of helplessness. The only hopeful American was President Roosevelt, who tried to bring encouragement to everyone through his weekly radio program when he shared what was being done to turn the country around.

But after his radio programs end, everyone is left to figure out how to feed their children for another week or even the next day. Keeping children sheltered from the increasing poverty and disasters touching families everywhere seemed a losing battle. Yet her struggles began before the depression hit.

The death of her young husband forced her to figure out not just how to survive and keep her children together, but how to salvage her children's minds which were touched so deeply by their father's love of life. Her effort each day wasn't only about her family getting through difficult times, but championing the exuberance toward life her husband intended them to have as they grew to be adults. The depression only deepened her determination to help her children get through it all.

Tominello broke the silence. "Well, ma'am, I just wanted you to know that Johnny left again."

Lucille noticed he'd gained his composure, perhaps at seeing how she had lost hers. She wasn't sure how long she'd sat with her thoughts, trying to come to terms with his words.

"I'm glad you let me know. I'll be thinking of Johnny and praying he stays safe. Please let me know if you hear from him."

"I'll do the same if I hear from Robert."

The sounds of her children nearing the house broke the conversation. "Kathleen took the kids on an afternoon walk." She'd just gotten the words out as they all bounded through the door.

The younger children raced toward her, dumping all the treasures they found in her lap, each talking over the other.

"Well, I need to be going."

"Oh, hello, Mr. Tominello," Kathleen said. "Did Johnny hear from Robert? Is that why you came?"

Kathleen stood near her mother's side, smiling at him in anticipation of some news.

"No, but your mother can tell you."

He rose from the chair. The abruptness of his move to leave startled Lucille. Nodding to her, he walked to the door, and left before anyone could show him out.

Still off balance from his abrupt actions, she shifted back around in the chair as her children tugged on her apron, vying for her attention. Kathleen sat across from her with an anxious look on her face.

"Johnny left him a note that he went to look for Robert, that's all." Lucille turned her attention back to the treasures filling her lap.

"Oh, yeah. I know."

Lucille glanced up to see her daughter catching herself for letting her words slip out.

"You knew?"

"Well, I didn't know Johnny would really leave. But he mentioned he might go when I saw him in town last week."

"Why didn't you tell me?"

Kathleen walked to the kitchen area, pulled out a pitcher from underneath the sink and set it on the counter. "Is it okay to make some lemonade?"

"Of course, just be sparing on the sugar we have left. We need to make it stretch for two more weeks. Did Johnny say he had some idea of where to look for Robert?"

Lucille watched as her daughter lifted the basket of lemons a neighbor had given them off the shelf. She could see Kathleen was taking as much time as possible to think about what she was going to say. She slowly slipped an apron over her head, and tied it behind her before turning to look at her mother. She crossed her arms in front of her.

"I was going to tell you after I had time to think about it. I was worried you would do something to keep Johnny from going after Robert."

Lucille started to reply, but the children's loud chatter about the treasures from their walk needed her attention. Emma's shiny silver and black rock, held two inches from her face and directly between Lucille's eyes, gave her the opportunity to drop the subject. Kathleen was right. She would have let Mr. Tominello know about Johnny's intention to leave.

Several minutes later there was another rap at the door. Their neighbor, Mr. Schmidt, stopped by to share his newspaper with them when there was big news, which seemed to be a couple times a week now. He and Kathleen were patient with Lucille while going through newspaper articles, helping her with words she didn't know, explaining the deeper meaning of the news when she asked, and calling attention to articles about issues sure to impact their family or community. Lucille was getting increasingly frustrated about having to rely on the two of them to keep up with the news that might affect her family, yet it was important if she was to keep life manageable as the changes hit.

Like all immigrants, she worked hard to improve her English. It was critical to protect their children from being teased or labeled immigrants. Learning to read English proficiently had become more difficult. With six children there'd been no time to learn to read more than everyday English words to get by. But with all the new words showing up in headlines linked to the country's economic downfall and new programs being created by Roosevelt's presidency, she pushed to keep up with it all by sparing a half an hour at a time to scan the paper with the two of them.

"This a good time, Lucille?" Schmidt asked. "Just thought you would want to see the news about the schools closing this fall. Well, maybe anyway. Seems there might not be enough funds to keep them open."

"Oh my goodness! Yes, come in please."

When Kathleen finished reading the article, she glanced over to her mother. "Ma, do you remember what the manager of the Five and Dime told me?"

"Yes, I do." Lucille looked away not wanting to discuss it in front of their neighbor.

Kathleen had been hammering her to leave school to take a part-time waitressing job paying twenty-five cents a day. After days of bickering and pleading, she persuaded her to stay in school for her father's sake, reminding her how he'd taken pride in knowing all of his children would be educated. But today's news was sure to prompt Kathleen to argue she should take the job before anyone else heard about it.

They finished going through the paper quickly with no other relevant stories, leaving Lucille relieved. Her German friend, Elsa, had come by with a copy of the *Berliner Tageblatt* earlier in the week. She had been shocked by the latest headlines, *GLEICHSCHALTUNG,* announcing the outlawing of any political party other than the Nazi regime. Unsettling her even more were pictures showing hundreds of Jewish merchants arrested in Nuremberg being paraded through the streets of Berlin. The paper a few weeks before had had a picture of Nazi soldiers burning books in the streets.

All this happening so far away left only sadness for her birthplace. But America was her home now and so were its economic problems and desperate situations, but she knew no matter how bad things got in America or how discouraging the headlines, life would never be anything like what people in Germany were living through.

Yet, the longer the depression went on the more preoccupied she had become with the growing inability to stretch money to buy enough food for the month and to pay utility bills. The added expense of buying coal for the winter months was getting closer.

Her children were growing so fast and needing new clothing made it even more difficult to manage her monthly allotment from the Widows Pension. She was now dependent on used clothing donated by charities, or family friends bringing clothes their children grew out of. The few laundry jobs friends gave her had slipped away completely as the economy worsened. Whenever she began to doubt her ability to manage it all, she would pause to be grateful for the Widows Pension, reminding herself of the true despair she'd face without it.

She recalled a recent photograph in the paper of a woman camped out in a field, sitting in front of a small, torn canvas tent surrounded by several dirty barefoot young children. Her face displayed extreme despair. When she saw the picture she looked away and tried to push it out of her mind before getting caught up in the disturbing image.

Needing to get her mind off concerns about schools closing, and the terrible news she'd read in the German paper earlier in the week, she walked to the kitchen to start potatoes and onions for supper. Wiping her brow with a dish towel every few seconds to keep sweat beads from dripping onto the potatoes helped keep her mind in the moment. The July heat was at record highs, and had been absolutely scalding for the last three days.

Lifting her head to look out the window when she heard the two o'clock train slowing to a stop, she watched, as always, in hopes of seeing Robert standing on the platform when the train pulled away. What she saw was a group of ten or so men disperse in different directions. Stinging with disappointment, Lucille fought to bring her concentration back to the potatoes she was slicing.

Voices on the porch grabbed her attention. Kathleen was talking to the letter carrier. Letting out a high-pitched squeal, she plunged through the door.

"A letter from Robert," Kathleen said, twirling around in delight. "I'll open it since your hands are messy."

Lucille hurried to wipe off her hands and smiled at Kathleen as she took the partially opened letter and sat down. Tears joined the stream of sweat beads dripping onto her face. "Kathleen, please make sure Marty is watching the younger ones, quick. I'll wait and read the letter out loud when you come back."

In less than a minute Kathleen was back, sitting in the chair across from her mother. Lucille took a few quick breaths to release the knots in her stomach and tension in her throat. She pulled the note from the envelope and began reading.

Ma,

I'm sorry I haven't written before, but this was the first time I got a hold of some paper and a pencil to send a letter. The city mission in Jackson, Mississippi, makes it available at no charge to people passing through. They even provide the post for the letters.

Yep, that is where I am and I'm okay and making my way home. If I get some work though, I may stop to take it. Don't be mad, Ma. I just wanted to earn some money to help out. Johnny should be back by now so he can tell you I can take care of myself. Hope you and the kids are okay. Miss you all a lot.

Your son,
Robert

"When is it dated, Ma?"

"He didn't put a date." Lucille turned over the envelope. "The post mark is June 18th. That's three weeks ago. The mission must have delayed mailing it," she added, trying not to sound concerned.

"Then he must have found work or he'd be home by now. Right, Ma?"

"Yes, I'm sure that's it. Why don't you walk up to tell Mr. Tominello that Robert wrote he was in Jackson, Mississippi, just in case Johnny calls him?"

"Okay, but it doesn't seem like he'd have money to call him, does it?" Kathleen said, looking puzzled. "Johnny never called when he was on the road with Robert, did he?"

She got up and walked toward the door, not waiting for a reply. Lucille shut her eyes once Kathleen pushed the screen door shut. Leaning back into the chair, she caressed the letter against her chest and prayed Robert would return safe. Within a moment, thoughts started to race through her mind. Maybe Robert does know how to take care of himself, how to stay safe and make it home, but the letter was written more than three weeks ago. Shutting off her thoughts for the moment, she gave into her tears of relief, too tired to fight them off.

All too clearly she remembered the recent headlines announcing the homelessness of hundreds of thousands of people in the country. Thinking about it helped her realize how much worse the situation could be for her family. She fought back fear of what could happen to her family and what might've happened to Robert since he wrote to her. Giving herself another moment to think about the letter and his encouraging words, she eased back against the chair.

She had learned to live one moment at a time by breaking the days into segments, starting from early morning when she rose until her children went to bed at night. She maintained a repetition through each segment, be it planning and preparing what was needed for each meal, moving through chores, managing play time for the children, or organizing the house to keep their small space clean and orderly. The repetition in each day she hoped would shelter her children from the chaos happening all around them. Wanting to protect her children, she couldn't allow them to see the despair she felt.

Going back to the kitchen to finish preparing supper would give her the distraction she needed to stifle her feelings until later when the children were asleep. Then she'd pull out Robert's letter from her pocket, hold it to her heart, and reread his words of confidence for his journey home. At least she had his letter now boasting he was safe and knew how to take care of himself. She'd reread his letter every day until she knew he was safe and really on the way home.

15

It was noon by the time Robert and Tucker got back to Marshall after spending all morning trying to thumb a ride from the Burketts' farm. They went straight to the town square, settled on the grassy knoll by the court house again, and pulled out the lunches Mrs. Burkett had packed for them.

"I'm sure gonna miss the three meals a day," Tucker said. "What about you?"

"Yep, that was something all right." He untied the twill from the sandwich wrapping. "Hey, it's chicken. After we eat, I want to find a map someplace. Then we can try to find information about work. Maybe we'll get lucky again."

"That would be some lucky, I'd say."

After spending the morning thinking about it, Robert wasn't any more decided about what to do next. Fifty dollars wasn't much to take home for being on the road so long. He debated writing home again when his plans were so uncertain, but his mother would have been pleased to know that the

Burketts thought so much of him that they offered him a chance to stay with them. *She'll be mighty relieved when I tell her that I said no.*

Letting go of five cents for a map was tough yet worth it. The train routes he'd taken south from St. Louis to Georgia were now vague and some of the names of towns he passed through forgotten completely. Scouring over the map, Robert could see that the railroad line going north from Marshall didn't go directly to St. Louis.

"Looks like the train stops in Joplin before heading on to St. Louis. I'd like to ask around again about work here in Marshall before heading north though. What are you going to do from here?"

Tucker acted surprised by the question. "Well . . . I'm sticking with you till I can't no more. I'm gonna have to find work until I can go looking for Al to sign up for those camps he told us about. That's my best bet, I figure, because the next thing you know I'll be living in one of those hobo camps. I'm not passing up Al's offer with helping me get in one of those camps."

Tucker leaned forward and touched his shoe. "I've kept that napkin he gave me with his information on it inside my sock. When I take my shoes off at night, I make sure it's still there. I figure someone might try to steal my shoes or my rucksack, but no one's gonna try stealing my stinky socks. Did you keep the half he gave you?"

Glancing up from the map, Robert grinned. "Yeah, I've got the napkin in my rucksack."

"You're taking a chance there, aren't you? I mean keeping it in your rucksack. You might need it someday."

Robert's eyes widened at Tucker's words. "Guess I might be."

"I wrote my dad from the town mission in Little Rock asking him to send a letter to Al in Ohio with my birthdate like he said he needed before I could get in one of them camps,"

Tucker said. "Then I sent my dad another letter from the Burketts' farm reminding him to send it just in case. I put the Burketts' address inside, and told him to write me there to let me know if he sent the letter to Al."

"Did he write you? I never heard you say anything about a letter."

"I asked Dexter if I got any mail before we headed out this morning, but he said no."

Staring at him, Robert was taken aback by Tucker's comments and his thought out efforts to get into a camp. He felt a bit deflated that he'd forgotten about the napkin with Al's information on it until now. It was careless even if he was too young for the camps. "Didn't realize you've been thinking about following up with Al. That's something for sure."

"So what's next? You figure out a route north yet?"

Pointing to the general store, Robert shoved the rest of his lunch into his rucksack and stood up. "The same old men are sitting in the rocking chairs over there. Let's see if anyone knows about any work? If they don't, let's try to get to Joplin tonight. We can ask about work when we get there."

—————

It had been lucky to catch a freight to Joplin with a few open cars out of Marshall early that afternoon, making the ride in the hundred-degree heat bearable. As expected, Robert noticed some of the men from the Burketts' farm in their car. It was reassuring when they looked over and nodded to acknowledge him and Tucker.

The wild shuddering of the open car and constant screeching of the steel wheels against the metal tracks made it impossible to talk. Men sat staring at nothing. Other men so weary from life on the road, and used to hearing the sounds banging in their ears, slept. Their heads jutted forward when the train tracks curved, and they eased back against the side of the car without opening their eyes as if easing against a pillow.

When the train notched down in speed for the first time, signaling they were approaching a station, Robert and Tucker jumped up to look over the edge of the car. Once the train started slowing again as they got closer to Joplin, it wasn't long before they passed by disturbing sights Robert had seen before.

Sitting yards back from the tracks were make-shift communities made up of rows of small, filthy, shredding tents, and lean-to shelters made out of cardboard boxes. Hopeless looking families sat on dirt or crates. The little kids, excited to see a train go by, jumped up and down, waving their arms wildly through the air, and yelping frantically when men waved back. The older kids began running along side the train until they couldn't keep up.

Tucker slid back down to sit, looking as if he couldn't watch them any longer. Several minutes later the train's speed slowed again. One of the workers from the Burketts' farm turned and yelled, "There are bulls on the tracks."

In an instant the option to stay put until they got closer to Joplin disappeared. All the men in the car bolted to the other side. Reaching for his rucksack, Robert turned toward Tucker, giving him a slight kick to get his attention. He pointed to Tucker's rucksack and leaned down into his face and shouted. "Come on, now."

Men from the open car in front of them were unloading at the same time the men in their car were leaping out. They all hit the ground hard, rolling over and then racing away as best they could into the nearby brush.

The last to jump off, Robert and Tucker rose unsteadily after hitting the ground, then scampered toward the high brush to reach cover before the train passed by and exposed them to the bulls. Tucker crashed down next to Robert, his chest heaving to catch a breath. "Been through this before, haven't we?"

Still too winded to speak, Robert gulped air until he could talk, responding in a breathless voice. "Yeah, but we're going to have to lay low until it's clear." He took another deep breath. "We'll know it's time to head out when the guys behind us start popping up. They can be the lookout. We'll start moving when they move."

The next half hour was quiet until everyone was sure the bulls weren't standing around waiting for men to spring up from the grass. There was no sound of boots coming toward them. If the bulls were waiting for the men to spring up, they would have to wait a long time. Robert had spent hours waiting it out in the brush like this, being still, listening for boots and voices.

Forced to lay quiet, Robert focused his mind on regrouping after the last few days at the Burketts and trying to relax from a state of anxiety. He'd been avoiding a decision about whether to head straight for home, and constantly forcing thoughts away of what happened the last night at the Burketts. Each time the image of the man on top of him pushed its way into his head, he felt the same helplessness and fear.

Then there was the constant twisting and turning around in his thoughts of whether to find more work harvesting somewhere. Going home seemed like such a simple decision, given how reckless it would be not to go, yet it was a decision he couldn't make. He'd made so little money.

The sound of boots against gravel started up and got louder. They could hear voices in the distance. Tucker hit Robert's arm, his eyes checking to see if he could hear them, too. Robert nodded as he listened to the sound of the boots. Voices were getting closer. He realized they were the last to fall into the high grass and would be the first to be sifted out. The boots stopped. The bulls' conversations continued, but the voices were too far away to understand what they were saying. Their voices suddenly stopped. The sound of the boots started up again but began to fade away. Tucker hit Robert's arm, giving him a thumbs up when it sounded as if the bulls were walking away.

It was another hour before they heard murmurs of the men behind them. They began to hear movement through the brush. Pushing Tucker's chest back down to the ground when he started to get up, Robert gave him a signal to stay down. They lay listening to the shuffle of men in the grass leaving every five minutes, waiting until he was certain the last of the men behind them had left, then Robert signaled a thumbs-up to Tucker.

"You as hungry as me?" Tucker asked, as he sprang up.

"You bet I am. Let's look for a place to get some sandwiches. We can check out the town after we eat. Doubt we're going to find any work though, with all the men who unloaded with us checking out the town, too."

It was a long walk into downtown Joplin. The size of the city wasn't what Robert had imagined, expecting it to be somewhat smaller. The hub of town was huge, looking as if it were twenty blocks long. Some of the buildings on the main street were four and five stories high with wide wooden sidewalks out front. Dark green awnings hung across the entrances to several stores and across many of the second- and third-story balconies. It reminded him of State Street in downtown Chicago.

They'd seen signs advertising zinc mines as they got closer to town. Not long after they noticed signs for lead mines, explaining the hustle and bustle of Joplin. Instead of one general store, barber shop, or market, they passed two or three of each as they walked blocks into the center of town.

A crowd was gathered on the side walk a few blocks in front of them, just the kind of place Robert watched for to search out information about work. As they walked toward the group clustered at the end of the second block, they passed a huge glass window with "House of Lords" painted in bold gold and black letters across it.

"That sure is a fancy place," Tucker said. "This is the first time I ever saw trolley cars running down the center of a street."

"The town is big all right. Let's see what's happening at the corner."

Men were gathered between a restaurant and a cigar store. Spotting a few guys from the Burketts' farm, Robert nodded to them as they walked by. "This probably isn't a good place to hang around. Looks like mostly men from the mines."

Just as they started to pass the cigar store, Robert noticed a "Wanted" poster tacked on the front of the building. "Hey, Tucker, see this? It's a wanted poster for that Barrows gang who were in Marshall before we got there. It's for Clyde and Melvin Barrows. Geez, look at this. They're wanted for murder here in Joplin. There's a thousand dollar reward out for them. Says they murdered the sheriff and constable on April 13. That was right before the shoot out we read about in Marshall."

"Look down here," Tucker said. "Says they killed them in a shoot out at the apartment they were staying in. Two women living with them got away, too. Says they made their getaway in a dark green 1932 V-8 Ford Coach automobile. Guess they like nice cars, huh?"

Robert pointed to their pictures. "That Clyde guy looks real young, doesn't he?"

"Yeah, he doesn't look much older than me. I wonder where the shoot out was. If we're in town long enough, do you want to try to find that apartment? I do."

Robert could feel someone standing close behind him. Stepping back against the building to allow room for the person to pass, he turned his head to see Arlie, the man who had jumped him at the Burketts' farm. He was swaying back and forth a bit, his eyes glassy, starring directly at Robert and holding a smug smile across his face.

Tucker had backed up against the wall next to Robert. When he saw Arlie he reached his arm behind Robert's back and gently nudged him toward the sidewalk. They kept their eyes on

Arlie as they stepped onto the street, edging their way to the other side.

"He's not following us," Tucker said with relief. "Let's head down toward the other end of town. I think he's more interested in the hootch he's drinking and getting drunk." Tucker looked over his shoulder again. "I'll keep checking if he's coming. Let's just keep walking."

He looked back every few minutes to see if Arlie was watching them until they were too far down the street to make him out. "Still don't see him coming behind us. Let's duck in some place just in case."

They spotted a small cafe almost at the end of Main Street with a menu painted on the windows advertising salt pork sandwiches for fifteen cents. After picking up a couple sandwiches to go they settled in a park several blocks away, not wanting to hang around the downtown any longer.

The clock on the Conquerors First National Bank showed eight o'clock by the time they started searching for a place to sleep for the night. Still unsettled after running into Arlie, leaving them leery about sleeping in the high brush or in an open prairie, they headed through the back of town to the residential area. They moved past blocks of small lots with two-story houses on them to larger ranch-like plots of land. Robert kept his head down as he walked, looking closely around the fronts of the property as they passed by.

"What are you looking for?" Tucker asked.

"Codes other guys left showing it might be safe to sleep on the property or in their barn. Help me look for them carved on fence posts, big boulders, or even trees as we walk by. Let me know if you see any kind of scribble carved on anything. I haven't seen any yet."

Just as they crossed the street onto the next block, Robert spotted a sign carved on a wood fence. "Here, this is what they look like." He pointed to three notched-out circles inside an oval. "That means only bread is given here. We're looking for one with a big T, a circle next to it, and a squiggly line across the top of both. That code means it's safe to sleep on the property."

"That's like finding a needle in a haystack, as the saying goes," Tucker said.

"Yeah, kind of but it's a big enough town that there should be codes for travelers somewhere. It's worth looking around for a while. If we don't see anything soon, I saw a hobo camp sitting back from the railroad tracks, probably half a mile from the station as we were walking in. We can check it out if we have to."

At the beginning of the next block there were several one acre-farm-like properties, all with two-story square homes and a shed or horse shelter inside the fences.

Tucker spotted a piece of fence post stuck straight up in the ground, a rectangle with a circle inside was carved on it. "Is this what we're looking for?"

"Nope, and we sure aren't sticking around. This code warns of danger. Someone put it here at the beginning of the block, so I'm not sure if it means to stay out of the whole area or just the first house. Seems if it's just this first one it would be placed somewhere in front of it."

"Great, now what?" Tucker asked. "I'm beat."

"I am too. Let's check out the camp, see if there's a code posted somewhere around it. I'd rather sleep there than in a park over night and take the chance of that whacky guy jumping me again, but he's not likely going to bother me with you around. He's probably really ticked off about being thrown off the Burketts' farm though, especially if he didn't get his last pay."

They started back toward the town. "Let's circle back around Joplin the opposite way we came through. Maybe we'll still get lucky and find a sign saying it's okay to sleep on someone's property."

The camp sat on the outskirts of Joplin, farther back across town than he remembered. Robert circled around as he usually did, spotting a code posted half way around.

"Look here, Tucker. That means it's a safe camp."

Seeing the skeptical look on Tucker's face, Robert paused a moment. "What do you say? You want to go in?"

Tucker shrugged his shoulders. "Guess so. Didn't have much luck entering the last camp though, did I?"

"Well, there's always the open prairie going back out of town if you want to walk a few miles more. I'd risk it, I guess. We might have to sleep out there anyway if that creepy guy is in here."

"Are you kiddin' me? I can't walk anymore. Let's look for the town mission tomorrow. The soles on these shoes aren't staying on much longer. I've been kicking out rocks ever since we leaped off the train."

A few people inside the camp glanced up as they walked by; most did not. The smell of dirty bodies and dirty clothes, enhanced by the high temperature, lingered around them as they walked through. There were rows of people, who like them, went days without a chance to clean up, leaving Robert thankful to have the chance to shower and wash his clothes at Burkett's farm.

They circled the outer area of the camp, then weaved in and out of the people in the center, scanning the camp as they walked through, hoping they wouldn't spot Arlie.

"I don't see the guy, but it's probably way too early for him to end the night." Tucker said.

"That's for sure. Well, given the code posted outside, this is supposed to be a safe camp. We'll see, I guess. Haven't slept inside a hobo camp before though."

They wrapped the straps of their rucksacks around one arm, shoving them underneath their heads. They left their boots on in case they needed to get up and run.

16

Robert woke to see two men from the Burketts' farm sleeping next to Tucker. The same men who nodded to them when they'd jumped into the open freight car the morning before.

In their thirties, he guessed, they were either brothers or friends because they always hung together on the strawberry farm whether out in the fields, in the bunks, or in the food hall. Most reassuring to Robert in seeing them again was remembering the two of them clapping, smiling, and showing excitement at the end of his violin performance. He'd been so focused on blocking out any thoughts of Arlie since the concert, he hadn't allowed himself to think of the performance or remember the positive responses to his music.

Tucker began rolling around, mumbling something in his sleep. Swift to sit up once his eyes opened, he grabbed his rucksack to check the inside. The man next to him heard the shuffling around and sat up just as fast to check his things, then shook the guy sleeping next to him awake.

Tucker took a quick look to see who was next to him. "Hey, Sheldon, right?" Tucker said, reaching out to shake his hand. "Glad you and Russell got off the train okay."

"Yeah, that was a close call, wasn't it?" Russell reached out to shake Tucker's hand, then leaned back to acknowledge Robert with a slight salute.

"Good to see the two of you again," Russell whispered as he peeked around. "We should get out of here before we wake everyone up. You two up for something to eat?"

After nodding a reply, they followed Sheldon and Russell out of the camp, glad to have some familiar company for once. Spotting a diner advertising eggs, ham, spuds, and a cup of coffee for fifteen cents a few blocks up, they all headed toward it. Scattered around inside the diner were six tables made out of square slabs of unfinished pinewood placed on top of two huge rain barrels, surrounded by smaller water barrels. Bunches of wild daisies in pint jars sat in the middle of each table, probably an effort to spruce the place up. The smaller barrels, meant to be chairs, were too low to be table height.

"Guess they don't want anyone to get too comfortable, do they?" Sheldon said as they sat down.

Robert laughed with the others, conscious that his small frame sitting on the barrel probably made him appear dwarfed.

"What are the two of you going to do in Joplin, or weren't you planning to get off the train here?" Sheldon asked.

Robert and Tucker waited for the other to answer.

"Don't know what we're gonna do," Tucker said. "Didn't have much time to figure it out yesterday, but we saw some signs for the lead and zinc mines walking into town. Do you know much about them?"

"Yeah, we do," Russell said. "We're going over to both mines right after we finish eating. Met four fellas last night who found some work at one of the mines a few months ago. Told us it wouldn't hurt to give it a try because men leave from time to time to go back home to check on their families."

Sheldon glanced across the table to Robert. "You look a little young to get in at the mines, don't you think?"

Feeling irritated by the remark, Robert turned away, taking time to think of a reply before turning back to Sheldon.

"Been told that before at the mines in Colorado."

"Well," Sheldon said, looking a bit impressed, "you've been around, haven't you? I was surprised that you got on at the Burketts' though. We've been working seasonally for them for a few years now, but never been entertained like the violin playing you did. Quite the treat, it was."

Robert gave him a slight grin, glad to have the conversation interrupted as the food was served, giving him a moment he needed to get over the blow of being told he could forget looking for work at the mines. Sheldon's followup comment about his music did little to help him recover. A job in a place like the mines was good money. He was eager to find more work right away so he could hang on to most of what he earned harvesting to take home.

Sheldon seemed to notice the somber expression on Robert's face. "Didn't mean to bum you out, kid, but we've worked the mines before. Never seen anyone even Tucker's age getting hired on. There's too many men traveling through to pick from. We heard when we got to town yesterday about some labor work for a couple of days though. You two interested?"

"Yeah, sure," Robert said, finally breaking a smile. He waited for Tucker to say something.

Sour faced, Tucker nodded, his own disappointment showing from Sheldon's comments about his chances of getting hired at the mines.

"Yeah, we'd be interested. I mean, if you think it'd be a waste of time for me to check out the mines."

"Oh, hey," Sheldon hesitated. "I assumed you were traveling together. I'm just saying what I've seen from working in the mines. Then again, like I said, I've never seen kids your age get hired on at the Burketts' farm either."

The same guy who took their order and prepared the food slipped the bill on the table. Sheldon pulled some change out of his pocket.

"Think I'll get this, sixty cents for four meals. That's a break, isn't it?"

Russell put another nickel on the table.

"Think I'll even shock them with a tip. That was a heap of good food."

As they walked outside, Sheldon put his hand on Robert's shoulder. "Good luck. Might cross paths again around town, huh? Either way, stay safe."

"Will do. Thanks for getting breakfast. It's sure appreciated."

"It sure is," Tucker added.

It was late morning by the time they got out of the Salvation Army. Robert took advantage of picking up a second shirt, gray twill, another piece of clothing signifying the uniform of the road. Tucker let loose of forty cents for a pair of work boots. He'd spent over thirty minutes picking through "a free table" looking for two matching socks with a little life still in them. Hitting the jackpot, he found two pair.

"Hey Tucker, look at the time on that clock on the back wall. Didn't Russell say the guy who owns the feed store needing some labor would be in by noon? It's after eleven. I'd like to head over early in case a line for the job starts out front. What'd you decide to do? You going to see if you'll have any luck at the mines first?"

Twisting the receipt for his shoes between his fingers, Tucker began to say something but held back, seeming puzzled by the question. "You're not going with me to check them out?"

"We got here with over twenty guys unloading from those open cars with us. Even more jumped off the closed boxcars. It's not like there's a chance I'd be taken seriously for a job in the mines anyway. I figure I might have a chance of getting the day labor job though. Had enough of those over the past months. But hey, going out to the mines might be worth your time."

Tucker stood staring into space rocking back and forth on his boots, as if thinking of what to say next.

"You should check it out," Robert said, trying to make it easy for him to go his own way.

"Yeah, but since I didn't go right over there this morning, it's not like it can't wait a few more hours until we see what happens with the labor job, don't you think?"

He held back a reply, wanting Tucker to decide for himself. He wasn't sure what he was feeling about them parting ways after all the time they had spent together. But he knew they'd have to split up at some point.

"I think you're right about checking out the other job first." Tucker said, as he spun around toward town. "Let's head out."

North of town they found the feed store Russell had told them about. It was locked. No line was forming and no one else was hanging around outside.

Robert stepped out to the street to look for a newsstand. Not seeing one, he started across the street to try his luck at plucking sections of a newspaper from the top of the trash container in front of the hardware store. "I'll be right back."

It had been more than two weeks since he read any news about what was happening in the country. Peeking at the headlines or skimming an old newspaper over the last months kept him at least a little in the know about if things were getting any better anywhere in the country. When he leaned over the trash there wasn't even one page of a newspaper inside. What was inside stunk and attracted a swarm of flies now buzzing around him as if he smelled just as tasty. The flies followed him off the curb until he shooed them away, making him sorry he didn't have time to take advantage of the soap and water available at the Salvation Army earlier.

A beat-up, rusted black Ford truck came to an abrupt stop in front of the feed store, leaving a vast dust cloud whirling around in the air. Tucker covered his face with his arm and walked toward the guy getting out of the truck, exchanged a few words with him, and was waved inside the store.

"So you're interested in trying to do the work yourself?" he asked, just as Robert came through the door.

"No, this is my buddy, Robert, we're both interested. What's the job?"

"It's mending some fence at my place that got knocked down in a wind storm some years ago. Haven't had the time to fix it, but I need the fence up for a cow that got traded to me last week. By the way, name's Darryl. You had any experience putting up a fence?"

"Yep, worked on a farm till my dad couldn't pay the money to farm it no longer. Robert here, he had a job in Colorado mending fences."

Robert held back any expression of surprise at Tucker's last comment just as Darryl glanced at him and waited for an answer. Robert tipped his head toward him as his reply. The expression on Darryl's face when he shifted his attention back to Tucker showed he wasn't sure about either of them. Watching him shuffle through a stack of papers laying on the counter behind him for an extended amount of time, Robert was sure Darryl was going to tell them to get lost without even turning around.

"Okay, it shouldn't take no longer than a day and a half, I reckon. If it takes any longer than that, I'll think you don't know what you're doing. Thirty-five cents an hour. My wife will give you a couple meals a day. You can sleep in the lean-to shed out back. That's if you need a place to sleep." Darryl hesitated for a moment. "You from that hobo camp at the edge of town?"

"No, sir," Tucker was quick to reply. "Sleeping in the lean-to would be much appreciated."

"I'm gonna be straight with you boys. The only reason I'm hiring you is you'll work cheap and look harmless to be working around the house and my wife. She's up at her sister's west of town right now, but she'll be back later in the afternoon. I'll be checking on you, don't think I won't. If you want the job, go check it out. Come back to pick up anything you need that's not already in the lean-to. It shouldn't be much."

He scribbled out his address on a note pad and handed it to Tucker. "The fencing is rolled up against the side of the shed."

Robert was stunned by how abruptly Darryl decided to hire them, and concerned about whether Tucker told the truth about working with fencing before.

Darryl's place was unkept, unlike the other homes they passed on the way. Paint was peeling off the house enough to show the gray weathered wood beneath it. The second step up to the porch was splintered-off half way across. The bushes on each side of the porch were dead. The entire lawn was choked by weeds.

Two large scrawny dogs ran from around back. They stood looking up at them from behind the side fence, growling, teeth showing, waiting for them to make a wrong move.

"Swell. Now what? Darryl didn't say anything about dogs," Tucker said, as he backed away from the fence.

Bending down to break branches off one of the dead bushes next to the front porch, Robert tore off what was left of the withered leaves. The dogs' growls intensified when he sauntered toward the gate until he began waving one of the branches back and forth in the air. "Let's check them out. Hey, fellas, want to play?"

The growling began to subside as they kept their eyes on the stick. Tails wagging now, they began going around in circles waiting for Robert to throw it. Raising it straight up, he sent the stick sailing yards behind the dogs. In an instant the two dogs raced to it, playing tug of war until one of the dogs claimed its prize and ran back to the fence, lifting his chin up for Robert to throw the stick again.

Robert glanced over his shoulder to Tucker. "Don't seem too ferocious now, do they?"

Slipping through the gate as he threw the stick soaring through the air again, he followed it fast with the toss of another one. "Come on, Tucker, it's okay."

They stood scanning the yard where the fencing was down, catching sight of the shed. "Let's walk out back and check what is in there first. See if we'll have to go pick up anything else," Tucker said. "Might get a good start on it before dark."

The dogs ran back, following close by Robert's side. Their bodies wiggled in excitement until he tossed the sticks again.

Tucker walked out into the middle of the field. "What do you think, forty, fifty feet?"

"I don't know. I guess we can walk it and find out. Looks like quite a few fence posts are down, too. I've never put up fence or fence posts before. Hope you were telling Darryl the truth about working with fencing, because one of us needs to know."

Tucker rubbed his chin and then let out a laugh. "Yeah, I kind of know how. I got us the job though, didn't I? Let's go check out what we have to work with."

Rolls of old barbed wire, coated with rust, were shoved up next to the shed. Tucker threw his hand up. "Crap, Darryl didn't tell us the fence was barbed wire, rusted yet. It's going to be miserable to work with."

Inside they found an assortment of hammers, shovels, and pliers lining the shelves. They were old yet usable, but coated with thick layers of dust and cobwebs. Tucker kept scanning the shelves. "I don't see any work gloves anywhere. We're gonna need those for sure with all the rust on the barbed wire."

It was mid-afternoon before they got back to the feed store. Darryl was helping two men load a truck. Inside, another customer stood waiting to buy an armful of goods.

Stepping outside to wait, they spotted Russell and Sheldon walking toward the feed store, and headed to greet them as they crossed the street.

"Hey, looks like you're following up with the job," Sheldon said.

"Yeah, we got it," Tucker said. "We're here picking up some materials to get started. What happened at the mines?"

"We start on Monday. They told us they're hiring four men to cover for workers leaving to go home for a few weeks. When they get back, our jobs are up unless someone else leaves. What's the job here?"

"Putting up a rusted barbed wire fence and several fence posts for thirty-five cents an hour."

Russell chuckled at Tucker's comment. "Well, that's a shitty deal, isn't it? We came to check it out in case you didn't, but lucky you, huh?"

Tucker laughed a reply. "Yeah, lucky us. At least it's something, not like we don't appreciate getting it. Did they hire the other two men at the mines?"

"They did. A couple of guys who worked with us at the Burketts' farm," Sheldon said. "They've worked in these mines before. We checked into The Miners Boarding House at the south end of Main Street. You two going back to the hobo camp tonight?"

"No, we got a sweet deal sleeping in a lean-to shed at Darryl's place until we're done," Tucker said. "Darryl seems to think a day and a half is enough to get the job done. Probably head out when we're finished, if we don't find something else." Tucker paused a moment. "I . . . I still might check out the mines after we're done with the job though."

"Why not give it a try?" Russell said.

Sheldon stepped closer to Robert. "Heard there's a community dance down at the corner of Main and Sixteenth Street tonight, if you've got nothing to do with your Friday night."

"Swell. That sounds like something different. Huh, Robert?"

Robert shrugged his shoulders, unexcited. He reached out to shake Sheldon's hand, and then Russell's. "We sure appreciate the tip on the job."

Sheldon kept his eyes on Robert as if waiting for him to say something else. When he didn't, he smiled. "Well, maybe we'll see you at the dance or maybe we won't. You should think about coming, Robert. There'll be lots of good music, though not the kind you played. Girls, too."

Robert ignored the comment. "All I can think about is getting up early so we can finish the job before he finds an excuse to fire us. I don't trust the guy after not telling us about the rusted barbed wire."

"Well, boys, anything else we can do for you?" Russell said.

"You helped us a lot. Thanks again," Tucker said as he turned back toward the feed store. Noticing Robert didn't move, he stopped.

"If you've got a little time right now, Russell, I . . . I can use some help at the bank a few blocks up."

"Oh hey, sure, I've got nothing to do until Monday," Russell said, seeming puzzled by the request.

Looking a bit baffled, Tucker broke the awkward silence when Robert glanced over to him. "Yeah, I'll get the materials and meet you back at Darryl's place then."

17

The sun began to cast a veil of shade over the field, a relief after working in the open for three hours. The temperature still registered ninety-seven on the gauge hanging from the corner of the shed. Robert stopped digging a post hole to wipe away the sweat dripping down his forehead into his eyes. "Think it's about six or so?"

"Got to be that, at least."

Tucker walked over to the well to pump another drink of water, splashing a handful on his face and neck. "How's the sledge hammer holding up?"

"It hasn't cracked apart like the first one did, as old and wobbly as it is. Lucky, too. We'd have spent the rest of the afternoon walking back to the feed store to pick up another one."

Darryl's wife called them for supper, handing each a heaping plate of spaghetti and two steaming hot biscuits with lumps of butter on top. "It's okay to eat right here on the back stoop, boys."

Tucker stared at his supper for a moment, and slowly looked up with a grin. "Thank you, ma'am. This sure looks tasty."

"Yes, ma'am, we sure appreciate the hearty serving, too," Robert added. Still smiling at their comments, she took a step inside, but quickly stepped back onto the stoop. "You boys can wash up at the pump, don't forget."

"Was just headed that way, ma'am," Robert replied.

When they came back up to the porch, a bowl of warm, fried apples was setting on the table by the spaghetti.

She'd given them a huge lunch when she got back from her sister's place, but they devoured the spaghetti as if it was their first meal in a week. When they finished eating the dish of fried apples, Darryl hadn't shown up yet.

"Guess we should keep working till dusk, don't you think? Keep Darryl happy?" Robert said.

It was near dark when they heard a truck pull up. Darryl came straight out to the field, yanked on each post as he walked by trying to get some movement, then pulled on the barbed wire fencing to test its tautness. Eying the busted sledge hammer laying next to one of the posts, he picked it up, holding it in the air.

"What happened here?" The slur in his few words was strong.

"The sledge hammer was loose when I started using it," Robert said. "Lasted a few hours of hammering post before it fell apart."

"Oh, yeah, wasn't busted when you started, was it? That's enough pounding for today. From the looks of things you should finish by tomorrow night, maybe. The wife will set food out on that wooden table on the porch in the morning."

He turned away abruptly, heading toward the back door. It wasn't long before arguing started inside the house.

Tucker slammed the shovel into the dirt, letting out a sigh of disgust as he began picking up the tools laying on the ground.

"What?"

"I wonder if he makes his own hootch. Let's get out of here for a while before he comes after us for something."

Robert picked up the broken sledge hammer and the shovel. "Great idea. The community festival is sounding pretty good right now. I'm going to wash up and put my other shirt on first."

It was easy to find the community festival. They could hear the music from Main Street several blocks away. Scanning the crowd gathered around, they watched as men, women, and kids of all ages danced in the street. Three fiddle players, one man on guitar, and one guy playing a washboard, were perched on a makeshift stage. A huge applause went up as they finished. The guy on the washboard walked to the center of the stage.

"This is a community festival. We know there are musicians out there wanting to be part of it. So who out there wants to be next?"

A young man stepped onto the stage and pulled out a harmonica from his pocket. The fiddlers began playing back up as the audience stomped their feet, clapping along wildly. As he played a few more pieces, the applause got louder and the crowd got thicker.

Robert beamed a smile as he tapped his foot along to the music. He watched the families dancing in the street, fathers with young daughters, mothers with sons, young couples, all of them grinning, their struggles set aside for the moment. The sight of everyone outwardly enjoying themselves uplifted his mood immediately, leaving him thankful for the opportunity to be part of it.

"See you decided to come down for some fun."

Robert turned to see Sheldon standing next to him. "Sure glad I did. They're all having a great time, aren't they?"

Russell walked up and tapped Tucker's shoulder to get his attention. "So what do you think?"

"Hey, this is something. Glad you mentioned it to us."

The harmonica player finished, bowed and stepped back into the crowd. A fiddle player walked to the front of the stage, holding his instrument in the air. "Hey, we must have some fiddle players out there. If you've got some tunes, we've got fiddles."

Sheldon nudged Robert's arm. "You're just dying to get your hands on one of those, aren't you? You fiddle, don't you?"

"Only a little. Hey, I'm happy watching."

"If you fiddle, I'll play my harmonica."

"What'd you say?" Robert turned toward Sheldon, but he'd already disappeared into the crowd. Within seconds he was on the stage talking to one of the fiddle players. The two shook hands. Sheldon accepted the fiddle the man held out to him, holding it up as he walked to the front of the stage.

"A violin player and fiddler, too, my buddy is going to join me in a piece. Come on up, Robert."

Rapidly turning to the crowd behind him, Robert hunted for an opening to squeeze through, but Russell's clutch was swift to turn him around just as whistles and clapping began. The crowd stood waiting, revving up their whistles.

Robert put a hand over his face. His heart pounded in his chest as he felt panic coming on.

"Go on kid; have some fun."

"Geez," Robert murmured, realizing there was no way out.

Russell cleared the way through the crowd for him. Hopping onto the stage, Robert leaned into Sheldon's ear to let him know the *Arkansas Traveler* was the only fiddle tune he knew.

"Let's go then."

Sheldon raised the harmonica to his lips. Robert raised the fiddle to his chin. The crowd roared the moment they recognized the tune. Surprised by such a response to the piece, Robert let himself look out at the crowd, watching as the dancing started. He felt touched to see such smiles of good spirits all around him, and humbled to be a part of it.

Applause went on and on when they were finished. Both of them beamed, bowing in appreciation. The crowd started yelling, "Play it again! Play it again!" just as Robert handed back the fiddle to its owner. A big grin spread across the man's lips as he gently pushed his instrument into Robert's chest.

"Go ahead, kid. Make them happy."

The second time around the dancers were winded at the end of the piece, applauding loudly but without the whistles and yelps.

"Looked like you were having fun up there," Sheldon said as Robert jumped off the stage.

"Yep, kinda did."

Russell and Tucker were waiting at the edge of the steps, so were two young girls about Robert's age, staring at him coyly. Feeling the usual blush rising up from his neck to his cheeks, he forced a smile, nodded, and skirted sideways to get away from them. The girls were quick to slip in front of him, blocking his way.

"That's one of the best songs to dance to. Can you play another tune later? Oh, I'm Hazel, and this is Dorothy."

Hazel wrapped her arm across her waist. Leaning in toward Robert, her long, blonde soft curls flipped forward over her shoulders. "Please," she whispered.

Before Robert could say anything, she was yanked to the side.

"Papa, I was just asking him if he'd play another tune."

"Told you to stay away from them hobo kind. Let's go, Hazel. Your mother is waiting. You too, Dorothy."

Both girls seemed embarrassed by the caustic remark. Glancing over her shoulder, Hazel shot Robert an apologetic expression before following her father.

Stunned by what he witnessed, Tucker let out a gasp. "You okay?"

Robert noticed the horrified expression on Tucker's face. "Hey, I'm fine; don't worry about it." He glanced away for a moment to hide his unsettled feelings after being called a hobo. "It wasn't the first time it's happened."

"Well, that sure was some good fiddling."

As people streamed by them, many stopped to thank Robert and Sheldon for the chance to dance to the *Arkansas Traveler.*

Sheldon put his hand on Robert's shoulder. "Hey, let me buy you a soda since I didn't give you a chance to say no to fiddling. We can listen to the music over there by the beverage stand. Didn't get a chance to ask you two how the job is going."

"We'll probably finish tomorrow, maybe, anyway. We want to get it done. The guy we're working for is scary, getting all hooched up and yelling at his wife."

"Let us know if he gives you any trouble."

Russell spun around. "Yeah, let us know. You know where to find us."

Darryl's house was dark when they got back. His truck was in the driveway. Several feet before the gate, Robert put his arm in front of Tucker's chest, signaling him to stop.

"I forgot about the dogs. Hope they don't start barking or crazy Darryl might come out with a shotgun. Better find a few sticks."

Walking up slow to the gate, Robert pulled the latch up, sticks in hand in case he needed them. Tucker followed close behind trying to ease the bolt down into the latch as Robert handed it off to him. The bolt slipped between Tucker's fingers causing a slight clink of metal against metal when it dropped, but loud enough to rouse the dogs. They tore around the corner of the house, growling, but eased up when they recognized Robert's voice.

He held up the sticks. "Hey guys, look what I have."

Excited by an offer to play, the dogs began to wiggle around in circles, eying the sticks with each turn, watching as they flew through the air in the glimmer of light from the half moon. It took awhile to reach the lean-to shed with Robert tossing the sticks every few feet, the dogs leaping after them, dashing right back for another toss.

Once Robert settled in for the night, the dogs snuggled around his feet, chewing on the sticks. Loud snoring from one of the dogs lying next to Robert's head woke him in the morning. The sun was just beginning to spread some daylight. Eager to get the day started and finish the work so they could head out, Robert tugged on Tucker's shirt to wake him. He sat up, glancing around as usual to see where he was.

"Hey, are those clean towels over there?" Tucker said, pointing to the corner of the lean-to.

"Yeah, it looks like it. She sure is a nice lady. Let's get going on the fence."

Two hours later, Darryl's wife put a breakfast basket of warm biscuits, jelly, salt pork, and milk on the table, and then shouted, "Hey, boys come and eat." Stepping onto the porch again at noon, she yelled "Lunch is ready, boys," waving to them as she set out a basket of cheese sandwiches and a pitcher of lemonade.

Darryl barged out the back door not long after and shouted he'd be back to check on them. All but three feet of fence was done when his truck pulled back into the driveway. He made his way to the back of the field, pulling on fence posts, testing the tautness of the fencing between each post again.

"It's five o'clock," he said, with a less recognizable slur than the day before. "Wasn't counting on having workers here tonight. We're going over to my brother's place for supper. You can sleep in the lean-to if you need to." He tested the sturdiness of a fence post as he walked by it. Stopping, he spun back around. "Come by the feed store for your pay tomorrow after you finish the job. You're gonna need to get your own supper."

"Okay, we'll be there in the morning," Robert said to Darryl's back as he walked toward the porch.

Tucker rolled his eyes when Darryl didn't bother to reply. "Let's get this done so we can get something to eat."

Not much later, the screen door slammed shut. They glanced up to see Darryl walking toward his truck.

The back door opened and shut again.

"Boys," Darryl's wife yelled, waving a basket. "Here's some supper."

When she walked to the truck, Darryl began flinging his arms around in the air like a kid having a tantrum, shouting something at her.

The job was finished by nightfall. The next morning a basket with breakfast biscuits and plums was sitting on the porch when they woke up. Beneath the rolls were peanut butter and jelly sandwiches tied in a cotton cloth.

Tucker peeked into the basket. "We're in luck. Darryl left already. That guy doesn't deserve a wife like her."

When they got to the feed store, it was closed. The stores across the street were open.

"We're waiting for our money if we have to sit here all day," Robert said.

Customers had come and gone by the time Darryl's truck pulled up. Taking his time to turn over the "open" sign, he leaned out the screen door and waved them in. Walking behind the counter, he pulled out two envelopes from a drawer and placed them down on the counter in front of him. Keeping his eyes on theirs, he slowly slid the envelopes toward them as if displaying a winning poker hand.

"I didn't deduct for the broken sledge hammer."

Robert picked up the envelopes and handed one to Tucker. Checking the contents, Robert was surprised it contained the pay Darryl promised. He waited for a nod from Tucker and then shifted back to Darryl. "Thank you." As they turned to leave there was no comment whatsoever from Darryl. He didn't even look at them.

Before Tucker took off to check out jobs at the mines, they agreed to meet up at The Miners Boarding House about one o'clock. Tucker was sitting on the steps of the boarding house talking to Russell when Robert walked up.

"How did it go?" Robert asked.

"Got laughed at a lot, just like you told me. Said to come back when I'm older, or when the waiting list of men looking for work is down to nothing. Like that'll happen."

Robert rested his hands on his hips, pausing before he said anything. "Did you hit all the mines near town?"

"Yep, I wasn't at one mine long enough to get held up from moving on to the next."

"At least you gave it a shot. Better than traveling across country with your hopes up to hear those same words, like I did."

"So what's next for you two?" Russell asked.

"I want to head north today yet," Robert said. "Think I'll hitch a ride this time after the close call with the bulls on the way in. Told Tucker I would hang around to see how things turned out with the mines before I go anywhere."

"Sounds like you two need to talk. I'm supposed to meet Sheldon at the Barrel House. You know where to find me if I can help with anything else. Be glad to."

As they walked through the downtown, not heading any place particular, neither of them spoke. Robert pointed to the park at the next corner, wanting to give Tucker time to think, figuring he'd talk about what was next for him when he was ready. It was awhile before Tucker said anything.

"Think I'll do what I was planning to do. Head up to Cincinnati to see Al to check on that letter from my dad to make sure it got there. If it's not there, I'll write to him again." Tucker laughed suddenly. "Maybe I'll find some kind of crap work while I'm in Ohio since I have experience in it now." Putting his hands behind his head to stretch, he was quiet for a few minutes before turning toward Robert. "Guess I'll head north with you tonight."

"Okay, but let's head out before it gets too late in the day."

Dark clouds hung overhead when they walked out to the county road north of town to hitch a ride. It wasn't long before a truck of migrant workers stopped to pick them up. The loud idle of the engine muffled the chance to say anything but "Springfield."

The driver put his hand up by the side of his mouth and yelled "Okay," signaling with his thumb to hop in the back. Two guys riding in the truck bed shifted their legs to make room, their dry, cracked hands, weathered to deep brown from the sun, looked like the withered leaves of fall. Having moved from harvest to harvest over the last five months, and just ending eight weeks of picking beans in southern Arkansas, the men were regulars working the harvesting schedule in the region.

"Where you headed next for harvesting around here?" Tucker said.

"Hate to shoot down your hopes of finding work around Springfield anytime soon, but the next harvesting in the area isn't until late August," one of the guys said.

The truck stopped across the street from the train station, which was really helpful. Walking by the driver, they saluted a thank you.

Grinning, the driver leaned his head out the window and shouted above the noise of the rattling engine, "You boys stay safe now."

18

Dusk began to settle over Springfield just as large, dark clouds raced in, expelling the last of the daylight. Robert and Tucker stood staring at the two-story, red brick Missouri Pacific Railroad station. The door was locked. It was quiet, with only a janitor inside sweeping the floor, a lamp sat in the middle of a long, wooden counter giving only enough light to cast shadows across the first floor of the building.

A train schedule taped inside a window pane on the door listed the first train to St. Louis leaving at 6:35 the next morning. The last evening train had just departed.

"From the size of the station, I don't think there'll be bulls around that early in the morning, but just in case we'd better catch out fifty yards or more up the tracks," Robert said.

Tucker glanced both ways down the street. "Where we gonna lay down tonight? I'm bushed."

Robert pointed in the direction they had just come from. "Let's find a spot across the road in the prairie we passed right before we turned off the highway. It'll be pitch black soon."

A drizzle began to fall as they crossed the road to step into the high prairie grass. Standing in the rain, they raised the palms of their hands out in front of them to catch the precious droplets of rain and began wiping caked-on dust from the long ride off their faces and necks.

"I was needing a shower, how about you?" Tucker laughed. "This feels great."

Before Robert could say anything, a heavy, pounding rain began pelting against them with such force it was difficult to talk about where to go. He waved to Tucker and started running in the direction they had just come from. Reaching the train station, he jumped onto the porch, allowing its cover to rescue him from the fierce, beating rain that felt like a bull whip striking relentlessly against his thin shirt.

"Wasn't expecting to wash my clothes, too," Tucker said, as he topped the porch steps. "Now what? I saw a couple of boxcars sitting on a side track not far up. Ever tried sleeping in one?"

"I saw them, too, and yeah, I've slept in cars along the tracks. These are kind of close to the station for my comfort, but if they're not locked, we can at least get out of the rain. We might get picked up if we hang around in front of the station too long."

In a fast dash to the end of the porch, Tucker jumped down. "Then let's go check them out."

The doors of the first car were shut. It took both of them to pull it open far enough to peek in. The odor from cattle dung smacked with such force they bolted back and rammed it shut.

"Whoa, let's try the other one," Robert said, sliding his fingers off the tip of his nose.

There was a slight opening in the door of the second car. Using more caution, Robert peeked inside. Smelling nothing, seeing nothing in the last light of the evening, they slipped through the opening. The hard rain pounding on the roof sounded like a jack hammer.

"Holy . . . !" Robert said, jumping back in surprise. "Didn't see you there ma'am."

Huddled in the back corner was a woman with two small children clinging to her. His sudden jump and outburst sent the youngest child's head into his mother's lap crying, setting off the other child's sobs.

"Sorry, ma'am, we're just getting out of the rain."

Her dark eyes steady on Robert's, she reached her arms around her children, pulling them closer, sheltering them as if they were precious eggs to be poached from a nest. She sat quiet, starring at him through questioning eyes. He waited for a reply, but she gave none. Sensing from her stillness that she was more startled than afraid, perhaps because of their age, he stayed at the opposite end of the car, sliding his back down against the wall to sit on the floor. Tucker slipped down next to him.

A large, dirty, frayed burlap bag that looked as if it was the bottom half of a feed sack sat next to her. It was open and he thought it was probably stuffed with what was left to hold her life together. The children had stopped crying. The sadness veiling their three faces chilled him more than the dampness of the rain still dripping from his clothes.

Darkness started to take its final descent, sending a creeping shadow across the car.

"We're just going to sit here until the rain stops, ma'am," Robert said. "No need to be . . ."

Before he could finish the sentence, a man jumped through the door, tripping over Tucker's feet stretched out in front of the opening. Turning quick to look at the woman, he shifted his gaze back to them. Cradled in his arms were several apples and a small bottle of milk.

"We just came in to get out of the rain, mister," Robert said. "It's coming down so hard out there."

The man, lean as a scarecrow and showing the start of a new beard, stood staring down at them for a moment and then nodded as he turned to walk to the other end of the car. The children circled around him as he pulled out a small round of bread from under his shirt. He handed it to the woman. The children's eyes stayed on the apples, their small frames each clutching one of his legs as they tiptoed up for the fruit.

"Come on, sit down here. Then you'll have some," he said, patting the floor next to him.

Robert was relieved to see they had some food. His stomach had been empty since breakfast. It grumbled at him during the long ride in the truck to Springfield, but he knew better than to start eating the cheese sandwiches he had picked up before leaving Joplin in front of the migrant workers. Reaching for one now, he was careful to keep the sandwich just inside the top of his rucksack, pulling tiny pieces at a time up to his mouth. Tucker watched him and followed his lead.

Rain poured down long into the night, pelting against the roof with vengeance. They fell asleep sometime during the night, but not before securing their rucksacks behind their backs.

Waking with the first rays of light coming through the door, Robert saw several new arrivals sleeping along the walls. He nudged Tucker awake, watching as he looked around to grasp where he was.

"We need to head down the tracks to wait for the train before any bulls come looking inside this car." Robert whispered. Jumping up, he reached out his arm to pull Tucker up. "Let's go."

Their boot heels against the wooden floor began arousing men in the car. Robert peeked his head out the door, checking both directions for bulls before jumping to the ground. It was still dawn. The clouds looked as if they were about to dump more rain, providing a dark cover to the morning. Behind them they could hear the sound of others in the car jumping onto the gravel and their boots following them down the tracks. Once they got far enough from the train station, they all started veering into the grass, stooping down twenty feet back.

"I'd let go of a nickel for some warm coffee and a bun," Tucker said. "The cheese sandwiches we ate last night sure aren't going to stay with me till the next stop."

"Yeah, well, everything is going to be closed for a few more hours, so we're out of luck."

Arriving the night before, exhausted, muscles aching from working at Darryl's place, Robert didn't think about going out in the heavy rain to pick up food before the stores closed for the evening. Over the past months, he'd made it some days with almost nothing to eat, but now he'd have to make it until they got to St. Louis.

Once they dropped down into the high grass, bodies kept walking by them. Robert caught sight of the man and woman with the kids as they settled into the grass next to them. They were quiet except for an occasional "shush" when one of the kids made a noise. Hearing the train approaching the station, they waited for the first whistle announcing its arrival and a second blast of the whistle signaling its roll out from the station. The explosive rumble of the engine noise and the screech from the steel wheels rubbing against the metal on the tracks were familiar sounds, providing a consistent timeline to those waiting for the right moment to seize a ride from the moving giant.

"Let's go," Robert said, as he brushed by Tucker's shoulder.

At least thirty men were heading down the tracks in front of them, leaving him anxious about ending up at the back of the train and missing a chance to catch on to a covered car. Robert broke into a slow run. Turning his head to see if Tucker was keeping up, he caught sight of the man and woman from the boxcar out of the corner of his eye, hustling along the track behind Tucker. They were each carrying one of the children, trying to keep ahead of the cars so they wouldn't miss their chance to load.

Robert stopped once he got to the midway point of the boxcar next to them when he noticed the doors were shut. Most of the men in front of him were filling the first two cars. The car rolling toward them was packed with cattle.

Tucker caught up to him just as the livestock passed by. Not far behind, Robert could see the woman straining to keep a tight grip on the youngest child, seemingly out of breath, looking as if she would collapse. Edging up closer, the man tried to prod her along as he battled holding on to the older child, and struggled to keep his grip on their belongings bundled inside the burlap sack.

Dark clouds loomed ahead of them for miles. Robert was still damp from the soaking the night before, so spotting the covered boxcar approaching was like a huge gift rolling down the tracks toward them.

Stumbling forward then sideways, the woman began to lose her footing as she ran along side the track trying to get in a good position to catch on. Robert bolted toward her, clamping one hand on her elbow and the other against her back. She gained her balance. Turning to look at him, she then glanced over toward the opening in the covered freight car as it began to pass by. Without hesitation she shoved the child into Robert's chest, walked closer to the tracks, grabbed onto one of the hands held out to help people trying to load and was lifted into the train. Swiftly, she swung her body around and leaned forward with her arms extended, ready to grab the child.

Immediate panic over came him at the possible peril of trying to hand off the child to her while the train was moving. Her husband came up behind him, threw the sack of their belongings into the car, put his hand on Robert's back and yelled, "Go!" with enough authority in his voice for him to obey.

Heart thumping in his chest he stepped toward the car, squeezing the child's back so tight it began to cry. Someone on the train saw what was happening, grasped on to Robert's free hand, then his belt, and slid him and the child into the car. Immediately a few guys leaned out to take hold of the other child and help the husband into the car. The woman leaned down, sweeping her child from Robert's arms, took hold of the other child's hand, and headed to the back of the train.

Bolting up quickly to look for Tucker, Robert saw him running along side the train waiting for an opportunity to jump on, but the opening of the car began passing by. Realizing he might miss his chance to load, Tucker immediately increased his speed to keep up with the opening in the door. Robert could see he was still going to try to grab onto the floor of the car to hop in. Moving back to the edge of the opening, Robert pressed one arm against the inside of the car to steady himself, and swung his other arm out ready to grip Tucker's hand.

The train gave its first major jerk as it shifted to pick up speed. Robert shook his head from side to side, his outstretched hand pointed toward the back of the train to let Tucker know he should catch the next car. He was too far behind the opening now for him to have a chance of boarding the car safely from where he was, yet Tucker kept increasing his pace until he got to the edge of the opening.

Reaching up to grab Robert's hand at the same time he tried to raise his foot onto the platform, Tucker's grip caught only the bottom half of Robert's hand. His toes were the only part of his foot to reach the opening, leaving him dangling above the ground. Within seconds, Tucker's grip slid off Robert's fingers, sending his body spiraling down onto the gravel.

As soon as his body stilled, Tucker jumped up and immediately jerked one foot back off the ground as if it had touched down into fire. Robert watched as he hopped around on one foot, arms groping up and down through the air like a bird trying to take its first flight. His torso teetered as he floundered to stay upright. Just when it seemed he would land face down in the gravel, he found his balance on one foot. Raising one arm up to his side and holding the palm of his other hand out directly toward the train, Tucker motioned for Robert to stay.

Stunned, Robert kept his eyes on him, trying to get his mind around what had just happened, not quite believing it couldn't still be undone. As he swayed forward, his instinct was to jump off the train. An arm reached around from behind him, enveloping his chest with such increasing pressure it felt like he was being torqued into place, unable to move in any direction.

Eyes fixed on Tucker, Robert watched until he disappeared from sight. Feeling the arm still firmly planted across his chest, he twisted sideways to see the man who shouted at him to load. Releasing his hold on him, he turned his eyes away from Robert's startled gaze, but not before they flickered regret for the mishap.

The woman sat at the other end of the car with her children clutching each side of her bony torso, watching as her husband walked back to them. Her eyes shifted past him toward Robert. She stared directly at him for a moment, then snapped her eyes shut.

Emotions shredded, Robert slid down against the wall of the car. The loss was immediate. The fright of not knowing what to do next began to overwhelm him, leaving his mind spinning with one plan after another. It'd be hours before they reached St. Louis. He could hop the next train back to Springfield, but it could be after nightfall when he got back, or depending on the train schedule, it could be sometime the next day. Thumbing a ride might get him there faster, but what would Tucker do if he couldn't walk? He might try to find help at a mission if he could get there somehow and risk getting his name on some agency list. Maybe he would lay low somewhere hoping his leg would get better? If Tucker could put weight on his foot he might hobble out to the highway to hitch a ride to St. Louis. If he did, then maybe it would be better to wait for him there a few days. But it'd be a slim chance to connect with him if he hitched a ride. St. Louis was a huge city. Tucker could be dropped off anywhere.

He kept tossing around one plan after another until the possibility that he would never see Tucker again started seeping in. The more he considered what to do once he reached St. Louis, the more he realized there was little chance of ever crossing paths again, or ever connecting no matter what plan he came up with.

Anger began bellowing through his mind for going against what he'd learned on the road. Travel alone. Don't get involved with anyone. It could lead to trouble, make travel complicated, and slow you down. He began banging the palm of his hand against his forehead as he remembered going against his instincts when he first met Tucker, and the worry he'd had about traveling with someone he didn't know. Then a rush of sadness overtook him as he imagined Tucker crouched someplace, hungry from being without food since the day before, unable to walk or limping around wondering where to go. He'd be an easy target for someone to rip off his rucksack, or roll him for money hidden in his clothing and shoes.

Realizing he was still banging the palm of his hand against his head, Robert stopped and glanced around the car. He tried to quiet his mind for a moment but caught the woman at the other end of the car staring at him again. He wasn't sure why, maybe because he'd been hitting his hand against his forehead. But he understood her maternal expression that made him think of his mother, and even about Tucker's mother not knowing her son was hurt. The contrast between the choices he had versus Tucker's choices seemed stark all of a sudden. He'd finally made firm plans to get home to see if his family was still together, but Tucker's plans had just been blown apart. The lingering dead-end thoughts made the burden of what to do when he reached St. Louis dismal.

Trying to sleep through the rain storm the night before left him worn out. Robert put his head against the wall to sleep, hoping his mind wouldn't float back into a spin. He woke to a boot nudging against his side, letting him know the train was nearing St. Louis.

19

It was a relief to step off the train as it slowed coming into St. Louis without the expected alert of bulls along the tracks. Robert still took caution by jumping off yards before the station, and heading into the brush toward the streets on the outskirts of town. Too worked up most of the train ride to think about having had nothing to eat since the night before, he began to feel weak from the heat of the day.

A makeshift food stand sat at the corner of the first street he came to. Two young boys sat behind a table made from stacks of concrete blocks with slabs of wood sitting on top. They jumped up when they saw him coming and raised a sign with one menu item. From the looks of the deteriorating houses all around, it appeared the stand was set up to get the attention of men hopping off trains, so hungry they might chance stopping to buy a salt pork sandwiches advertised for ten cents. "Free water" scrawled at the bottom of the sign ended any thought of walking on.

Robert unwrapped the sandwich, smelled it before taking the first bite and decided it might be safe enough to take a chance on. The scrawny, short-haired dog following along behind him seemed to think so too.

He headed toward the train station to check the schedule thinking it might help him sort out his options. The next train to Springfield didn't leave until close to evening. A train to Chicago left in two hours. If he took the train to Chicago, he could be home by the next day. If he waited to take the train back to Springfield, it would be dark by the time he got there, diminishing the chance to connect with Tucker that night.

Robert tried again to sort out what Tucker might do. If he could walk by now, Tucker might already be on his way to St. Louis. If he couldn't put weight on his leg, then where would he begin looking for him? It wasn't likely he would have stayed along the tracks. He felt helpless by the choices. None of them seemed hopeful in ever knowing what happened to Tucker.

Needing time to walk off his frustration and to clear his mind, he headed for what he thought would be downtown St. Louis. But he went in the wrong direction and wound up on the outskirts of town. He stood on the side of the main highway. Signs for Springfield stared at him, so did signs for Chicago.

It took Robert only a moment to decide he would leave the decision of what to do to chance. He crossed the highway and stuck out his thumb, knowing if he didn't catch a ride soon, he was sure to get into Springfield after nightfall. Worse yet, if he wasn't lucky enough to get a ride with someone going directly there, he could get himself in a position of being dropped off on the side of the highway, trying to hitch another ride or maybe more to Springfield after dark.

The first truck that came by pulled to the side of the road just past him. A farmer and his wife were headed west to Sedalia, Missouri, straight north of Springfield. Robert had just seconds to decide after he heard "hop in the back" if he'd take the chance of ending up in the dark on the side of the road.

Robert crawled over the tailgate to see stacked up crates of chickens. They didn't like the intrusion. Once the ruckus from the chickens settled down, he decided to enjoy the upside of the day by taking in the lush, rolling hills of the Ozarks as they got closer to Sedalia. Yet most of the ride he beat himself up for leaving what to do to chance. But by the time they dropped him off at Junction 65 east of Sedalia, he'd realized going back to look for Tucker was the right thing to do even if he didn't find him. Recalling their recent conversation with him about his determination to get into a CCC training camp to get some skills so he wouldn't end up in a hobo camp was impressive. Not making the effort to help Tucker would stay with him for a long time.

The last sight of Tucker was holding his hand up, signaling for him to stay on the train. Not expecting that he would come back to Springfield to find him, Tucker could be at any number of places in the area by now. But where?

Heading out on foot toward Springfield, he put his thumb out as cars approached until he caught a ride with a couple going to Joplin. As they drove farther south, his tensions eased in seeing the Lake of the Ozarks surrounded by picturesque dense woodlands, a setting he knew he'd remember forever.

The sun was just beginning to descend when they dropped him off by Springfield. Standing by the side of the highway, it was as if his legs were stuck to the road. Finally, after taking the time to formulate a plan, he headed into town to find the mission or a Salvation Army. He found both but not Tucker. Next on his plan was checking out the parks, thinking Tucker might hang out in one without anyplace else to go. Seeing two parks on a small map of the town tacked up outside the post office, Robert headed for the largest park and walked through it twice. The second park was not far from the train station. It was almost dusk when he finished circling through it a second time. Disappointed in not spotting Tucker yet, he felt at a complete loss of where to look for him next. If there was a hobo camp in

Springfield, he'd have to wait until the next morning to walk through it. Dusk was settling fast. Finding a place in the prairie to sleep before it got dark was critical, so he headed toward the highway to settle in the tall grass on the other side of the highway.

He came to a sudden halt, almost tripping over his feet. It was as if someone walked by and thumped him on the head, realizing now where Tucker might be, still unable to walk or not. Taking off in a run he passed the train station, stopping to catch his breath when he reached the freight car they'd slept in the night before. He leaned in to see the shadows of several men propped up against the side walls.

"Tucker, you in there?"

"Hey Robert, I'm back here."

At the far end of the car he could see an arm waving, barely visible in what little light was left. As he stepped into the boxcar, he noticed Tucker didn't move to greet him as he walked toward him, he sensed an immediate concern.

"What the hell! . . . Geez, Tucker. You're kind of a mess."

Tucker let out a slight laugh accompanied by a gasp of pain. "Well, that makes me feel better."

Robert slid down next to him. He had a bruise on his cheek, blood crusting at the corner of his mouth, and several bits of broken skin at the edge of his chin. Looking down to check out his leg, Robert noticed his left boot was off, but he didn't see it laying around anywhere.

"What happened to your face? All that from the fall? How about your leg? Were you able to walk here on it?"

Tucker scratched his head, looking as if he was thinking of what to say.

"You're kinda of a dope for coming back. You know that, don't you?"

Robert smirked but held back saying anything, even in a joking way. "So, what happened?"

"Okay. After my grand exit from the train, I hobbled back here on one leg, using the tip of my boot on my bum foot to keep my balance. The car was empty when I got here. Then some creepy, little old man came in, saw my chin cut up and boot off, and got the idea I was hurt pretty bad. When he bent over to reach for my rucksack, I kicked him in the crotch with my good leg. I got him good, too. It left him doubled over, so he tried kicking me in the chin, hoping I'd let go of the rucksack to shield my face. When I didn't let go, he tried to reach for it again, but I had both my arms wrapped around it and hung on tight. Figured he was still hurtin' from the first kick in the crotch, so I got him again. Guess he didn't want to take a chance on a third kick because he jumped back, spit on me, and snatched my boot before he left."

"Good fighting for a gimp. What about your leg? Did you try to walk on it since this morning?"

Tucker pointed to two guys at the other end of the car.

"Those two helped me outside so I could take a piss when they saw me struggling to get up earlier. Tried to put my foot down then but it hurt something awful, way more than it did this morning when I got here. Haven't tried to stand on it again, but it looks like the swelling's gone down some."

"You eat since yesterday?"

"Eat? Thought about running into town but . . . "

Robert jumped up. "If you can joke about it, you might be okay. I'll be back. Don't go anywhere."

Tucker laughed. "Yeah, that's a scream all right."

Half way up the block, Robert spotted Tucker's boot thrown to the side of the road. The inside sole lay next to it, leaving Robert curious about whether Tucker had hidden any of his money inside.

All the shops were being swept out when he got into town or already closed for the night. Robert walked into a small food market just as the owner was about to flip the open sign to closed. He let him in and sold him a couple of day-old meatball sandwiches for a nickel just to get rid of them. Robert let go of another nickel to buy a pint of milk. When he got back to the car it had filled up some.

"I got lucky finding a place open, Tucker. I ate mine on the way back."

The light was filling the car when Robert woke the next morning. Tucker was already awake, propped up against the wall looking miserable. Robert pulled Tucker's boot out of his rucksack.

"Thought I'd have to shop for boots for you, too."

Tucker grinned as he patted the inside sole firmly back into the bottom.

"That old man must be really dumb to think I'd take my boot off and not take the money out."

"How's your foot?"

"Not sure but it ached all last night. Don't think I'm gonna be hopping any trains today."

"Yeah, I think you're right. Let's get out of this stinking car for a while."

Tucker reached for his boot and eased it over his foot.

"Well, it's slipping on better than it slipped off last night, but not by much."

Tucker pushed himself up with one arm while Robert pulled him up by his other arm. Leaning against the sidewall, Tucker lowered his foot to the floor.

"I'll give it a try."

Shifting his body around to face the sidewall, he leaned against it as he hopped sideways on his good leg to the opening of the car, wincing at every step. Robert jumped down onto the gravel, waiting to see how they'd manage getting him out of the car.

Tucker stood in the opening sizing up what was next. Robert raised his arms up for him to brace against while he hopped down, but with his short height against Tucker's tall body, it became clear the attempt could be risky. "You'll have to jump, then I'll grab your arm."

Once he was down and steadied against Robert's side, he tried to put his foot down. "Oh, crap, that hurts."

Leaning on Robert's shoulder, he set his foot down only long enough to steady himself so he could hop forward on the other foot. Once they got to the park by the station, Robert helped settle him under the shade of a large maple. Tucker's face was flush from the heat. He was breathing heavily from the three block walk.

"Is it hurting even more now?" Robert asked

Tucker winced when he stretched out his legs in front of him. "Yeah, but not like it did yesterday." He bent his leg again and began rubbing the top of his ankle.

None of the stores were open yet. Robert tried to figure out the day and how long they'd be around Springfield. He was curious if Tucker was thinking about heading home. Stay or leave, it would be a struggle for him until he could put weight on his foot again.

"Where do you think you're going from here, Tucker? Heading home until you heal your leg or hanging out here?"

"Go home and be more of a burden to my dad. Are you kidding me? I'm heading to see Al so I can check if my dad sent that letter. Don't want Al to forget me."

"You sure about going to Ohio? That's a long way from Missouri"

"Yeah, I'm sure. I'm getting in one of those camps."

Robert grinned, surprised again by Tucker's fortitude.

"Okay, how about I go into town to pick up some day-old doughnuts or something? You going to be all right here?"

Tucker started to take money out of his rucksack. Robert put his hand up to stop him. "Hey, don't be pulling money out in the open. We'll settle up later."

Waiting for the stores to open, Robert walked up to the mission. Not sure what he was looking for he shuffled through all the tables, finally finding a long sleeved cotton shirt that had all the buttons and no rips for only five cents. The shirt he worked in for days at Darryl's place stunk and was getting thread bare. He kept looking around until he noticed the shops across the street were flipping the closed signs over.

Tucker was asleep when he got back, still sitting upright against the tree, his boot off and rucksack strapped behind his back. The park had filled with guys hanging around waiting for the next train. Two young kids stood about six feet away eying Tucker. They were quick to scoot away when Robert sat down next to him. He worried how long Tucker would walk at a snail's pace. If he needed to see a doctor, it could be sorry trouble for him.

Tucker snorted, waking himself up. "You back already?"

"Yeah, glad you woke though, didn't want the milk to go sour in the heat."

"Well, that's a treat, milk two days in a row."

"Figured you needed it right now. Here's something else that might help." Robert handed him an old, nicked-up black cane. "Couldn't find any crutches."

Tucker turned the cane around in his hands and broke into a broad grin. "Think it'll work for my new hop-a-long walk?"

"I'm thinking you should get a cot at the mission for a night or so."

"You think they'll have a cot open? Seems like they were always full up in the other missions we walked through."

"I checked, they do. Eat up so we can head that way."

20

The cane did little to help Tucker walk the eight blocks to the mission. Robert's shoulder acted as a crutch the entire way, leaving him hoping there'd still be an empty cot for Tucker by the time they arrived. A man with a green twill cap and white hair cut below his ears was standing by the rows of cots.

"You look worn out, boy. You must be wanting a place to rest for a while?" He put his hand on Tucker's shoulder as he spoke. "I'm Jeb, the volunteer who tracks this area most mornings."

"If you've got an empty cot, I'd sure be grateful."

"Well, you got lucky. There's still a cot open."

Jeb gave a quick wink at Robert before he began questioning Tucker. "Do you know what's going on with your ankle, or is it your foot?"

"It's my ankle. Not sure what's wrong, but it don't hurt as much as it did yesterday."

"We can have the nurse who volunteers in the afternoon look at it. What do you think?"

Tucker grinned. "That would be swell."

"We'll need to get some personal information from you."

Tucker hesitated for a moment. "Yeah . . . that'd be okay."

They helped Tucker down onto a cot. "Oh, man, does this feel good." Just minutes after putting his head against the canvas, he dozed off.

"And what about you? There's a couple of chairs against the back wall. If you want to get off your feet, sit for a bit, I'd claim one. Place fills up fast this time a day."

"You bet. I'll get one now. Thank you, sir." He bent down and grabbed Tucker's rucksack he'd slid under the cot.

Robert had traveled enough in the last few days to wear him down. His arm muscles still ached from pounding fence posts into the ground at Darryl's place, and now he felt intense pain in his right shoulder from Tucker's weight pushing down against it.

Shoving the rucksacks under one of the wooden chairs, he noticed the clock above it showed ten o'clock. Leaning his head against the wall as he settled onto the chair, he felt thankful for a place inside to rest.

It was twelve thirty when Robert woke, surprised he didn't remember nodding off. Jeb was walking toward him.

"Your buddy hasn't moved since he fell asleep. I was hoping you'd wake up before I left for the day. Ralph works the afternoon shift."

"Will the nurse be coming in then, too?" He was eager to find out how long Tucker would be laid up.

"She gets here around two. Why don't you have some soup while you're waiting? I'll walk over with you on my way out and take you to the head of the line so no one accuses you of cutting in. That way you can get an extra bowl to bring back for your buddy."

Tucker was just sitting up when Robert came back. "I figured you were looking out for my rucksack."

He handed Tucker a bowl of soup and a thick slice of bread. "Sorry, it might be a little cool by now."

"I'd eat it if it was frozen."

"Jeb says a guy named Ralph works the afternoon shift. He should be around here somewhere. Nurse comes in at two."

Tucker didn't look up until he finished the soup. "Barley. It's filling, huh?" He started to say something else but pulled back to think for a moment. "I don't mean to hold you up. What are you going to do now?"

Robert scanned the room. "I'm going to find Ralph. Oh, it looks like he's coming over here."

A tall, thin, red-haired man was walking toward them. He looked as if he could be related to Tucker. "I'm Ralph. Jeb left a note to check in with cot 26. You're Tucker?"

"Yes, sir. This is Robert."

"You're on the list to see the nurse. I need to get some information from you first."

Robert was eager to check out the center of town, so he broke into the conversation. "What time should I come back?"

"I'd say late afternoon. The nurse has two people to check on before Tucker. He won't be going anywhere before then."

"I'll be back later, Tuck."

Robert walked toward the center of Springfield unsure of what to do. The main street was similar to Joplin with trolleys running back and forth through the city. The business area was smaller than Joplin's by several blocks, but he felt it was going to be just as hard to find information about work. He kept walking, hoping he'd find a spot where he could at least sit and listen to the locals.

The downtown was a bustle of activity. Men in suits darted in and out of businesses. Women strolled along the sidewalks holding parasols to shade them from the sun. They didn't give any hint of bad times unless they took notice, as he did, of the large numbers of transient people sauntering along the streets, none of them looking as if they were heading to a destination. For some reason the thought hit Robert hard. The need to find a lead on work seemed less urgent for the moment, replaced by the need to find solitude somewhere.

Robert kept walking, roaming really, until he came upon another park at the edge of a lake. Spotting an area not crowded with people, he sat taking in the glimmer across the water. It was the first chance in weeks to be alone, to have quiet, a place to just think.

Thoughts and images of the last few days burst randomly through his mind. The woman handing her child to him, and then reaching out to grab the kid back as the train was moving, the girl's father calling him a hobo at the festival and dragging his daughter away, Darryl's belittling comment about not charging for the crappy sledge hammer, and Tucker's grip slipping from his fingers.

Images kept rushing through his mind, one after the other until he couldn't allow one more thought to slip in. Jumping up, he darted closer to the lake, trying to focus on its beauty and the birdsong around him. But his thoughts went back to the desolate situation of the family in the boxcar sharing a loaf of bread and a few apples, their whole life in a beaten-up, dirty, burlap sack. Thoughts of his mother, his brothers and sisters poured in, and what he might not know about them since he left home. Were they still together? What if the people came back who talked to his mother about having the younger kids live in other people's homes? It had been almost five months since he'd left. Dropping down onto the grass he leaned his face into his hands, wondering what might have happened to his family since then. *I should be with them. Not worry Ma anymore about where I am.*

Suddenly, his family being forced to sell most of their belongings to assure they'd be able to buy food, and having to exist in a stark, two-bedroom home seemed unimportant now. He'd seen over the past months how truly devastating survival was for some families, stripping them of laughter, a simple smile, and worst of all their dignity.

Robert tried to make sense of what he'd been doing the past months, and what he should do next, unsure now of how to justify continuing on the road. *I need to get home. I need to know if they're together.*

When he got back to the mission it was five o'clock. Tucker wasn't in his cot, leaving Robert feeling anxious about whether he'd been asked to leave. After several minutes he spotted him coming out of the bathroom with his rucksack on his back, hobbling along with his cane. Relieved, he headed toward him.

"Hey, you look steadier walking with that cane. They fixed you up already?"

"Kind of. The nurse taped up my ankle before she left. I sure need to sit down though."

Ralph noticed Robert across the room and put his hand up to get his attention. He met them at Tucker's cot.

"Your buddy looks better, huh? The nurse checked him out. He's got a sprained ankle. We see a lot of those . . . and sometimes worse."

Robert knew Tucker was lucky that his ankle wasn't broken. He remembered hearing about people who broke their legs hopping trains being dropped off at a state line to fend for themselves.

"So what happens now?" Robert wasn't sure who to look at for an answer. Tucker shot him a puzzled look, so he waited for Ralph to say something.

"The nurse told me he needs to stay off of his foot for another day. Seems he doesn't have any place to go, so we're going to let him keep the cot at least until tomorrow."

Tucker reached up to shake Ralph's hand so fast it startled him. "Thanks, Ralph. I'm so grateful."

Putting both of his hands over Tucker's, Ralph gripped it for a moment. "Well, glad it wasn't anything too serious. Not sure who could help you if it was."

Ralph pointed to the soup line. "They've started serving soup again. The crowd out front is shoulder to shoulder waiting to get in. Robert, you'd better get over there. Oh, and Tucker, Chester works the evening shift. I left him a note about you."

When Robert got back with food, Tucker was stretched out on the cot. "Hey, you're not asleep, are you?"

Tucker bolted upright. "No, that was fast."

"Looks like you got lucky about a place to sleep."

"Yeah, what are you going to do tonight? Did you scout around for work today or find somethin'?"

"Scouted around, yes. Found something? No, I'm going to try to bed down in that prairie across from the train station again. Weather looks good this time."

"Well, there's one good thing about me being laid up here."

Robert gave him a puzzled look. "What's that?"

"We both get soup." Tucker gave a faint grin. "Sorry I'm slowing you down like this. You don't have to wait around for me, you know."

Shifting his eyes away from Tucker's, he didn't quite know how to reply. "We'll see what tomorrow brings. Hey, I think Chester's coming over."

He stood up as he approached them. "Evening, boys." Robert gave him a nod of acknowledgement. Chester glanced at the notes in his hand, then at Tucker.

"How you doing? Tucker, right? Ankle any better?"

"It is. I walked to the toilet earlier. Doesn't hurt as much to put my foot down wrapped up like this."

"Good. Well, you have the cot for the night." Chester shifted his eyes toward Robert. "You two traveling together?"

Surprised a bit by the question, Robert hesitated before answering. "Yes, sir."

"Ralph said to let you have a cot if one opens up. That's if no one sick or hurt comes in needing one. We won't know until the mission closes for the night and we've locked the doors."

A broad smile spread across Robert's face. "That'd be great."

"We can't let anyone sleep on the floor, but if you think you can sleep upright in that chair, you're welcome to it. You can set it against the wall and lean your head back. But a cot might come open."

Chester caught Tucker's grin and winked at him. "You see, the notes say you need to stay off that foot for at least another day. If your buddy's here, he can help you out."

They watched as he walked back to his desk. Robert noticed Tucker's face was pale. "You need to lie down?"

Tucker rubbed his chin, as if thinking about it. "Kinda. Do you mind?"

"Of course not."

Seeing Chester settle behind the desk, Robert watched as he started shuffling through papers. He didn't want to bother him again so soon but he needed to ask him some questions. Taking Chester's advice, he picked up the chair he'd slept on earlier in the day, and sat it by Tucker's cot so no one would claim it. Chair or cot, he was glad for the chance to sleep inside for the night.

"What can I do for you?" Chester said, as he glanced up to see Robert standing in front of him. "Did you have a question? Why don't you have a seat?"

Robert began talking before he settled into the chair. "Tucker needs to get to Ohio for a job. Hitchhiking, I mean. He doesn't know the route and neither do I."

He wasn't sure Chester was the person to ask, but he needed to start somewhere. Tucker had mentioned he didn't know the way to Ohio, and Robert couldn't remember where Cincinnati was situated in the state.

Shifting back in his chair, Chester took a moment to think. "I couldn't tell you the route offhand, but I can sure ask around about it. What kind of job is he heading there for?"

"We met a guy traveling a few months ago who said he works for the government. Told us training camps are opening up to put young people to work. Gave us his information in case we need it."

Chester gave him a questioning look. "You think the guy was on the up and up? Ohio is a long ways from here."

Robert shrugged his shoulders. "Think so."

"Well, I sure hope he was if your buddy's heading there with his ankle like it is." Chester opened the desk drawers and began shuffling through them. "I think I might've seen something about a program like that. We usually get that stuff. I'm not seeing anything in here though. I'll keep looking."

He slipped a pen out of his pocket. "Tell you what, I'll leave a note for Jeb and Ralph that you're looking for the route. See if we can get directions for you."

"It sure will be appreciated."

Robert found himself smiling the next morning as he stretched out on a cot, not yet over his luck about getting one for the night. Sitting up to check whether Tucker was awake, Robert saw him wave from across the cot area and headed over.

"I'm going to wash my face. After that I'll go get some buns or something for us. Want to hop along with me?"

Tucker laughed. "Yeah, sure."

"I meant to the toilet."

"Oh, you bet I do, if you're sure you don't mind me hanging on your shoulder again."

When Robert got back with buns, he noticed Jeb behind the desk.

"Say Tucker, someone might be asking you questions about going to Ohio. I talked to Chester last night about you needing to know how to get there."

"Jeb knows about it. When he checked me in, he asked me why I was on the road and where I was going."

Robert didn't know what to do with himself while Tucker was lying around, or what he'd do if he couldn't travel for a while. His plan was always to part ways when they got to St. Louis. He'd head northeast to Chicago and Tucker east to Ohio. There were too many ifs to decide whether to wait around for Tucker, so he spent the morning reading *The Return of Don Quixote*, one of the used books scattered on a table by the cot area.

"You haven't had your nose out of that book all morning. Must be a good one."

Robert lifted the book up so Jeb could see the cover. "Oh, that's a great story."

"I'm on my way to check on your buddy. Chester's note says he's still planning to go to Ohio when he leaves."

"That's his plan."

"Well, I've put him on the list for the nurse to check on." Jeb headed toward Tucker, pausing to look back. "If you don't finish the book before you leave, take it. You can drop it off at another mission when you're finished."

"Swell. I might have to do that."

It was mid-afternoon when Robert noticed the nurse by Tucker's cot. He was taking steps up and down the cot area with the cane. She watched as he tried walking without it. Robert headed over when she left.

"What'd she say about how you're doing?"

"Didn't say much except it's getting better and that Ralph will come by before he leaves."

"Hmm." Robert didn't know what to say. "They're selling apples two for a nickel around the corner. I'll get one for you."

When he got back, Tucker was lying down. Both Ralph and Chester were at the desk. Robert backed away from Tucker's cot, not wanting to wake him. He noticed Ralph waving him over.

"We just chatted with Tucker. He was happy to hear the nurse suggested he keep the cot for another night."

Robert couldn't hold back the huge smile spreading across his face. "I've been worried about finding Tucker a place to bed tonight."

"Glad we can help him out," Ralph said. "Chester has been asking around about the route to Cincinnati. We've come up with a plan to get you part of the way. Seems the evening cook's brother, Wendell, does deliveries in St. Louis three days a week. He can give you a ride there in the morning. How does that sound?"

Speechless, Robert's eyes widened. The relief was overwhelming. "Really?" He ran his fingers through his hair, still not believing what he'd heard.

Seeing the expression on Robert's face, they both slipped him a slight grin. Chester handed him an envelope. "Give this to volunteers at the mission in St. Louis. It asks to give you the best route from there to Cincinnati."

Robert's jaw dropped open. "Oh, that's going to help us a lot. Thank you."

"Well, you seem like good kids. Wendell will be by when the mission opens at seven. Look for a white truck."

Leaning forward in his chair, Robert reached his hand out to shake Chester's hand, and then Ralph's.

"Thanks, we'll both remember this . . . and you."

"Well, good luck to you," Chester said. "You know the drill about the chair or cot for the night."

As soon as the light seeped through the front windows, Robert stood up to go shake Tucker awake, but he was already sitting on the side of his cot. They headed out the front door at seven. A white delivery truck was parked just to the right of the mission. Wendell saw Robert point his way and hopped out of the truck.

"You boys my riders to St. Louis?"

"Yep, we sure appreciate you helping us out. I'm Robert. This is Tucker."

Wendell watched as Tucker leaned on his cane and came forward. "We're sure grateful for the ride, sir."

"Glad I can do it. Maybe you should sit in front. Robert can hop in the back."

21

Two days after the local newspaper announced the Illinois schools could be affected by government funding shortfalls, Kathleen took the job as a waitress at the Five and Dime. When she arrived home, she dreaded breaking the news to her mother. Oliver was nestled on Lucille's lap. "Thought you would be in town with your friends longer."

Not knowing how to begin, she took a deep breath and blurted it out. "I met with Mr. Granger and took the waitress job. If school isn't delayed or closed in the fall like the papers say, I promise I'll quit the job and start school, but at least I can work until then. Maybe Mr. Granger would let me work on weekends if the schools stay open." She knew her tone sounded like a plea. "I got the job because Mr. Granger knew Pa. He'd be pleased I was his first choice, don't you think?" Without waiting for her mother's reply, Kathleen went on. "Anyway Ma, we need the money. Winter is coming in a few months, and we'll need coal. Mr. Granger wants me to work five hours a day and five days a week. I want to help out in case we need the extra money. Really I do."

Kathleen paced back and forth in front of her mother, arms crossed at her waist as if thinking what next to say. "I took it just in case schools might not get funded for fall. I know you want me to stay in school, and Pa would want me in school, too, but if things weren't so bleak for everyone then it would be different. I think he would understand."

Lucille felt sabotaged. Kathleen had taken the job before asking her. It was clear she'd prepared well before presenting her case. She was becoming a woman too early, just what she had worked so hard to prevent.

"Please don't be mad. Mr. Granger hired another girl in my class. You see, I'm not the only girl who took a job."

Uncrossing her arms, Kathleen kept her pace back and forth steady. She stopped suddenly. "Mr. Granger said I could start on Monday, if I wanted."

At a loss of what to say, Lucille needed time to work through the blow to her pride. Her daughter was right to protect the chance for a job to help out if the schools closed. They both knew Robert had run off because he couldn't find a job in Elmhurst to help the family. Kathleen could sense the tightening of the budget, and see the cutback of certain foods for meals as she planned for the extra costs during the winter months. It was the possibility she wouldn't return to school at all if the economy worsened that left her heart sick, so much so, the only reply she could give her daughter for the moment was a nod of the head.

Marty was next in line to help with the younger children. Lucille was surprised by his enthusiasm, showing pride in taking charge when she asked him. By the end of the day he presented her with a written plan for activities and games for each day of the week. The neighborhood kids making their way over every day gave Marty plenty of back up to keep the younger children busy.

After Kathleen started working, Lucille kept Oliver by her side much of the day to make sure he didn't get knocked over by the mania of all the feet scurrying around the yard. Emma had learned to navigate among the kids well enough to stay on her feet.

Even with Marty's eagerness to pitch in and take charge, Kathleen working half a day, five days a week added to the burden of balancing the household and children. A major hurdle to contend with the first week of Kathleen's job was keeping the cupboards stocked with basic but critical staples. To make money stretch, she bought twenty-pound bags of potatoes, ten-pound sacks of flour, five-pound bundles of spaghetti, and quart-size cans of tomatoes.

Just the size and weight of the staples needing to be transported in their wagon meant a couple of trips a week to the store. It was Marty who always walked with her to the general store to help pull the wagon load of groceries home while Kathleen watched the children. Now the trips would need to be taken in late afternoon, after Kathleen was home from work, changing the entire schedule for baking bread for the day and meals for supper.

Worsening the impact of her scheduling problem were the sacks of the neighbor's apples filling the porch that needed to be canned. With the ongoing high temperatures, the apples would go bad soon. It was critical to spend the large part of the week bottling them up. Apples were their main fruit during the winter.

Before they could begin the long process of canning, the jars currently boxed up in the shed needed to be washed in hot soapy water. The actual canning process would have to be done in the afternoon when Kathleen was home and after the kids were in bed.

The next morning, Marty came up with a plan for moving the canning supplies from the shed to the porch to be washed. It would be one of his activities for the day. Each kid who helped transport and wash the jars would get half a piece of homemade bread with apple butter when the job was done.

"Okay, Ma?" Marty asked after he presented her with the plan. With a hug and a wink to approve, Lucille knew it would be worth her time to prepare extra loaves of bread and use the few jars of apple butter left from last year's canning.

By the time they finished sealing all the jars six days later, she was worn down and achy. Kathleen looked exhausted too, although she did her best not to let it show. Twenty-seven jars of apple sauce, thirty jars of apple butter, and twelve jars of pickled apples sat on the floor. The last chore to finish the process was moving the jars onto the shelves in the storage room inside the shed, a job she didn't have to worry about. Marty organized the transport as an activity for the next day.

Trying to soften a week of steady work canning, Lucille gathered the children around her. Often tired by evening, she'd found story telling somehow energized her. As she pulled from childhood memories in Germany or shared Nicolas's tales of Italy to weave a story, her words always seemed to captivate them, and by the time she finished, their smiles and almost dream-like gazes let her forget, just for a moment, any concern of what needed to be done the next day.

Oliver woke in the morning fussy from a stuffy nose. By mid morning his cheeks were red and he was warm to touch. She spent a good part of the day holding her five-year-old son on her lap, gently rocking him and watching his eyes as they gently closed. Just as she was slipping him into bed for an early nap, a loud rap on the door startled him awake, crying. She tried to calm him before answering the door, and his head dropped against her shoulder as he nuzzled himself back to sleep.

The second loud rap startled her, woke Oliver again and left her anxious about what the urgent knocking might mean. Mr.

202 • Jeanette Minniti

Tominello stood on the porch. Her heart started throbbing in her chest just thinking he might have heard news about Robert.

"Come in, please."

"No, don't have time. I was in the bank this morning. Mr. Hurst saw me in line and asked if I'd tell you he needed to talk to you. Said to come by when you can." He blurted it out as if there was no other way to say it.

"Thank you, Mr. Tominello. Have you heard anything from Johnny?"

He glanced away for a moment before giving a reply. "Johnny got home yesterday. He stayed in St. Louis watching for Robert in the city and around the train station where they parted, but he never spotted him. He'll come over to see you by himself later." Finally, he raised his eyes to hers. "Looks like the little guy needs a nap. You should tend to him."

After he turned to leave, she rolled her eyes at his frank comment about tending to Oliver. Relieved he hadn't come with tragic news about Johnny or Robert, her concerns turned to what Hurst might want, hoping it wasn't about lack of government funding for her widow's allowance. There hadn't been anything in the newspaper, but she'd had to skip going through the paper with her neighbor during the week of canning. It'd be a few days before she could get to the bank. Kathleen wouldn't risk taking time off from her job this soon. With Oliver sick, she would just have to care for him and try not to worry about what Hurst had to tell her.

Oliver's stuffy nose continued into the next day. Keeping him cool in the heat of the day and trying to keep him resting inside when he wanted to play outside, consumed most of her energy. On Kathleen's day off, she was too tired and worn out to walk into town to the bank. But having a break in the day with Kathleen to help with Oliver, she began to work herself up about why Hurst wanted to see her.

The following day, Oliver had recovered enough to take him to the bank with her along with Emma. She trusted Marty to keep an eye on Del. By the time she got to the bank, she was sure he wanted to talk about the pension. It terrified her to think of how she would keep her family together if it was cut.

When they arrived at the bank, Hurst asked his secretary to bring some paper and pencils for the children. After he settled into the chair behind his desk, he smiled broadly as he picked up a large brown envelope.

"I was planning to drop this off when I didn't see you this week. It came addressed to me." He held it out to her. Sitting the envelope on her lap as if it was a delicate platter, she pulled out several folded sheets of paper and found a long white envelope tucked inside.

Hesitating for a moment, she looked at Hurst not knowing what to think. Giving her a reassuring grin, he gave a nod toward the smaller envelope. Lucille opened it and found four ten-dollar bills and a note from Robert written on stationery from The Miners Bank.

Ma,

Thought you might need this before I got home. My friend Russell went with me to The Miners Bank and helped me get Mr. Hurst's address to send this so it might be safe getting to you. Hope you are holding it in your hands. I earned the money working harvest. I am working my way home and am okay. Don't worry about me. I miss everyone and hope you are all doing okay.

Your son,
Robert

Covering her eyes for a moment, she felt thankful it wasn't anything negative. Mustering up a smile for Hurst, she handed the larger envelope back, noticing the return address was from Missouri. Just as she started to ask him how far away Missouri was, Oliver and Emma started fighting over the pencils. She got up and gently took the pencils, letting them know it was time to leave. Oliver reached up, got a grip on the pencils, and tried to wrestle them out of her hand.

"Oliver, we have to leave these with Mr. Hurst." He began pulling harder on the pencils.

"Please, let them each have one to take home." Hurst leaned down to pick up their drawings, slipped them on top of several blank sheets of paper still on the floor, and handed the sheets to Lucille.

He walked with them through the lobby to the door. "Don't you worry now, he'll be home in no time."

"Yes, Robert wrote he was on his way so he should be here soon," she said, knowing her words sounded hollow. "Thank you for being so kind."

On the walk home, feelings of relief that Robert might still be safe turned to frustration, as she tried to understand why he would go to the bother to mail the money if he was on his way.

22

It was mid afternoon when Wendell dropped them off at the city mission in St. Louis. Robert wasn't sure where to go when they walked through the door but figured the cot area was the best place to start. With no one at the desk in the corner, they stood scanning the area trying to get an idea of who was in charge. The cots were full.

"I say we just wait to see if anyone sits at that desk or asks us what we're standing here for," Robert said.

Just as he was beginning to think no one was in charge, an older woman wearing a nurse's cap sat down behind the desk. Robert elbowed Tucker. "Well, let's give it a try."

As they approached she kept her eyes on Tucker's cane once she noticed it. Her expression was stern when she raised her eyes to Tucker's. "I bet I can guess how that happened."

"You'd probably be right, ma'am."

Robert reached into his rucksack, pulling out the note from Chester and Ralph. "Ma'am, this is a note from two volunteers at the mission in Springfield. They told us to give it to someone here."

Eyes fixed on his as she reached for the note and slipped it out of the envelope, she finally took her eyes off of him as she unfolded it. "Well, let's see what this is about."

Once she finished reading it, she glanced at Tucker. "Cincinnati, Ohio? Not sure I can be of much help, but since they took the trouble to send the note, I guess we should try to find someone who can give the best route. I'm Lillian, by the way."

Tucker nodded, "Thank you, ma'am. This is Robert."

Seeming to let her guard down after reading the note, an amiable smile appeared. "I probably should check your ankle before leaving for my shift at the hospital. Have a seat in the chairs against the back wall while I check on the others on the list waiting to see me."

It was late afternoon before she came by to examine Tucker's ankle. She watched as he walked back and forth across the area a few times. "I don't think you're going to be walking very far on that ankle today. It's healing, but put too much weight on it too soon, it'll swell right back up again. Wait here, some cots are supposed to open up by the end of the day. I'm putting you on the list for one. Grady will be over to let you know."

Stopping at the desk now occupied by two men who were going through some papers, she chatted with them a while before leaving. Robert wanted to get up and stretch. More than that he wanted to go through the soup line when it opened, but he didn't want to be gone when someone came over to talk to them. Finally, the elderly of the two men at the desk walked toward them.

"Hello, boys. I'm Grady. You must be Tucker given the cane you're holding."

"Yes, and this is Robert."

"The nurse just gave me an update. We just checked someone out so we have a cot open. Follow me." He turned to Robert. "I'd like you to come over to the desk when you're done eating. I have a few questions for you."

Grady's comments left Robert curious about why he wanted to talk to him instead of Tucker. When he saw him at the desk, he headed straight over.

"We've been trying to find the best route to Cincinnati. That's quite a ways from here. You going there, too?"

Robert stared at him, stumped as to what to say. He was planning to head to Chicago. It was almost a straight shot north from St. Louis to his home in Elmhurst. That's the route he took to St. Louis with Johnny. He didn't know the way home from Cincinnati. He didn't even know the way *to* Cincinnati.

Grady picked up a map sitting on top of the desk and spread it out. "There's no easy route, so it means maybe several rides if he's hitching, and a couple of days to get there, if he's lucky. That's why I asked if you were going. Look here."

Robert's eyes followed Grady's pencil as it slid over the map from St. Louis, east across southern Illinois and southern Indiana and then north to Cincinnati. When his pencil stopped, Robert was quick to scan the map to see where Chicago was from Cincinnati. He'd end up farther east of Chicago, but also farther north from where he was now, which might level out the distance to travel home from either St. Louis or Cincinnati.

Grady lifted his pencil off the map. "He's going there for a job in a government camp, the note said. I've seen articles in the paper over the past few months about training camps the government is opening. 'The Civilian Conservation Corps,' they're calling the program. We just had another camp open in Missouri. Why's Tucker going to Ohio? Is he from there?"

"No, he's from Georgia."

"There are camps opening everywhere."

Robert thought about what Grady just told him for a moment before replying. "We met a guy traveling who said he'd help Tucker get in one."

"That's risky, going all the way to Ohio on the word of someone you met on the road."

"Well, Tucker's bent on going. He even had his dad send a letter to the guy saying when he was born, because he told Tucker he can't get in a camp without it."

"Do you or Tucker have the pamphlet or what he gave you about the camps? I'd like to take a look at it."

"He just wrote out his name and address on a napkin."

"What?" Grady slid a hand over his mouth without trying to hide his reaction to Robert's comment. "He didn't give you anything besides what he wrote on a napkin?"

"No."

"And what about you? You're too young for the camps."

"I'm going home." Robert hesitated before adding, "West of Chicago."

Grady turned his eyes back to the map. "Well, we'll write out a route for him, but he's going to look pretty pathetic standing on the side of the road with that cane trying to get a ride. He'd be ripe pickings for anyone passing by with ill intent if he has much of anything in his rucksack."

Robert stood up to leave. "He'll appreciate the help, sir."

"There's another cot coming open. The man is not back from eating yet. When he clears out, I'll let you know."

Robert grinned at his good luck. "Thank you, sir."

Seeing Tucker already lying on his cot, Robert went to sit down and wait. He couldn't shake Grady's comment about "someone you met on the road" after getting a similar reaction from Chester when he'd told him about Al. "You think he was on the up and up?" as Chester put it.

Trying to sort out their options, Robert thought about Tucker's first. After seeing the map, he was a lot closer right now to Cincinnati than he was to Georgia. Tucker already said he wasn't going back home, but he didn't know camps might have opened there. If Tucker went to Cincinnati to find Al and he wasn't who he said he was, it would be devastating. Yet if he did find Al, it was possible he might help him out like he told him he would.

Taking a deep breath as he leaned back against the wall, Robert mulled over his own options. He could hop the train from St. Louis and be home in a day or so. That's what he wanted to do, needed to do, get home to his family. The thought of finding his way back from Cincinnati felt weighty.

Leaning his face into his hands, he tried to think out what was bothering him about his choices. There were only two. Catch the train to Chicago from St. Louis or go with Tucker to help him out.

Robert closed his eyes trying to force the answer. What shot into his mind was how close Tucker had come to being swept under the train as his fingertips slipped from his grip. The vision of two boys flipping off the ladder to be ripped apart under the train raced back into his mind. He tried to hold back other images, mishaps he'd seen while traveling with Johnny, leaving people helpless with injuries. Robert knew he'd been lucky riding the rails over the past months, but for the first time traveling, he seriously questioned how long his luck would hold out.

Hoping to get his mind off more dreary thoughts, Robert pulled out *The Return of Don Quixote*. Making a decision about what he'd do would have to wait until he had a chance to talk to Tucker anyway.

Grady came over to point out the open cot. He handed him an envelope with the route and told him to be sure to check in with Ben at the desk the next morning before they left.

When Robert finished sharing what he'd learned from Grady about camps opening in Georgia with Tucker the next morning, he was firm that his best bet was to find Al, camps opening in Georgia or not. "Traveling back to find out if they have any and where they are, then trying to get in one could take months. That's if I get in. Al said the camps were filling up, and once they're full then you have to wait until someone leaves. I just don't want to be left wandering around again."

Robert decided to hold back telling him he'd become skeptical about Al after talking with Chester and Grady. But if Tucker didn't find Al in Cincinnati, he'd be in the same wandering around and fending for himself situation, but in an unfamiliar place.

The next morning, Robert waited for someone to sit behind the desk. He tapped Tucker's shoulder. "Grady said to check in at the desk today. Looks like now's a good time."

As they got closer, Robert thought the guy behind the desk looked too young to be in charge and wondered if his thick, bushy beard was supposed to make him look older.

"I'm Ben, Grady's son. You must be Tucker. I noticed your cane and just finished reading some notes my dad left. How's the ankle?"

"It feels better. I can put more weight on it today."

"Seems you're going to Cincinnati. My dad mentioned giving you a ride out to the highway going east. It's several miles from here."

Tucker's eyes widened. "Really? That's sure good of you to do."

"Hey, it's nothing. I live out that way, but you'll have to wait around till noon when I leave for the day."

Ben turned to Robert. "You heading that way, too?"

He had thought about what he'd do if Tucker decided to go on to Ohio, but he still hesitated. "Yeah, I am." What Grady said about Tucker being an easy target for someone had stuck in his mind. *I can't just leave him like this, not knowing for sure if he got there okay.*

"Guess we need to find a couple chairs while we kill time, Tucker. I'll go get some doughnuts or buns. Try to find some apples, too."

Grady was right when he told Robert it'd take two days to get to Cincinnati hitching rides. But they were fortunate in being picked up by good people wanting to help, though a young couple passing a flask back and forth to each other during most of a ride was scary, especially when the guy driving reached back to share the flask with them and let the car swerve off the highway into a ravine.

Based on the address they had for Al, a truck driver making deliveries in Cincinnati dropped them off south of the downtown area. "Now you boys just head east for five blocks. You'll hit Central Avenue. Head north to Fifth Street from there, and you should find it easy enough."

It was the farthest Tucker had to walk in the two days they'd traveled. He'd burrowed in the brush on the side of the road while Robert got them rides. With the additional two days of keeping weight off his foot, his limp was minor.

Spotting a one-story office building matching the address, Robert felt relieved. Department of Labor was printed in large, black letters across the glass window on the door. "This must be it."

Putting his arms up over his head as he usually did when he got worked up, Tucker stood staring at the building. "I'm kinda nervous. What if he doesn't remember us?"

"Let's go in and find out if he even works here."

"What? This is the address."

Without answering, Robert swept through the door. Across a large black and white tiled foyer were two oak-paneled doors. Nervous himself, he walked to the drinking fountain situated between the restrooms. "Let's freshen up before we go in. Maybe change into our spare shirts."

The office was chaotic. Desks were crowded together in the center of a large, open room. A constant loud tapping noise came from typewriters being used in the back rows. Two young women sat at desks opposite each other at the front of the office typing, not seeming to notice they were standing nearby. One of them finished what she was working on and glanced their way as she stood up. "Who are you looking for?"

Tucker froze. Robert stepped forward. "Al Thurman."

"Mr. Thurman works with the Department of Labor camps. I haven't seen him come back in yet this afternoon. Do you have an appointment?"

"No, we don't, ma'am."

"Oh, then let me find one of his clerks for you, have a seat." She seemed glad to hand them off.

After several minutes, a tall, blonde headed kid who looked about Tucker's age came over to them. "You're here to see Mr. Thurman?"

Robert glanced at Tucker, waiting for him to say something, relieved when he finally began to speak.

"Yeah, Al, I mean, Mr. Thurman, gave me his address. Said I could contact him about training camps. I asked my dad to send him a letter stating when I was born. Mr. Thurman said he'd need it. Came to check on if it got here."

The young man didn't seemed phased by Tucker's rambling comments. "Mr. Thurman won't be back for another hour. I'm Jimmy. I take care of most of his mail." Pulling a small notepad and a pen out of his shirt pocket, he held it out to Tucker. "Why don't you write down your name and your father's name. Since you don't have an appointment, I'm not sure Mr. Thurman can meet with you today, but I'll look for the letter while you're waiting."

"Sure would appreciate that. I really want to find out if my dad's letter got here."

At three o'clock, Al came through the door and rushed right by them. At three-thirty Jimmy came back. He seemed uneasy, unlike before. "He has a few minutes and can see you now. Just follow me."

Tucker slipped the cane under the seats as he got up. When they walked into Al's office, Tucker started toward his desk, stopping when Al looked up. The lack of response from him showed he was wondering who he was. Al shifted his eyes to Robert as he stepped from behind Tucker. Leaning back against his chair, he tossed his pen onto the middle of his desk. "You didn't go home yet?"

Robert shrugged his shoulders as he gave a meek smile. "I'm on my way home."

Al shook his head from side to side as he glanced away for a moment. "Have a seat," he said, as he motioned to the chairs in front of the desk.

"Okay, let's start with you, Tucker. Jimmy couldn't find the letter. You sure your dad sent it?"

"Well, I wrote him twice. Once asking him to send it to the strawberry farm I . . . we were working at in Arkansas. When it didn't arrive at the Burkett's farm before we left, I wrote my dad asking him to send a letter here."

"Hmm, well, I can't do anything without a letter. Seems I remember you weren't eighteen when we talked about the camps. Am I right?"

"Yes, but I will be in less than three weeks. What you told us about the camps made me think it's my only chance to make something of myself."

Reacting with a slight grin, Al was quiet for a moment as if pondering something. "Jimmy, is it possible it could be misfiled? "

"Maybe, I'll check again. Your appointment should be here, sir. Do you want me to have him wait?"

"You caught me at a bad time, boys. I have a meeting in a few minutes. After that I have a report to review. It needs to be sent off to Washington by the end of the day. You've got a place to stay tonight?"

Robert spoke up. "People at the mission in St. Louis gave us a note to give to the one here asking if they would put us up if they have any room."

"Good." Al took out his calendar. "What were you doing in a mission? Have to do with that slight limp, Tucker?"

"Yes, sir."

"I can meet with you tomorrow at ten."

A blush started to crawl across Robert's cheeks when Al turned and stared at him with a questioning look. "Robert, wasn't it?"

"Yes, sir."

"Well, I'm glad to see you're okay. Jimmy will give you the directions to the mission."

Al stood up, letting them know it was time to leave. Robert stepped toward his desk, holding out his hand. Tucker followed him forward.

As they started toward the door to the foyer, the woman who helped them at the front desk earlier called them back. She nodded to Tucker and then the cane he'd left under the seats. "You might be needing that."

Tucker slid it out from underneath the chair. "Hope I won't, but thank you, ma'am."

When they got outside, Robert caught the beaming expression on Tucker's face. "I just knew he was a good guy."

"Well, let's see what tomorrow brings," Robert replied, feeling relieved himself. "Let's hope they find that letter."

"Yeah, I hope so too. I've already asked my dad twice to send one."

23

Cincinnati felt massive compared to the cities and towns Robert had stopped in during his months on the road. Criss-crossing through the downtown on their way to the mission, they passed posters displayed in the windows of businesses showcasing the newly constructed Cincinnati Union Terminal built at the edge of town.

Stopping suddenly, Robert pointed to a large billboard on the roof of a block-wide city building advertising the station's size, art deco design, and the restaurants and retail shops located inside. "Look up there. See the length of that entryway up to the terminal. Must be two blocks long? Don't think there're too many guys trying to hop a train out of that place. Think you'd try it?"

Taking another look at it, Tucker mulled it over. "Not unless there's a way to enter the freight yard from the back."

"Well, this is as close as I'm getting to it. It has to be swarming with bulls."

The next morning they arrived fifteen minutes early for their ten o'clock appointment with Al. Robert was as nervous going into the building as he'd been the day before, but for a different reason. Al being all business when they'd met threw him off. He was expecting the casual guy they got to know riding the rails. Tucker seemed just as anxious, working himself up about whether his dad had sent the letter, and if he hadn't, why.

They'd been waiting to meet with him for forty-five minutes by the time Al arrived at ten-thirty. "Sorry, boys, my meeting ran late. Jimmy will come get you in a few minutes."

Tucker rubbed his hands together nervously as Al walked down the hall. "Whew, I was starting to worry he wouldn't show up. Should've known he would."

Al was reading something when they were escorted into the office. "Tucker, seems you owe Jimmy a big thank-you. He worked extra last night until he found the letter from your father."

"Oh, that's swell." Tucker jumped up, reaching his hand out to shake Jimmy's. "Sure appreciate you finding the letter. It means a lot."

"Just glad I found it for you."

As Jimmy turned to leave, Al pointed to the chair against the wall. "Jimmy, I'd like you to stay for a minute."

Lifting the letter off of the desk, Al looked it over again. "It was misfiled, all right. Seems it was forwarded here from the Burkett Strawberry Farm with a note inside from the manager, Dexter Black. Looks as if you made a good impression on him while you were there. He says you'd be a good worker."

Al shifted his attention to Robert. "Says you would be, too." Robert smiled meekly as he shrugged his shoulders.

Reacting with a tough luck grin, Al turned back to Tucker. "I said I'd help you out, and I will, now that I have a confirmation of your birth date." He wrote something on a pad and handed it to Jimmy. "Can you get on both of these right away?"

Jimmy scanned what he wrote. "You bet, sir."

Leaning his arms onto his desk, Al looked directly at Tucker. "First, I need to explain the serious labor going on in the camps. It is back-breaking work on projects controlling soil erosion, planting trees, and building or rebuilding bridges and roads. You up for that kind of hard labor?"

Tucker's smile gave Al his answer. "I'd work real hard, sir."

"Second, you need to know it's a tightly run operation, much like the army. Men get a bunk, three meals a day, and get paid thirty-dollars a month. The men get to keep five-dollars. The remaining twenty-five dollars is sent directly to their families."

Letting out a gasp, Tucker sat quiet for a second. "I didn't remember the part about the money, but that's really something. My dad lost his job just before I left."

"Do you know if he signed up with a work relief agency?"

"He never said. Could have though."

"If he did, it'd be an easy process to transfer you to a camp in Georgia."

Jimmy rapped lightly on the door. "Sorry to interrupt you, sir." He held up the paper Al had given him.

"Any luck?"

He slipped the note on Al's desk. "Yes, sir."

"Let me finish up with Tucker. I'll be ready in a few minutes."

Seeming as if he was going to continue with Tucker, Al swiveled his chair around to Robert again. "I know this must be tough on you, but the economy isn't getting any better. The camps are going to be around for a while. You'll have your chance if you need it."

Robert acknowledged Al's encouraging words, then shifted his eyes to Tucker. "I'm just glad it's going to work out for Tucker. He really wants this."

Al began again. "The report I reviewed after you left yesterday was a list of how many men are placed in camps and where. There are two camps with openings here in Ohio. Camp Shawnee is southeast of here near Friendship, Ohio. You'd be working on a state forest project. The other project is in a state park, straight north near Waterville."

"If I get this chance, you won't be sorry," Tucker said.

"Good."

Abruptly, Al stood up. "We'll finish over lunch. You two hungry? It's almost noon." Seeing the expression of surprise break out on their faces at the same moment, he couldn't help but chuckle. "Well, you boys came all this way, and Tucker with a limp. I can at least buy you lunch. There's a good diner a block from here. Jimmy, why don't you join us."

It was as if the atmosphere in the diner transformed Al into the casual guy they knew before. He was interested in what had happened to them once they parted ways, and glad to hear that his lead on work near Marshall worked out.

Tucker told them about Robert's violin playing at the Burketts' farm. "He's real good, too."

Al leaned forward as he glanced across the table to Robert. "Really?"

A shrug was Robert's only reply. Quick to change the subject, he told them about the fencing work they'd done for Darryl. "We did a great job for him."

They laughed over Tucker's story about heading to Marshall to find out the Barrow gang had just been there shooting up the place and could still be hiding in the area.

When the waitress started clearing the table, Al checked his watch. "I've got to get to another meeting, so we need to finish up. Jimmy's made some calls to check on a few things that will help you both."

Al stopped the waitress as she passed by to ask for the check, then turned his attention back to them. "Tucker, we have a few ranchers that work with us in cases like yours. There's a horse ranch west of town with several stables, and a large barn with cots inside. If you're willing to help the other employees maintain the stables and premises, you'll have a place to stay until we can transition you to a camp. There will be serious hard work and no pay."

"You bet I'm willing. Thank you, sir. Having a place to bed is worth a lot."

"We'll need a day to set that up. You might have to stay at the mission another night if they'll let you." Al paused as the waitress put the check on the table. "Tucker, why don't you walk back with Jimmy. He'll get you started filling out paper work for the camps so it's ready when you turn eighteen." Al slipped money on top of the check. "Robert, you can walk back with me."

Outside, Jimmy tapped Tucker's shoulder and headed toward the office. Al handed Robert a business card. "Is home really next for you?"

Slipping his hands into his pockets, Robert fixed his eyes directly on Al's. "Yes, sir. I'll figure out a way to help my ma when I get there."

"I'm sure it'll help her enough to see you're safe."

A bit of a grin appeared on Robert's face as he tipped his head toward the sidewalk. "I know."

"I've been working with government programs for a while now. I started out in the agricultural department, but when I heard President Roosevelt was starting the CCC program to get youth off the freight trains, I asked for a transfer. You see, my young nephew died riding the rails." Al paused, "I think you've seen first hand the risk you've been taking."

He put his hand on Robert's shoulder for a moment as they walked back to his office. "Jimmy checked on an army transport truck taking men and equipment from the CCC camp southeast of here in Friendship to the camp north near Waterville. It's scheduled to leave Friendship at eight o'clock tomorrow morning. It'll pass through Cincinnati about ten o'clock."

Robert tried to sort out what he was hearing and what it meant.

Al went on. "Waterville is just shy of Toledo. From there it's a straight shot west across Indiana to Chicago. You interested in catching a ride with them?"

"Oh . . . yeah, it'll help me out a lot."

"Good decision."

They stepped inside the foyer as Jimmy and Tucker were coming out of the restroom. Al waited for them in front of the office doors. "Glad I caught you two. Jimmy, would you call to confirm the transport trucks coming through from Friendship for a ten o'clock pick up in front of the building tomorrow?"

"I will, sir."

Al stopped in front of his office. "I'm going to grab my valise and head to my meeting. Jimmy can handle any hiccups that come up. Robert, this might be goodbye. I have a meeting out of the office in the morning."

Robert reached his hand out. "I sure appreciate everything. Won't ever forget how you helped us out."

"Glad I could help. You know where to find me. Stay safe traveling home. Tucker, I'll probably see you again." He gave a quick wave as he walked into his office.

Jimmy stepped forward. "Let's head back to the last row of desks. I'll get Tucker started filling out forms. After that, I'll make that call for you, Robert."

The next morning, Tucker walked with Robert to Al's office for his ride north. He was catching a ride to the horse ranch with another of Al's clerks at eleven. They got to the office at nine-thirty, a half hour before Robert's pick-up time.

After checking in with Jimmy, Tucker came back outside to wait with him. "Hate to leave you traveling by yourself."

"I'll be okay. Getting a ride north is a big break."

"I've got your address. I'll keep it in my sock just like I did Al's." Tucker pulled a note out of his shirt pocket, holding it out to Robert. "I asked Jimmy to write out the address of the ranch I'll be working at. Once I get to a camp, I'll send you that address. You gonna write me back?"

"Yeah."

"You sure?"

"Yeah, I will." Tucker kept staring at him seeming not to be convinced.

"Have to find out how you like taking orders."

"You sure I gave you enough money to settle up?"

"Tucker, you gave me plenty."

"You'd tell me if it wasn't, wouldn't . . ." He paused and pointed at something. "Hey, take a look."

An army truck had just turned the corner, followed by a large military truck covered in canvas. A second truck just like it pulled up behind. Robert walked to the curb to wait for one of the drivers to make contact. The driver of the second truck jumped out, waved, and stepped onto the sidewalk. "You our pick-up?"

"Yes, sir, I'm Robert."

"I'm Sam. You'll ride with me."

"Well, this is it, Tuck."

Grasping Robert's shoulder, he held it for a moment. "I'm never forgetting how you helped me, never."

"You'd have done it for me."

Breaking away from Tucker's grip to catch up with the driver, Robert waved as he climbed inside.

Sam talked of nothing but the camps while driving. He'd been assigned to heavy equipment operations and maintenance and spoke with pride about recently completing his maintenance training. "I'm pushing to get some supervisory experience while I'm here, too. They're pretty good about passing around duties and responsibilities if you show them you're serious about doing a good job for them."

The convoy pulled off the road in front of a large grove of beech trees to eat lunch. It'd been awhile since Robert had been in a group of guys who were spirited about their lives, grinning as they spoke, not holding the desolate, empty looks he'd become accustomed to while traveling. After they ate, they started a game of catch using an orange as the ball. In fun, they tried to trip each other up throwing fast balls and curve balls or turning fast to sail it over to someone unexpectedly.

Robert felt the tension in his body release for the first time in days and wanted to be a part of the fun longer when one of the guys shouted, "It's time to head out."

As they came to the signs for Waterville, the other two vehicles turned left onto another highway as Sam drove straight ahead. "Toledo is another nineteen miles. Been told to drive you there."

Passing the outskirts of the city, Sam followed signs to the downtown area, pulling over alongside a public park. "Is this okay? Don't know Toledo."

"You bet. Thank you. I sure appreciate the ride all the way in."

"Oh hey, glad to do it. You be safe getting home now."

Stepping out of the truck, an immediate emptiness swept over him. Forcing a smile, he held it until Sam pulled away. Trying to figure out what to do next seemed beyond him for the moment. Perching on top of a wooden table in the park, he pulled out the extra lunch the guys gave him earlier, focusing on the only thing he could, peeling an orange. He'd hang onto the sandwich for later.

It was early evening. Dusk would be setting in soon. The weight of trying to find a place to sleep was enormous, yet the choices for heading out of Toledo would leave him traveling into the night. But risky or not, he wanted to head for home. Just as he was about to shove the last wedge of the orange into his mouth, he heard a train whistle not far away signaling its arrival. Knowing the window of opportunity to hop a train before dark was short, he leaped up in a rush to find the station, hoping the whistle he heard was from a freight pulling in.

After seeing the pictures of the sleek new station in Cincinnati, he was surprised by Toledo's old, run-down terminal. It would be easy to hop a freight given the station's layout. The schedules weren't posted outside. Not seeing any bulls around, Robert went inside the terminal.

The depot was crowded with people, signaling a passenger train would be departing soon. He found the westbound schedule tacked up on the wall across from the ticket counter. The first to depart was a passenger train going to Chicago, leaving in fifteen minutes. The first freight going west wasn't due for three hours, which meant trying to hop on after nightfall.

It would be dangerous to try to catch a train in the dark, but he'd felt overcome by a sudden sense of loss and loneliness. Watching the guys play around at lunch, joking, even laughing, brought on a longing to be back home with his brothers. Whether his family was still together had kept creeping into his thoughts, gnawing at him now that he was finally on his way.

As the thought struck him to buy a ticket on the passenger train, he stood frozen in place, struggling with a decision to spend money to have the surety of getting home, possibly that night. Taking the chance of hopping a freight in the dark he knew was stupid, but finding someplace to sleep as night cast its shadow in a town he'd been in for less than an hour, called for a swift decision.

He found himself standing in the ticket line. The fare to Chicago in coach was less than expected. Heart pounding, he stepped out of line, slipped the ticket into his shirt pocket, and tried to think out riding inside a passenger train for the first time. Deciphering the signs listing information about where and when to board seemed unclear, so he followed the crowd out to the platform. People were walking in all directions, yet barely moving.

Figuring coach would be the cars at the back of the train, he stepped around the crowds of people walking in that direction. Stuck behind a large group of Amish people who weren't moving at all, he shuffled around them, keeping his eyes focused on the passenger cars to his right. Realizing he was passing by the last car of the train, Robert stopped to see two husky bulls standing several feet away. One bull's pistol was in clear sight. He had one hand resting on the club clipped to his belt. The other bull was holding a rifle straight up and was yelling at several men lined up in front of him.

"Your free ride on the top of this train is over," he shouted. "Those of you with money will be allowed to keep one half. The rest of it will go to pay for your ride here. If you don't have any money, we'll see about you later."

The bull closest to him was standing in front of a boy about eighteen who was claiming he didn't have any money. The bull leaned forward, sticking his face a few inches from the kid's face. "Are you sure?"

The kid stiffened, nodding his head fiercely up and down.

"Let's see those pockets."

The kid pulled out the lining of his front pockets, then turned around showing the bull the lining of his back pockets.

"You're sure you don't have any money?"

Not waiting for an answer, the bull reached for his cap and counted the bills he found tucked in the lining, giving some back to the boy. "Take off those shoes." Yanking out the inside soles, the bull threw them onto the platform in front of the kid when he didn't find money inside.

Next in line was a man who hesitated before pulling out a small roll of money from his trousers. The bills were barely out of his pocket before the bull snatched them.

"Twenty dollars," the bull said, as he slipped half into his shirt pocket. Ripping the man's hat off, he ran his fingers completely around the edges of the inside flap, exposing tightly folded bills tucked inside. After counting the money, the bull took half, handing back what was left. "Take off that belt." The bull dropped the belt in front of the man when he didn't find anything tucked inside its fold.

As the bull walked away the man yelled, "I earned that money working in the fields. I need it for my family."

The bull put both hands on his rifle, staring back at the man as he walked on.

"You don't have to take that much," the guy shouted.

The bull walked back to where he stood and smacked him across the face with the butt of his rifle, sending blood gushing down his chin and neck. "If you want to stay out of jail, I think you'd better keep your mouth shut."

Frightened by being that close to railroad detectives, Robert wasn't sure what to do. Instinct sent him slowly walking backward, away from them, stopping when he bumped up against someone. Turning as he said excuse me, he found himself facing the chest of another bull. Heart pounding, he glanced up to see a stone-faced burly man. Stepping sideways, he began walking around him but the bull took hold of his arm, yanking him back. "Trying to get away, boy?"

"No, I . . . I've got a ticket."

The bull let out a sarcastic laugh, hitting him in the abdomen so hard with his club, Robert collapsed onto the platform. "Get up, kid."

With the breath knocked out of him, he struggled to stand up and collapsed back down. The bull gripped the back of his shirt to pull him up, ripping the front of it open as buttons snapped off and scattered across the platform. Once the bull stood him upright, he shoved him against the terminal wall. One of the other bulls noticed and walked over. "Who's this?"

"Another free loader. Caught him trying to get away. Says he's got a ticket."

"Oh, he does, huh?" He leaned into Robert's face. "We'll see when I get done here because you sure don't look like you'd have a ticket, now do yah?"

Feeling a throbbing pain in his gut, Robert looked down and snapped his eyes shut, squeezing them tighter as he heard the first boarding call for the train to Chicago.

The bull walked back to the last guy lined up. "How about you? Go on, dig it out."

Reaching deep into his front trouser pockets he handed him a few bills, then turned around and pulled out his back pockets, leaving them hanging inside out.

"Two dollars? Not likely. Hand me that cap. Take off those shoes." Finding nothing more, he asked him to take off his belt. Opening up the seam inside, the bull slipped out bills folded all along the inside, counted the money, and handed some back to him. He walked to the front of the line. "Listen up now. If you only got a few bucks left, you can start walking. The rest of you, I suggest you go inside and see about buying a ticket. Your free ride is over."

The bull turned, keeping his eyes fixed on Robert as he walked over to him. "So you have a ticket, huh? Let me see it."

Feeling his hand quiver as he reached into his shirt pocket, a panic overtook him. *He's gonna keep my ticket, take my money, and leave me with nothing to take home.*

The bull leaned in. "Well, let's see it."

Pulling it out of his pocket, Robert kept the ticket close to his body, pinching his fingers tight against it, afraid to let go.

The bull's smirk changed to a questioning look when he saw the ticket. Feeling Robert's grip holding on to it, he yanked it out of his fingers. The last boarding call for the train to Chicago was shouted out.

After taking a swift glance at the ticket, he brought it closer and read it again. When he shifted his eyes back to Robert's, the smirk was back on the bull's face. Stepping in closer, he stood inches from Robert's face, staring down at him for a moment before handing over the ticket, and then yelled sharply, "Go on, now."

Taking a deep breath to steady himself, he stepped away from the two bulls cautiously, and ran to the conductor standing by the last car. Too shaken to speak, he held out his ticket. The conductor walked him one car back.

"Here you go, young man," he said, holding a smile until Robert stepped in.

Not sure of where to sit, he sank into a seat next to a window. Clamping his eyes shut once more, an overwhelming sense of relief shuddered through him. He leaned forward to press his hands down hard against his knees to stop them from shaking.

24

With the arrival of the first cool day in Illinois for weeks, Lucille took advantage of Kathleen's day off to walk in to town early with Marty and Emma to pick up groceries, and stop by to see her German friend, Elsa. The visit would give her a chance to catch up on the latest news in the *Berliner Tagebatt*, and give her children a chance to play on the wooden swings Elsa's husband had built for their children.

Sitting on the porch with her friend, watching the children take turns pushing each other on the swings, she felt pleased with herself for getting the two children away for the morning. It gave Marty a break from managing play time activities for his siblings and Emma an uninterrupted morning with her.

For Lucille, visiting with her friend allowed a bit of relief from the stresses over the last weeks with Oliver sick, enduring the intense schedule to complete the canning, and her constant worry over why Robert hadn't returned yet. Since sending the letter saying he was on his way, surely there had been enough time for him to get home. Each day that passed gave her more reason to worry.

Elsa seemed to understand she needed the support and re-assurance of a friend. Bringing out a tray with coffee, Elsa pulled back a napkin covering slices of applesauce cake.

"I bought this at the church bazaar on Sunday and have been waiting for the right moment to slice it."

Lucille clutched Elsa's hand. "You're so kind to serve me coffee and cake. It's such an unexpected treat."

"Well, I want you to just sit here and enjoy your coffee. I'll get lemonade for the children. We'll surprise them with the cake."

Moved by her kindness, she did just what Elsa said to do and what she needed to do, enjoy a cup of coffee, and think of nothing else for the moment. Feeling her shoulders relax, the tightness in them easing for the first time in months, she decided to wait to read the German newspaper. More news about Hitler's rise to power and his aggression would only bring her spirit down.

On the way home later that morning after a much needed stop at the market, Emma walked next to Marty as he pulled the wagon load of groceries. Listening to their excitement about playing on the swings, and having applesauce cake made her feel content about accomplishing what she had intended for the morning.

Enjoying the refreshing breeze blowing across her face after weeks of high temperatures seemed like an added blessing. Marty began walking backward as he pulled the wagon. "Ma, do you hear that music?"

"I do hear it. Beautiful, isn't it?"

Emma wrapped her arms around her waist and stopped. "I miss hearing music. Let's just stand here so we can listen to it."

Her mother gently nudged her forward. "We'll have to listen to it as we move along. Kathleen is meeting her friends when we get back."

Marty turned around again. "Sounds like that one piece Robert used to play, Ma." "You're right, Marty, it does. It makes me miss him even more."

They walked another few minutes before turning onto their street. Marty stopped abruptly, dropping the handle on the wagon as he swung around to face her.

"Ma?"

Her hand was covering her mouth. Her son began running down the road, stopping again to look at his mother. Stretching her arm out toward their house, she signaled him to go ahead. "I'll bring the wagon."

He caught hold of his sister's hand. "Emma, it's Robert."

Letting out a screech, she pulled her hand back from his, clapping as she jumped up and down, and spun around in circles. He took her hand again. "Come on, Emma."

Watching as her children raced toward the house, Lucille picked up the handle of the wagon only to drop it again to get a handkerchief from her purse. Walking on, she kept her eyes on Emma and Marty as they bolted through the screen door.

The music stopped. All of her children burst through the front door in one big huddle. Marty darted back down the street to get the wagon. Robert followed him for a moment but stopped. Positioning the violin under his chin, he began playing as he walked to meet his mother. Embracing her son, there was only silence as his siblings gathered around the two of them. All she could manage to say through her tears as she looked at him was "You said you'd get home safe." Squeezing his arm, she led her family inside.

Robert put the violin on the table, gently placing the bow next to it as he turned toward his mother. "When I came in the house and saw my violin . . . well, I was so happy. Not just to have it again, but maybe that you got it back meant you couldn't be mad at me."

Slipping her hanky into her pocket, she replied with a smile, hugging him again. "Moms don't stay mad long," she whispered in his ear. "I bought the violin back so it would be here when you came home. I know it was something special between you and your father. When I came home with it, Kathleen told me she overheard you telling your father you'd like to pursue a musical career one day." She leaned in again to give him another embrace. "I'm so sorry that I wasn't here this morning. How long have you been home?"

"Since late this morning. I bought a train ticket from Toledo to Chicago so I could get back today. Sure glad I did." Hearing his voice get shaky when he mentioned the ticket, he glanced away just as he caught the concern in his mother's eyes.

"Let's all sit around the table." She took his arm. "So you got home this morning?"

"Well, no. I got in late last night on a bus from Chicago. I didn't want to wake everyone so I went by Johnny's, tapped on his bedroom window and slept there. We stayed up for hours talking. I told him to wake me up early, but he didn't. When I got out of the shower this morning, he insisted I borrow this shirt."

"Did Johnny tell you he went to St. Louis looking for you?"

"No, he didn't say anything about that. I sure surprised Mr. Tominello this morning though. When he saw me he got all choked up. Even hugged me." A grin spread across Lucille's lips. "Really? I would like to have seen that."

She turned to her children. "Everybody stay seated. We're going to have a celebration that Robert is home. I'm going to boil some spatzle noodles and sprinkle them with cheese."

Marty bellowed out a laugh. "That's Robert's favorite dish."

Placing her hands on Robert's shoulders before walking to the kitchen, she took a moment to enjoy seeing all of her children sitting around the table. "Maybe Robert will want to play more music for us after we eat."

She let her children enjoy him the rest of the day, knowing it would be after they were in bed before she'd have time to sit with him and get details on his long time away from home. Waiting would give her the time she needed to get her emotions in balance after seeing the deep strain on Robert's face. It left her uneasy noticing how he winced each time Emma slipped her arms around his waist and squeezed him tight. His body looked right for his age, though thinner, but his eyes were so much older. *I can only imagine the horrible things he has seen over the months.*

By bedtime the kids were so worked up from the excitement of their brother being home and being able to listen to him play the violin again, he and Kathleen had to stay with them until they quieted down and fell asleep.

Robert came out of the bedroom first to sit with her. When he began to speak, his shaky voice surprised her. "I . . . I'm sorry Ma, for leaving. I just wanted to help out. It scared me when those people came to the house asking about having the kids live somewhere else."

"It upset me, too."

"I just thought Dad would want me to do something to support you."

"You did, son. Your father would be proud of you. He'd be even prouder that you got yourself back home safe."

"I should have come home with Johnny, but I . . . I didn't want to come home with nothing after leaving you to worry like that."

"You didn't. I have the money you sent tucked away for when we need it."

"So Mr. Hurst got it okay. I was worried he wouldn't."

Robert stood up, reached into his trouser pocket and pulled out the money he had left. "I kept a little of the money I earned harvesting with me in case I needed it traveling home."

"That was a good decision. We'll tuck this away with the rest. I'm proud of you for bringing it home. I hope you used what you needed for yourself."

Seeing a slight grin appear for just a quick moment, Lucille knew she had said the right thing.

"It feels good to be home, Ma."

She sat quiet, thinking of what to say to reassure her son they'd be all right.

"After you left I started getting a small widow's pension. It's a program President Roosevelt started for families like us. Mr. Hurst told me about it and helped me fill out the paperwork to sign up for the program."

"Really, that's so good to hear."

Kathleen came out of the bedroom, picked up one of the wooden chairs around the table, and slid it next to Robert. "Really what? Did you tell her already?"

He rolled his eyes as he looked over to Kathleen. "No."

Lucille watched the glances go back and forth between them. "Tell me what?"

Robert stretched his arm out toward Kathleen. "Go ahead."

"Mr. Moretti comes into the Five and Dime every once in a while with his kids. He stops when he sees me to say hello and always asks about Robert."

"Well, he was a close friend of your father's. It's kind of him to ask about Robert."

Kathleen put her hands on her lap, staring down at them for a moment. "Mr. Moretti mentioned the last few times he came in that he's planning to hire another bus boy at his restaurant."

"And?"

"He said Robert should come by to talk to him about it when he gets home."

Lucille caught Robert's eyes shifting to her. Needing time to collect her thoughts, she peered out the window. "The newspapers say if they have to close the schools, it won't be until

January now. They'll be starting up again soon. You've already missed some school."

Robert slid his chair closer to her. "Ma, Mr. Moretti told Kathleen it would just be on the weekends. I want to help."

Turning away again to think of how to answer her son, it didn't take her long to realize the job might keep him from leaving again. "Okay then."

Breaking into a smile, Robert glanced at his sister. She nodded back as if coaxing him to say something more. "Go ahead, tell her the rest."

"Mr. Morreti told Kathleen he wanted to hire me because I play the violin."

Kathleen interrupted. "Ma, he told me he heard Robert playing for dad a few times while he sat outside the bedroom door waiting to visit with him."

"And?" Lucille said.

"He'd like me to play for his customers a few hours on Friday and Saturday evenings, and he'd pay me a higher wage for the hours I play my violin."

She felt taken aback by what they had just told her. "Is it something you want to do? Play your violin in front of people? You've always shied away from that."

"It really is. It would give me a chance to keep practicing my violin, learn new pieces, and maybe even give lessons someday. Pa would like that, don't you think?"

"Seems it's settled then, isn't it?" She eased back into the comfort of the high winged chair. It had been a long time since she could just sit, relax, and not have her mind wander off to worry about her son. "Do you want to tell us about your travels? Maybe what you did after Johnny came home. If you don't want to talk about it now, I don't mind. It doesn't sound like you had much sleep last night."

"Yeah, I spent a long-time telling Johnny about everything. Some of what we talked about can help him it turns out. I want to tell you about my buddy, Tucker. I've been traveling with him over the last months. Johnny wants to meet him."

"So where is your friend now? Did he go home, too?"

"Maybe I should start with when I hooked up with him." He began by telling her about his luck stepping off the train with Al and Tucker following him. But he was careful to leave out any details that might upset his mother as he shared his stories.

After explaining what Al told them about President Roosevelt's program to train youth, he went on to talk about following up on the lead Al gave them on harvesting work in Arkansas. When he spoke about getting the job because he mentioned playing the violin when Mrs. Burkett noticed him staring at a violin that had belonged to her son, Lucille covered her eyes for a moment. "My goodness."

"She asked me to play for the two of them, and I did. It meant so much to the Burketts to hear violin music again. And later on she asked if I would play for all the workers. It really scared me thinking about playing for strangers but I couldn't tell them no."

"I'm proud of you. It was the right thing to do."

"Yeah, it was what I needed to do for the Burketts, and Tucker made sure I told them yes."

Kathleen spoke for the first time since Robert started talking about his travels. "Is that why you didn't hesitate when I told you Mr. Moretti wanted you to play for his customers? You surprised me when you said you'd like to."

"Yep, that's why, but it took me playing my music for other people a few times before I enjoyed the opportunity to share my music."

He went on to tell them about traveling to Ohio to find Al so Tucker could get into a training camp. "The neat deal is he gets a bed, meals, and pay to send home to his family. When I told Johnny about the program, he got all revved up and wants to get into a camp when he turns eighteen in a couple months.

He wants me to write Tucker a letter asking him to find out from Al how he can get signed up for the program, too."

"Do you think this man can get Johnny into a camp?" Kathleen asked.

"I think so. Ma, I want to include an invitation for Tucker to come visit sometime to hear me play my violin since my playing ended up helping both of us. He'd like that, I know."

"It did help you both, didn't it? I'd like to meet your friend."

The next morning, Lucille's heart warmed as she listened to the sounds of play in the yard. She'd peeked out the window a few times already to get a glimpse of Robert. The excitement he was home safe was still whirling around each time she looked outside. It helped her to see at breakfast the nervous tension so bold on his face yesterday had subsided a little.

The hollers and loud clapping outside drew her attention from the kitchen to the window again. Robert was teaching Oliver how to kick the ball. When he managed to move the ball forward, even a foot, the kids burst into applause. She laughed softly as she watched Oliver clap his hands in delight each time they cheered him on.

Walking back to the kitchen, her smile faded away when she realized the serious economic problems in the country had caused her young son to become a man much too soon. Another burst of loud cheers brought back her smile. But for now, Robert could be a fifteen-year-old boy, playing kickball with his brothers.

Acknowledgments

I owe a heartfelt thanks to many people who supported me during the writing of this novel. I appreciate each and every one of them.

Members of my critique group were the first readers of many chapters of *The Only Way Home*. I am sincerely grateful to Marylin Warner, coordinator, Barbara Bowen, Barbara Gibson, Annette Kohlmeister, Rose Salcetti, and Mary Zalmanek. Their feedback and insight was invaluable.

I feel fortunate to have had Jack Adler, editor, read the final manuscript. His writing experience as an author and editor provided the perfect guidance for the final copy.

Finally, I appreciate the ongoing, loving support of my family and friends. To my husband, Bill, you made what is often a solitary journey of writing and rewriting easier. Thank you for your ongoing proofing as needed, and most of all my deep appreciation for all your endless encouragement.

Printed in Great Britain
by Amazon